CW00496492

BACKWATERS

Chris Crowther

Backwaters copyright © 2024 Chris Crowther

All rights reserved. No part may be reproduced, stored in a retrieval system, or transmitted in any form or by any means, electronic, mechanical, photocopying or otherwise without the prior permission in writing of the author.

The right of Chris Crowther to be identified as the author of this work has been asserted by him in accordance with the Copyright, Designs and Patents Act 1988.

taleweaver@chriscrowther.co.uk

First published 2024

Taleweaver
Hoveton – Norfolk – England – NR12 8UJ

www.chriscrowther.co.uk

ISBN 978-1-9998111-6-7

Illustrations by Sarah Rogers
Cover aerial photo by Mike Page - enquiries@mike-page.co.uk
Cover design by Jane Dixon-Smith – www.jdsmith-design.co.uk

Other books by Chris Crowther

Prologue

1943

The North Sea in winter is never particularly inviting, but on this war-torn night, viewed from the cockpit of a badly-damaged aircraft whose single-engine was giving all the indications of imminent failure, it was looking positively deadly.

For the tenth time in as many minutes, the pilot scanned the instruments; not an easy task with all electrics shot to hell and the oil pressure relentlessly falling. Not to zero yet, but how much longer would it keep supplying the engine's lifeblood?

Hopefully long enough to reach the blessed English coast just appearing on the western horizon. No lights, of course, in this wartime blackout, but the moonlight occasionally piercing the broken stratus might be enough to make some sort of landing. It owed him that after very nearly being his Nemesis. For it was as he was heading home over the Dutch coast that the night-fighter had caught him.

Up to that point the mission had gone well. Having reached the Zuider Zee, he had successfully map-read his way to the rendezvous seventy miles into occupied Holland. Just what reception would be awaiting him there, was the question every Special Operations pilot asked himself when making a night-time r/v behind enemy lines. He was soon to find out as a coded signal, flashed briefly from the small wood on the edge of the landing field, told him somebody - friend or foe - was there and ready.

No lingering was the name of the game for this stage of the operation and, as he positioned for approach, three small pinpoints of light in the form of an inverted L marked his landing area. They would only be torches, hopefully held by Dutch resistance fighters, with the single nearest marking the spot he needed to touch down. The other two showed the far end of this short strip. Thankfully, the old Lysander needed little landing run and he was soon down and ending his rollout with yards to spare, swinging right around that light and then fast-taxiing back to the first light for the pickup.

There, shadowy figures were waiting, thankfully in the garb of working Dutchmen who immediately swung into a well-practiced drill that would take seconds rather than minutes. And every second saved was one less for enemy soldiery doubtless already hot-footing it towards the sound of his 860hp Mercury. Not that the waiting Resistance needed any prompting; already figures were running to his aircraft, brave men who would disappear back into hopeful anonymity as soon as this pickup was complete.

Only one of them would be taking this ride back to England, and he was already beside the aircraft, throwing a large bag up into the rear cockpit and instantly following it up the ladder permanently fixed to its outside. The canopy shut, a quick thumbs-up, full-power, and then they were roaring along the strip, getting airborne in two-hundred yards, building speed and then rolling into a steep-turn westwards for home and safety.

Knowing enemy radar would already be searching, the pilot kept low, just a hundred feet above the flat Dutch countryside that looked deceptively peaceful in the sporadic moonlight piercing the low stratus above him.

It was as they were flying back over the Zuider Zee, just beyond the threat of anti-aircraft ground-fire, that 30mm cannon shells suddenly slammed into the fuselage, followed immediately by a Messerschmitt Bf 110 night-fighter flashing by and already banking over for another pass. Equipped with airborne radar, it must have locked on to his lumbering Lysander soon after take-off. Whatever, it had scored some hits on the electrics and, judging by the immediate loss of power and increase in vibration, also the engine. With the enemy now set to deliver its *coupe de grace*, it was a time for quick action.

With no defensive armament and less speed than his attacker, his only chance was the thickening stratus ahead. Praying that the aircraft held together and the engine kept running, he brought the nose up and zoomed into the blessed overcast.

Thankful that at least some of his instruments were still functioning, he levelled in the total white-out and prayed the 110 wouldn't lock onto him again. Its radar had only a range of three miles at the most, so it was just a case of hanging in there for ten nail-biting minutes before cautiously letting down to contact again with the rolling North Sea.

A quick scan of the surrounding night sky showed no sign of his attacker, but with a hundred miles of forbidding water ahead on an engine with faltering oil pressure and rising temps, this was going to be no joy-ride.

With the intercom also dead, he spared a second from the instruments for a glance behind to check his passenger in the back. What he saw was far from reassuring, for the man he was supposed to be flying to safety was now slumped head-down in his seat, seemingly lifeless except for his scarf whipping and fluttering spookily in the slipstream roaring through the shattered plexiglass.

Nothing he could do now to help the poor fellow except get him to England and possible aid. And so he pressed on, nursing his crippled ship for another forty tense minutes until the white line of surf breaking on an East Anglian shore went sliding under the nose.

Now at least he'd be home when the engine, with its temps now hitting limits, finally seized for good. He needed to land sooner rather than later and the nearest place would be the very strip where they had trained for this mission. Small familiar lakes he knew to be the Norfolk Broads were now appearing below and guiding him in. Over the largest he turned just a tad west of north, and another minute had the strip in sight.

Being only a satellite field, it would be unmanned and with no lights to help, but that was the least of his challenges as the engine died its last breath and they glided silently down. Turning to line up with the strip and easing back his airspeed, he was relieved to feel the automatic flaps lowering as the boundary hedge went under the nose and, seconds later, the blessed feel of wheels touching grass and rolling to a stop just in front of a wooden barn.

Thinking only of the passenger, he jumped out of his own cockpit and up to the rear one, sliding back the shattered canopy, pulling away the bag the Dutchman was still gripping and throwing it out onto the ground. Even as he unbuckled the harness, he was checking for signs of life and, just as quickly, realising there were none. There he sat, the man he should have brought to safety, but now with his lower body black with blood that had pumped from the gaping wound in his chest where a cannon round or flying splinter had passed right through.

The pilot dropped off the cockpit ladder onto the ground, any satisfaction at having brought his aircraft home effectively neutralised by the realization that this was one mission with no good ending. He turned to walk away from this tragic scene and, as he did so, his foot hit something on the ground.

It was the Dutchman's bag that he had tossed down from the cockpit.

On hitting the ground it had burst open, strewing some of its contents across the damp grass.

The pilot bent down to examine them.

Chapter One

Eighty years later

'Are you *sure* that thing's safe, Jack?'

Standing in a field just south of the city of Norwich, Audrey Fellows was staring with some trepidation as a young team unfolded an enormous deflated balloon and spread it carefully over the ground.

'Of course it is, Aud.' Jack's suppressed excitement allowed little sympathy for his wife's mounting anxiety. 'Just think, we'll have a bird's eye view of all the places we know so well. You'll love it once we get going. It'll open up a whole new world to us.'

'I'm perfectly happy with the one I'm in and with my feet firmly on it, thank you Jack,' replied Audrey, hoping her rather forced smile disguised the reservations she was feeling, especially as a sudden roar filled the air and a flame from the basket began inflating one side of the balloon. Everyone watched in awe as it expanded into a huge colourful sphere while rising slowly like an awakening leviathan.

'Don't worry, Mum.' Standing close by and holding the hand of her five-year old nephew, William, Amy put a supportive arm around her mother's shoulder. 'It'll be fine. Hot air balloons are governed by the same safety regulations as any other aircraft.'

'Amy's right, Mum, and we know you'll just love it once you get up there,' added sister Jo, hugging her three-year-old daughter, Amanda, ever-tighter while trying to cover the little girl's ears against the blast of the burner. 'If we didn't think it was safe, we wouldn't have arranged this flight as your anniversary surprise.'

With Jo's husband away on a business trip and Amy's flying long-haul to the Far East, it had worked out perfectly for the Fellows' two daughters to spend this special Ruby Anniversary weekend with their parents in Norfolk.

'And very generous it was of you,' acknowledged Audrey through tight lips, 'as long as we're still alive to celebrate another next year.' It was at this

5

moment that little Amanda chose to dissolve into a welter of uncontrolled howling, frightened by the noise, flame and gigantic billowing balloon expanding before her. Forgetting her own fears, Audrey quickly gave her granddaughter's hand a consoling squeeze. 'Don't worry, Mandy, it's perfectly safe. Just watch the pretty colours as it fills with air.'

'And you'll soon be able to wave to Granny and Grandpa as it takes us high up in the sky,' added Jack, clueless as to why his well-intentioned words only seemed to be making the screaming worse.

Audrey gave a barely-concealed roll of her eyes. 'Just you watch your balloon with William and Amy, Jack, and leave Mandy to us. She'll be fine just as soon as that roaring stops.'

Which it soon did as the balloon became almost fully inflated and the burner was shut off. Clearly things were almost set to go, a prospect that seemed to be filling the other waiting passengers with varying degrees of enthusiasm. For Jack, though, this was a dream come true and he could hardly wait to get boarding.

Except he might have to wait just a little while longer, judging by the slightly-concerned expression on the face of the young member of the balloon team he spotted striding towards them.

In his late-twenties with rugged good looks, dark curly hair and a muscular frame stretching the *SKYRIDES* logo on his dark-blue tee-shirt, the young man smiled apologetically. 'Good afternoon, folks, I'm Stuart Steadmore, in charge of the ground-crew.' He nodded back to the multi-coloured balloon swaying and nodding in the gentle breeze wafting over the field. 'We're pretty well set to go, but I hope you won't mind a slight delay for a quick photo-shoot. It won't take long ... Ah, here comes Kathy.'

Having finished checking the balloon, a young woman wearing a jumpsuit in the same dark-blue as the ground crew, came jogging across the grass to join them, though looking slightly agitated.

'Hi everyone, I'm Kathy Caterall, your pilot today.' All eyes fixed on this slim, attractive-looking woman with a long auburn pony-tail tucked through the opening at the back of her logoed cap. 'I'm sorry for this slight *unscheduled* delay, but I hope we can get going very soon.' The exasperated glance she gave her ground chief and her following words gave the impression she knew exactly who to blame for this. 'So, where is she, Stuart?'

'Here any minute now, Skipper.'

'Hmm, that's assuming she even knows the meaning of a minute.' Kathy gave an exaggerated sigh. 'The only thing you can rely on with *her* is that she'll be late. Okay, I'll crack on with the passenger briefing while we're waiting.'

Putting her obvious irritation to one side, she welcomed the passengers with a mix of seriousness and good humour before briefing them on their boarding order, in-flight procedure and the brace position they would be adopting on landing in case the basket turned over. Seeing looks of wide-eyed concern, she was quick to reassure them this was all part of the fun and in no way dangerous.

Jack listened intently to it all before being slightly distracted by the sight of a chauffeured sleek black Audi coming through the field-gate before easing to a halt close by the balloon.

This had to be the mystery "*her*" arriving for the "publicity shoot", and soon everyone's attention was diverted to catch a glimpse. Heavily-tinted windows gave no clue as to who it might be, but now an earnest young man in dark suit and sunglasses was jumping out from the driver's seat to hurriedly open the rear passenger door while, at the same time, talking on his mobile phone. As he helped out his charge, he was scanning the waiting bystanders with a pompous concern as phoney to Jack as the striking female emerging theatrically from the back.

Clad in tight-fitting white jump-suit and cowboy boots, she paused just long enough to give her onlookers a condescending wave. Jack did not wave back but instead glanced at the faces of the others around him, their admiring expressions turning to gasps as they recognised the identity of the woman brushing long blonde hair back from her heavily made-up face.

Noticing her father's blank expression, Amy leant closer and whispered, 'Don't you see who it is, Dad? It's Tracy Goldman.'

'Tracy who?'

'*Goldman*, Dad. She's the new singing sensation who won *A Star is Born* a few weeks ago.'

'The hit talent show on Saturday night TV, Jack,' chipped in Audrey. 'The one I can never watch because it conflicts with your true-crime series.'

'Oh, her.' Jack vaguely remembered the local news item featuring the winning contestant who had generated such excitement by being a Norwich girl. 'So, who's the twerp fussing around her then?'

'Probably her manager-cum-minder.'

'Minding what?'

'That her adoring fans don't get in the way, I expect. And this is probably the rest of her team arriving,' explained Amy as a second vehicle pulled into the field and stopped behind the first to disgorge a long-haired man with cameras, followed by another young female. The latter immediately began titivating Tracy Goldman's make-up and well-spruced hair. After just a short discussion, the photographer sprang into action, clicking off multiple shots of the singing star lounging sexily on the balloon basket while affecting a well-rehearsed pouting look. Although none of the balloon passengers had so much as moved, the scowling minder now advanced towards them holding up a halting hand. 'Not any closer ... thank you.'

'Why would we want to?' asked an increasingly-irritated Jack.

'Shush, Dad!' warned Jo with a frown.

Skipper Kathy had other concerns. 'Does that stupid girl know not to touch anything, Stuart?'

'I'm not sure ... but I'll go and tell her.'

'Don't bother, I'll enjoy doing that myself.'

Certainly, Kathy Caterall's determined stride back to her balloon carried enough bristle to have the photographer lower his camera and Tracy Goldman to abandon her ridiculous pose. Now the two young women stood toe-toe and, although Jack couldn't hear the actual exchange, it was animated enough to leave little doubt as to its tone and final enough for the singing star to angrily wave off her photographer before stomping towards the watching group.

Managing to swap her scowl for an affected sugary smile, she greeted them all by saying, 'Hi everyone, sorry to keep you waiting, but I hope it was worth it.' Jack let out an impatient groan, and got a severe dig in the ribs from his wife. Pretending not to have heard, Miss Goldman continued undeterred. 'And because I've held you all up, please let me make amends by offering you complimentary tickets to my next show in Norwich.' She turned to her hovering minder. 'Jarvis!'

The young gofer immediately swapped his mobile for a wad of tickets which he began handing out to the star's grateful admirers. However, when he offered two to Jack, the ranger shook his head. 'Thanks anyway, but not my sort of thing.'

'Well, speak for yourself, because I'd love to go,' jumped in Audrey, leaning over her husband's shoulder to grab the proffered offerings. 'Thank you, Jarvis, we'll look forward to a night out.' And, before Jack could offer further dissention, she quickly added, 'I think it's great to have a local girl win like that. Have you worked for Tracy very long?'

'Almost since she started performing really.'

'How exciting.'

'Oh, it certainly is.' Unused to anyone actually striking up conversation with *him* rather than his celebrity boss, Audrey's nosiness was having a loquacious effect on the young man. 'Tracy's a wonderful girl, and being offered the chance to be her manager, was beyond my wildest dreams.'

'Manager!' Unfortunately, the "wonderful girl" herself was within listening distance and now bore down with forbidding anger voiced in a slight Norfolk accent. 'You don't "manage" me or anyone else, Jarvis, so don't go getting ideas above your station. Just stick to doing the running around you get paid for which, right now, means checking that car seat is clean enough for me to sit on again.'

'Oh ... right ... sorry Tracy.' The red-faced Jarvis scuttled off.

Realising she'd let slip her charm, Tracy Goldman turned back to the now star-struck gathering with a re-fixed smile. 'Sorry about that, but I hope to see you all next week at the show ...' she turned to glance at the balloon, '... assuming you live long enough, 'cause there's no way I'd go up in that thing.' She gave a humourless chuckle before turning to Steadmore standing close by. 'Thanks for arranging the shoot, Stuart darling, and don't let that bossy flying bird get you down.' She was leaning forward seductively to give what was obviously going to be a heartfelt kiss when a sudden roar from the balloon's burner and Skipper Kathy's glare caused her to think twice. She drew back with a regretful shrug. 'Ah well, some other time, Stu.' Then she headed straight for her Audi where the waiting Jarvis was already holding open the passenger door. Ignoring him completely, but with a final wave, she was soon being whisked swiftly away through the gate, followed shortly after by the publicity team.

'My goodness,' said Audrey, turning back to her family with a shake of the head, 'I guess that's the world of show business for you.'

'If it is, you can keep it.' Jack's eyes had already returned to the balloon where Kathy had just given a wave and thumbs-up for the first passengers to board. 'Our turn next, Aud, so let's go and get our aerial view of Broadland.'

*   *   *

Already speeding the Audi back into the city, Walter Jarvis felt Tracy Goldman's manicured finger jab his back, followed by a sharp order. 'Pull in at the next pub we pass ... I need a drink after all that.'

Another mile brought them to a thirties-style establishment on the city outskirts. 'Will this do?'

'It'll have to, and park here where there's less chance of me being recognised,' she ordered, pulling a navy linen coat around her shoulders and putting on her oversized sunglasses.

With a less-conspicuous Tracy seated at one of the outside tables, Jarvis scuttled off to get her a large glass of Beaujolais and an apple juice for himself. Returning with the drinks, he was rewarded with the merest nod of thanks as he tentatively handed Tracy her glass, knowing full-well what was to come. Sure enough, after just a sip, she wrinkled her nose and snapped, 'What do you call this? Certainly not the French red I asked for.'

'No, they don't stock it, Tracy, but it is their best house wine.'

'It'll have to do then. I need something after that bloody awful session.'

Even Jarvis was reaching the limit of his patience. 'Well, don't blame me for that fiasco back there. I made the arrangement with Stuart Steadmore and just assumed you'd cleared it with Kathy Caterall.'

'Of course I hadn't,' retorted Tracy, 'that's your job.'

'Not for much longer ... now you've signed up with that management agency.'

'Yes, well, I don't pay their extortionate fees for organising second-rate photo-shoots for the local paper when they need to be setting up recording contracts and nationwide tours.' She took another disparaging mouthful of wine. 'Unfortunately, I'll still need someone for all the mundane day-to-day stuff and, for the time being, you'll have to do.'

'Thanks a lot.' Jarvis felt, perhaps, it was time to appeal to his boss's conscience. 'It hasn't always been like that Tracy. Back in your early days you relied on me a lot.'

'What, fixing up second-hand sound and lighting systems at all those pathetic village hall gigs?' She rolled her eyes at the memory. 'Days long gone, thank goodness. Next time I need that sort of backup, it'll be at top venues with professional crews who know what they're doing.'

'Yeah, well there's a few things you'll need to sort before you start counting your millions,' said Jarvis. 'Song rights being one.'

Tracy looked up abruptly, her glass halfway to her lips. 'How do you know about that?'

'Steadmore told me.'

'Did he now.'

Jarvis felt a little smug at the thought of dropping *Skyrides*' crew chief right in it. That could mean even precious Stuart Steadmore might soon be on the receiving end of Tracy Goldman's viper's tongue. Perhaps this was a good time to make a move of his own as he gulped down the last of his apple juice and leant a little closer. 'Look, Tracy, now you're an up-and-coming star, you need someone like me you know you can trust. Once you're coining in real money you'll never know if blokes want to be with you because they really like you or just because you're rich and famous. I've always fancied you and no-one could be more loyal than me and I was wondering if ...'

But she cut him short. 'Oh God, Jarvis, don't tell me you're going to ask me out! You *must* be joking.' Tracy put down her glass with a guffaw. 'No chance ...' but before she could add insult to rejection, the roar of a burner giving a burst of flame caused her to glance upwards to where the brightly-coloured *Skyrides* balloon was rising above the urban skyline. 'And as for Kathy Caterall, don't worry, I know how to deal with her.'

Chapter Two

'Oh my gosh, Jack, this really *is* wonderful.'

Audrey Fellows didn't often admit to being wrong but, as their balloon floated birdlike over the rivers and marshes of Broadland, she did concede she was loving every minute. With only the occasional burst from the burner as Kathy maintained the envelope's hot-air lift, their passage so far had been as peaceful as it was enthralling.

And now they were approaching the large broad close to their home, allowing Audrey to marvel at the watery world and its surroundings that she knew so well: the narrow river flowing out of the broad, passing the small hamlet in which they lived, and allowing her to spot their own little cottage snuggling there on the outskirts. 'My goodness, doesn't it all look so much neater and cleaner from up here?'

'Yeah, even the garden,' agreed Jack.

Audrey could imagine her husband wishing it looked as tidy at ground level, but his summer job as a ranger gave him few spare hours for gardening, a situation that undoubtedly suited him perfectly, for Jack would always prefer to be out patrolling the waters of Broadland sniffing out miscreants, than cutting lawns and tending borders. After years in London's Metropolitan Police, Audrey knew he missed the challenge of detection and was never happy unless he had some great mystery to solve. The Broads, though undoubtedly possessing their own air of mystery, were thankfully low on actual crime, but that did not stop Jack being ever-watchful for it.

Added to that was the fact that he always seemed far happier in recollections of the past than the hurly-burly of modern life. That was one reason she had tried to enthuse and put aside her own misgivings when the girls had made this trip their anniversary gift. Looking at Jack now, standing in complete contentment as Skipper Kathy skilfully manipulated their progress over the magical area he loved so much, she could see he was indeed at peace with the world.

*   *   *

Jack was indeed feeling free from all earthly cares as they drifted silently over the broad. Not that there were too many problems within the Broadland boating community, but what there were inevitably fell to a ranger to sort out. Looking down at the motor boats and sailing yachts criss-crossing the broad's length and breadth, all looked serenely peaceful, as if of another world from which he felt a blissful sense of detachment.

It was an ethereal feeling that had begun from that moment of lift-off as they waved cheerio to the girls and the balloon became airborne and gracefully glided over the field's surrounding trees. Gradually they had gained height to the west of the city before the slight surface breeze steadily increased with altitude to south-west and their track accordingly more north-east. Standing close to Kathy as she cleared their flight-path with Norwich Air Traffic on VHF and levelled the balloon at fifteen hundred feet, Jack was delighted to see they'd be flying right over their own patch of Broadland.

With the GPS showing a groundspeed of eighteen knots, fifteen minutes had them clear of Norwich's urban sprawl and drifting under the influence of wind alone over familiar rivers, dykes, marshes and broads. He was glad to see that Audrey was equally enthralled as they floated over this watery expanse, though that did prompt one question to their skipper.

'Typical Broadland, Kathy, but not too many places to land a balloon?'

She turned and smiled reassuringly. 'Not here, for sure, but just a bit further north it gets more agricultural with plenty of fields to put down in.'

'Don't the farmers mind you dropping onto their land?'

'No, they're very understanding and know I always avoid fields with crops in them. The trick is to put down close to any road or track where we can recover with minimum upset. There's actually one place that fits the bill perfectly which I always try to make for.'

'Will we be landing there today?'

'I hope so. It depends on wind, of course, but I do have some control of our track by altering height.' She nodded to the altimeter set on the basket's edge. 'In fact, it's time to start going down now so we're not too high when we reach it.'

Leaving Kathy to her descent, Jack went back to sharing their remaining flight time and this idyllic scene with his wife.

'Not long to landing, Aud.'

'Oh, that's a shame.' As the balloon steadily lost height, Audrey joined the other passengers in calling down and joking with people in the boats below. 'How wonderful that they can actually hear us.'

'The glory of silent ballooning,' smiled Jack, pausing to return a mock salute from the crew of a large sailing cruiser churning across the shimmering water. He shrugged. 'In a few days I'll be down there amongst them again, but this certainly gives a whole new perspective to my work-place.'

'And with none of its hassle.'

'Absolutely.'

They were reaching the northern edge of the broad now, passing over extensive reedbeds as they slowly lost altitude. Jack peered down, taking in an area he had passed countless times in his patrol launch, but whose extent, beyond the outer fringe, was largely invisible at water-level and virtually inaccessible. Or so he had always thought, until something caught his eye.

Was that really what it seemed? Surely that was impossible? Jack leaned over the edge of the basket for a better look and then, as it slid out of sight beneath, quickly glanced at the balloon's GPS before turning back to his wife. 'Have you got a bit of paper, Aud?'

'What for?'

'I'll tell you later. Just give me something I can jot some figures down on before I forget them.'

'What figures?' persisted Audrey as she extracted an old receipt and pen from her purse and handed them across.

'Oh, just something I might check up on later,' hedged Jack as he jotted down twelve figures and slipped them into his pocket.

Audrey gave him a questioning look, but got no answer in return and so, with a slight shrug, turned her attention back to enjoying the final stages of the flight.

As the balloon continued down, Jack too put the unexpected episode behind him, moved close to his wife and, placing his arm around her shoulder, gave her a loving squeeze. 'Well, what a truly amazing experience it's been. One we'll never forget.'

'Yes, wonderful. It's been absolutely fascinating.'

And in more ways than one, Jack thought to himself, as river and marsh gave way to pastoral fields and Kathy prepared the balloon for landing.

*　　　*　　　*

Sadly, this trip would soon be coming to an end as the coast of north-east Norfolk drifted ever closer and Kathy continued the balloon's steady descent.

'The trick here is to find the right field before we end up over the North Sea,' she quipped with a grin for the benefit of some of the slightly-concerned passengers. 'If we don't, it'll be a long trip to Norway.'

Little chance of that, however, as they had come down to just a few hundred feet and were skimming over the trees and rooftops of a small hamlet where the locals waved and shouted greetings as the balloon drifted slowly and silently overhead. Once they had floated past, the slightly backing wind was taking them a little more westerly towards open farmland as Kathy gave a short burst on the burner. 'Good, this should take us nicely to Wildmarsh Farm.' She nodded ahead about a mile distant. 'It's a perfect landing site and one I've used before. During the war it was a small diversion field and you can still make out the old landing strips from the air.'

Jack could see the area they were heading for. 'Obviously the present owner doesn't mind you putting down on his land?'

'Actually, there hasn't been anyone living on the farm for years.' The edge of this open area was passing beneath the basket as Kathy made slight adjustments to the burner to control their rate of descent. 'Right ... Landing Positions!'

Settling down into their wicker seats and adopting the landing brace they had been shown, the passengers could only wait with varying degrees of apprehension for the landing. It might have been a more tense time were it not for the calm but concentrated expression on the face of their skipper as she counted down the height. 'One hundred feet ... fifty feet ... okay ... standby to touch down.'

Almost immediately there came a jarring lurch as the basket touched ground, bounced just once, touched again and came to rest. A second to realise they were still right-side up and then, as Kathy vented some of the envelope's hot air, spontaneous clapping broke out from the passengers for a job well done. Their wonderful trip was over and they had returned to earth safe and sound.

*   *   *

Climbing out of the basket, Jack paused to take in their surroundings.

They had landed on a strip of reasonably level grass, not large enough to be called "a field", but certainly wider than a mere track. Close by was a leaning clapboard barn next to a run-down farmhouse with dirty small-paned windows looking out on overgrown gardens and dilapidated outbuildings. The fact that no-one had emerged to greet their airborne arrival seemed to confirm abandonment and long-time neglect. So, this was Wildmarsh Farm.

From the farmhouse stretched a driveway, weed-strewn and potholed, but useable enough for the Land Rover and trailer of the *Skyrides* recovery team now bouncing towards them in a cloud of dust. Jack realised they must have been following the balloon throughout the flight and been given final landing details from Kathy as she made the approach. The way Stuart Steadmore unhesitatingly drove the rig straight up to the balloon reaffirmed the fact they had used this location before. Once out from behind the wheel, he opened the Rover's rear door and hauled out a large wicker hamper.

Kathy barely acknowledged him as he brought it over and lifted the lid, producing bottles and glasses. 'Right, everyone,' she instructed, 'a glass of Prosseco to celebrate a successful end to your adventure.'

With corks popping and all the balloonists on a high, they toasted Kathy before finishing off their bubbly and getting to know each other better. Jack, though, noticing Steadmore walking off to start preliminary work disassembling the balloon, slipped away to join him.

'Quite a bundle of fabric to fold up, Stuart.'

The young ground-crew chief paused in laying out the now completely deflated balloon, seemingly pleased at some friendly distraction. 'Yes, but it's a well-practiced procedure ...' he gave a wry smile, '... which you'll all be lending a hand with when you've finished celebrating.'

'All part of the experience, Stuart, but where exactly do you store the balloon between flights?'

'Not far from here actually ...' Steadman nodded to the north-west, '... a boatyard nearby.'

'A boatyard!'

'Yep, the *Watercraft* yard.'

'Didn't that used to be *Cecilian Cruisers* way back?' queried Jack, recalling something he had heard of a boatyard he was vaguely familiar with.

'Yes, but long before my time. Mr Turnberry took it over thirty years ago, just when the smaller yards were going bust and the ones with large fleets were getting even larger. He just lets the moorings to private owners now and concentrates on hiring out dayboats and canoes.'

'Mr Turnberry?'

'Yes, Alec Turnberry. He still owns the yard.'

'And agreed to store a hot air balloon there as well?'

'Yep, for the last two years, since Kathy turned up looking for somewhere to base her new venture. We had a bit of spare room in one of the sheds, so we did a deal that included general back up for the whole operation. Now I look after bookings as well as leading the ground crew for her.'

'You said "we", Stuart. Does that mean you're involved with the boatyard in some way?'

'Yep, I've been manager there for six years. In fact I hardly ever see Mr Turnberry. He lives in London and pretty much allows me to run the business as I want.'

'Which is how you've been able to be such a support to Kathy,' concluded Jack before glancing around and slightly lowering his voice. 'I know it's none of my business, Stuart, but I couldn't help noticing that she seemed a bit put out when Tracy Goldman was all over you at the photo-shoot. Would I be right in thinking you and Kathy are more than just colleagues?'

'That obvious, was it?' Steadmore blushed slightly. 'But, yes, Kathy and me hit it off from the start. You've seen what a great girl she is. I fell for her big-time and it was wonderful ... until recently, that is, when things turned sour.'

'Because of Tracy Goldman?'

'Yes, but it isn't what it seemed,' said Steadmore, shaking his head sadly. 'Just after Tracy won on *Stars*, Walter Jarvis, that so-called manager of hers, contacted me to ask if they could use the balloon for a promotion shoot. With all the publicity she was already getting, and being from Norwich, I was all for it and jumped at the idea. I suppose I should have asked Kathy first, but I thought it would be brilliant free publicity for *Skyrides*.'

'Not the worst of decisions I'd have thought. Does Kathy normally over-react to things?'

'Not at all but, in this case, she seemed to get it into her mind that Tracy and me had something going between us.'

'What made her think that?'

'Just the flirty way Tracy carried on when we met up to discuss details.' Steadmore glanced in the direction of Kathy and the rest to ensure they were all out of earshot. 'Okay, I was a bit flattered that someone like her was coming on a bit, but I didn't take it seriously. After all, she could have any bloke she wanted since winning *Stars*, so I knew she was just leading me on.'

'But Kathy didn't see it that way?'

'Unfortunately not, but she and Tracy's fallout goes way back, so she probably thinks the worst anyway, even when there's nothing in it.'

'"Fallout"?'

But further explanation would have to wait as Kathy's rapid approach and sharp call of, 'Is that balloon ready for folding yet?' were enough to silence young Steadmore who, with a shrug, went to rejoin the rest of the group waiting patiently to help pack the balloon.

'You seemed to be deep in conversation with Stuart back there, Jack,' said Audrey, putting her empty glass down beside the hamper. 'Anything special?'

'Oh, just asking a few questions and, as always, raising a few more. Nothing that important though.'

'Well, we've all been hanging around waiting for Stuart to show us how to fold the balloon, so you'd better put your back into helping to make up for the delay.' Audrey wasn't best pleased with her ever-curious husband as Kathy waved them over.

'Fair enough,' accepted Jack, philosophically, as he ambled back to the balloon with the others.

*　　*　　*

The next twenty minutes saw everyone, under Stuart Steadmore's good-humoured direction, enthusiastically lending a hand to meticulously lay out and then fold the huge envelope so it could be heaved, together with basket and burner, onto the trailer. Just as they finished, a minibus arrived to take all the passengers back to the Norwich field and their cars.

Seeing that Kathy and Stuart would be towing the balloon back to the boatyard, Jack wandered across to thank them both before they went. There still seemed to be some frostiness between the two, but they accepted his thanks with gratitude and he had just shaken their hands when something unexpected happened.

It was the sudden appearance of a tall, slim, middle-aged man with grey close-cropped hair who seemed to have materialised from nowhere. Although he spoke impeccable English, it was with a foreign accent.

'Hello, please excuse my intrusion, but I was cycling your roads when I saw your balloon. I have a great interest in ballooning and so I followed it here for a closer look.'

'Ah, that's a shame,' said Kathy, 'but you're twenty minutes too late because, as you can see, it's packed and ready to go.'

The stranger shrugged. 'Yes, my fault for not cycling faster, and please forgive me if I'm intruding on private land.' He nodded back to the derelict farmhouse. 'Do you actually own and live in this property?'

'Good heavens, no,' laughed Kathy. 'As you can see, it's uninhabitable. In fact, the old place gives me the creeps.'

The stranger frowned. 'Oh, really ... in what way?'

'I don't know, but it's always given me the shivers ... even on hot days.' She shook away uneasy feelings and gave a quick glance at her watch. 'But is there something else I can help you with Mr ...'

'...Van Heiden ... Hans van Heiden ... and, yes, perhaps there is. I've already enjoyed some balloon flights in Holland, but one here over your Broadland would be something I would very much like to do. Would it be possible to book one with you, Miss ...?'

'Caterall, but please call me Kathy,' she emphasised with a smile, 'and, yes, we do regular trips, but when were you thinking of?'

'It would have to be this coming week, Kathy. Unfortunately my time here is short, as I return to Holland next weekend.'

'Ah, that's a problem then,' explained Kathy, 'because we're fully-booked for the rest of this month.' She gave a regretful smile. 'A pity, because I would've loved to have given you a flight over our Norfolk Broads.'

The Dutchman looked equally disappointed. 'More my loss, I think, because rarely is it possible to fly with such an enchanting and attractive pilot.' Van Heiden gave a smiling, chivalrous bow.

'Oh, goodness ...' Kathy took off her cap and ran a taming hand through her loosened auburn locks, '... but there might just be a solution, because we do have a group charter later this week and they might just have a spare place remaining. Let me check with them and get back to you.'

'I don't think they'd want an outsider joining their party,' interrupted Stuart Steadmore. 'It wouldn't be right to even ask them.'

'Oh rubbish!' Kathy was in no mood for contradiction, especially from Stuart Steadmore. 'They might well be delighted to have an extra passenger chipping in to the cost.' She turned back to the Dutchman with a smile. 'Give me a contact number and I'll let you know.'

'That would be good.' Van Heiden took out his wallet and extracted a card. 'You can call this mobile number any time.'

'I certainly will,' she promised, 'but there's a ballooning event you might want to return to Norfolk for in July when I'm planning to re-enact John Money's epic 1785 flight from Norwich. Surprisingly, very few people know about it even though it was one of the very first long-distance balloon flights. He did it all those years ago to raise money for the Norfolk and

Norwich Hospital, and so we are doing it for the same good cause.'

'I too have heard of this man,' said Van Heiden, 'but I would be interested to find out more.' The Dutchman raised questioning eyebrows. 'Perhaps we could discuss it over a meal together and work out how I might support your event financially?'

'Oh, that sounds great,' enthused Kathy. She glanced again at the card in her hand. 'It says here you are an Art Historian? Is it art that brings you to Broadland, Mr Van Heiden?'

'Mainly, yes, researching a paper I'm writing on the influence Dutch 17th Century landscape paintings had on the Norwich School of artists ...' he glanced around him at the surrounding Broadland landscape, '... but also to enjoy a little wandering of my own to appreciate the countryside and scenery that so inspired those painters in the first place.'

'Then I hope we can give you an additional perspective by getting you airborne,' gushed Kathy.

Stuart Steadmore took a meaningful glance at his watch. 'Kathy, time's going and we need to get the balloon stored and the crew away.'

'Yes, I'm sorry to have held you up,' apologised Van Heiden, 'but give me a call to arrange that meal together.'

'Yes, I'll certainly do that,' promised Kathy smilingly while completely ignoring the black look on Stuart's face.

Sensing Steadmore was about to say something he'd regret, Jack stepped forward and offered his hand to the Dutchman. 'Sorry to butt in again, but I've always had an interest in the Norwich School of painters myself ... erm ... especially John Crome.' Thinking quickly to recall which of the artist's works he had noticed in Yarmouth's Time and Tide Museum, he managed to add, '... *Removal of Old Yarmouth Bridge* ... have you seen that one?'

'Sadly, no, not that one,' admitted Van Heiden, returning the handshake, but frowning slightly. 'Perhaps you could tell me where I might view it, Mr ...'

'Fellows ... Jack Fellows.' Jack took out a card of his own and handed it across. 'Perhaps we could meet for a drink and chat.'

'Yes ... perhaps ...' Now it was Van Heiden's turn to study a card. 'So you are a "Broads Navigation Ranger". That must mean you have a great knowledge of this area and its past?'

'I like to think so.'

'Then I'd be delighted to have that drink with you, Jack. I'll call you when I have some free time later this week.'

'Thanks. I'll look forward to it.' Jack, glanced towards the mini-bus where all the other passengers sat patiently waiting. 'Right, mustn't hold them up any longer, but thanks, Kathy, for a great trip today ...' he paused just another second, '... but, before I go, Stuart, can you just spare me a minute?'

Thankfully, this time it *was* just a minute and Jack was soon on the mini-bus and easing himself into the seat next to his rather put-out wife. 'Yet again you've held us all up with your chatting. I just hope it was worth it.'

'So do I,' admitted Jack, enigmatically. 'It's not often you encounter three mysteries in one day.'

*   *   *

Not far behind the *Skyrides* minibus, Stuart Steadmore swung the Land Rover, towing trailer and balloon, out of Wildmarsh Farm's drive and onto the main road for the *Watercraft* yard. Beside him, sitting with arms folded and eyes firmly ahead, pilot Kathy was clearly not in a mood for talking.

Usually, returning to base would have been a time of cheerful banter over a job well done, but Steadmore was finding this sullen silence unbearable. Deciding to at least try and lighten the mood, he turned and forced a smile. 'Your passengers certainly seemed to enjoy their trip, Kath.'

'Did they?' She made no effort to return the smile. 'Lucky for us then that they didn't complain about the late departure.'

'What? That fifteen-minute delay for the photo shoot? Actually, I think they all rather enjoyed seeing Tracy Goldman in the flesh.'

'Not as much as you seemed to do.'

'Oh, for crikey's sake ...' Steadmore banged the steering wheel in frustration, '... you're surely not jealous just because I spoke to the girl. And as for that photo shoot, I genuinely thought it would be some good free publicity for *Skyrides*.'

'Except, you didn't think to mention it to me first.'

'No, because Walter Jarvis gave me the firm impression that Tracy had already cleared it with you.'

'But you know damned well that she and I don't talk to each other anymore.' Kathy did at least steal a glance at Steadmore, be it one of incomprehension. 'So why on Earth did you think we'd arrange anything between us?'

'The only thing I'm thinking is that I'll never understand women,' he grumbled, slowing in preparation for the turn off the main road. 'Actually, I thought you two *were* talking now, at least about *one* bone of contention.'

'Which is none of *your* business ... or anyone else's,' snapped Kathy as they drove into the yard and pulled up by the doors of the main shed, 'so just remember that when you're next chatting to your Miss Goldman.'

'And what makes you think I *will* be "chatting" to Tracy ... or anyone else?' queried Steadmore as he switched off the engine and turned to face his accuser. 'What *are* you talking about?'

'I'm talking about the way you two seemed so chummy this morning, Stuart. I'm sure you're flattered at having TV's latest heart-throb drooling over you, but don't come running back to me when you find she's just been playing you along.'

'I have no intention of "running" *away* from you in the first place and I can't believe we're having this conversation, Kathy. Where have you got these stupid ideas from? You're the only girl for me, and that's how I want it to stay.'

'Sorry, but some time apart would probably do us more good right now.' Kathy shrugged. 'I think we both need a bit of space from each other.'

'In other words, I'm being given the shove.' Steadmore nodded towards the shed where the *Skyrides* balloon was stored. 'And does that go for all the help I give in operating the balloon as well? How about this re-enactment fundraiser you've got planned for July? Who's going to help you with that?'

Kathy shrugged. 'I'll find someone.'

'Yeah, like this mysterious Dutchman who suddenly materialised at Wildmarsh this afternoon. You didn't waste any time agreeing to go out with *him*, even though I was standing there beside you.'

'And why shouldn't I, when you'd been flirting with the lovely Tracy in front of everyone at the publicity shoot? How do you think I felt then? Anyway, that's pure business, because, as you heard yourself, Van Heiden seems keen to invest in the scheme, and some cash is what I need right now to literally get that idea off the ground.'

'That and the fact that you're flattered by his attention,' countered an unconvinced Steadmore.

'Well, perhaps I am, Stuart ... perhaps I rather like the idea of going out with someone who's interesting and more mature than men my own age.' Kathy nodded towards the adjacent shed. 'So, let's finish this conversation, get the rig stowed away and then you can leave me to sort some other ground support arrangement.'

And with that, the owner of *Skyrides* climbed out and started sliding open the boatshed doors.

*   *   *

In spite of Kathy's favourable first impression of Hans van Heiden, the Dutchman was already showing himself to be somewhat economical with the truth. Two miles down the road, in the opposite direction to *Watercraft*, he was not on a bicycle, but stopping his hire car in a lay-by to make a call on his mobile.

'Hi,' he greeted to the voice at the other end, 'not much success this afternoon. Would you believe some hot air balloon came and landed before I could even get started. Luckily, I'd stuck the car in the barn and told them some story of being out cycling, but I don't think it'll be wise to return too soon. On the plus side, though, I've got a new lead.'

After a short further discussion on future strategy Van Heiden finished the call and drove off back to his hotel. He had another call to make which could well make this day worthwhile after all.

*   *   *

'Right, you two, sit yourselves down,' ordered Jo as, later that day and back home, Amy poured drinks while William and Amanda played happily in the garden with Spike. The Fellows' adored Border Collie had been less than happy at being left out of the day's excursion, but any feeling of neglect had soon been forgotten with abundant fuss and treats from the grandchildren.

Also contented after a day fulfilled, Jack and Audrey were only too happy to relax as ordered. 'I must say,' admitted Audrey as she took her G&T, 'that the idea of a balloon flight had filled me with dread, but instead it's been one of the most enthralling days of my life.'

'Oh, that's great Mum,' smiled Jo, raising her glass, 'so here's to many more anniversaries shared.'

'Amen to that,' responded Jack, drinking the toast. 'So, what for next year, Aud? Bungee jumping?'

'I think I'd need a few more of these to do that,' giggled Audrey, feeling a little light-headed already. 'And anyway, I can't see anything topping today, what with even meeting Tracy Goldman in the flesh.'

'You mean *that* was the best bit?'

'I'm not saying that, Jack, but she is the flavour of the month on TV and it did give us an insight into the celebrity world.'

'If only to show it being an artificial one of false glamour and bitchiness,' said Jo, tutting with disgust. 'The way she bossed her poor assistant around.'

'Walter Jarvis, you mean,' said Jack. 'Manager in his eyes and dogsbody in hers.'

Amy could only agree. 'How could any self-respecting man allow himself to be treated like that?'

'*And* still believe he'd landed the best job ever,' added Audrey, incredulously.

'But that was obvious, wasn't it?' Jack allowed Jo to top his drink. 'Couldn't you see that the poor chap's hopelessly in love, thinks she's wonderful and is quite happy just to be near her?'

'You're probably right,' conceded Jo with a cynical smile, 'but it won't be for long once the big boys start getting their claws into her.'

'Good luck to them, I say,' muttered Audrey. 'Talk about someone fancying themselves. Did you notice the way she was so obviously flirting with that nice Stuart Steadmore?'

'Who could miss it? She was hardly subtle was she? And you could tell Kathy wasn't happy about it. In fact, our lovely pilot was pretty jealous.'

Audrey nodded. 'Yes, and it was very obvious that Kathy was upset at that photo-shoot business to start with.'

'Oh, it went further back than that,' explained Jack. 'From the minute Kathy introduced herself to us, I knew that there was no love lost between her and the person we were all waiting for.'

'How on earth did you work that out, Jack? Tracy hadn't even arrived at that point?'

'Simple. Kathy said something about "she" always being late. How would Kathy know that unless they'd met before?' Jack shrugged. 'And, anyway, there was bad blood between them long before today.'

'Over what?'

'I wish I knew. Stuart was about to tell me more when Kathy stepped in to get us all folding the balloon.'

'Ah well ...' Audrey finished off her drink, '... probably over some chap, seeing how Miss Goldman behaved today.'

'Possibly,' acknowledged Jack, 'but I'm not sure it would have been completely one-sided. Our lovely skipper isn't too backward at coming forward when she meets a man she fancies either, going by the way she latched on to that mysterious stranger this afternoon. It got poor Stuart's blood well and truly up.'

'I bet that's why she did it, love ... to get back at him for flirting with

Tracy.' Audrey took another sip of her drink. 'By the way, did you find out who that man was and what he wanted?'

'A Dutchman called Hans van Heiden, who reckoned he's here researching the Norwich School of Painters.'

'When you say "reckoned", Dad, does that mean you didn't actually believe him?' asked Amy, always aware of her father's inherent suspicion of anything beyond the norm.

'Just that telling a lie is always easier if you base it on a real truth.'

'And you thought he was lying?'

'Not totally, Amy, but for starters there was something strange about the way he just turned up like that ... seemingly materialising from nowhere.'

'You're right, Jack,' agreed Audrey. 'Now I think about it, none of us actually *saw* him arrive.'

'He reckoned he'd cycled up, but he certainly wasn't dressed for cycling and didn't have a bike with him, or anywhere else, as far as I could see.'

'Hmm.' The girls shared questioning glances and frowned. 'So what's the explanation?' asked Jo.

'The only one possible ... that he was actually there when we landed.'

'Where?'

'Probably in the farm buildings. For a man who said he'd been peddling after our balloon, he seemed remarkably sweat-free, so my guess is that both him and his wheels had been in that barn some time before we arrived.'

'Then why didn't he come straight out to watch us land and talk to us then?'

'Perhaps worried he'd be in trouble for trespassing until he was sure we weren't actually the farm owners.'

'Or perhaps he was up to something more sinister in the barn,' suggested Amy, 'although it's doubtless something about nothing.'

'Of course, Amy's right,' agreed Jack, 'but I'd still like to find out what lies behind our mysterious Mr Van Heiden.'

Audrey raised questioning eyes. 'And just how will you do that?'

'Quite simply, actually. I told him how I had an interest in the Norwich School of Painters, suggested meeting up for a drink together and he accepted.' Jack produced the card from his shirt pocket. 'He wasn't over-enthusiastic at first, but changed his tack and gave me his number when he found I was a ranger.'

'*You ... art ...* The Norwich School of Painters!' exclaimed Audrey, in disbelief. 'Jack Fellows, you haven't the slightest interest in art or paintings. I've never managed to drag you into a gallery once.'

'No, but I had to have some excuse for talking to the man.'

'But all you'll do is make a fool of yourself, Dad?' warned Amy. 'You know nothing whatsoever about the subject?'

'No, but I can read up about it,' defended Jack. 'I'll call him later in the week to arrange the meeting and at least try and find out what he's really about.'

'Poor man,' groaned Audrey, knowing her husband's doggedness when it came to digging into people's lives and motivations.

'But you told Mum there were *three* mysteries today, Dad,' queried Jo, in an effort to move on. 'You've given us this enigmatic Dutchman, plus some long-time bad blood between Kathy and Tracy Goldman, so what's the third?'

'Not so much a mystery, actually, as just something I've never heard of before.'

'Which is ...?' asked an increasingly intrigued Amy.

'An epic balloon flight that apparently began in Norwich back in the seventeen hundreds. Kathy is planning on doing a re-enactment of it in July and this Van Heiden showed an interest in donating money towards it.'

Jo grinned. 'No wonder she was keen to have a date with him then.'

'I think you're probably right there,' agreed Jack.

'Yes, well, it works both ways and she might find that Van Heiden is only using that as a carrot for other favours,' decided a suspicious Audrey.

'Which is why I just want to get the measure of the man. In the meantime, I plan to find out more about this epic balloon flight Kathy's re-enacting to raise money for the hospital.'

'Ah, well, I'm glad to hear she has decent principles even if her judgement of men is a bit shaky. For her sake it's probably a good thing you're going to be checking out this Van Heiden.' Audrey sighed. 'And to think I was worried we'd feel flat once the girls went home. Instead it seems you'll have your mind full of sleuthing while I'm looking forward to our other treat.'

'"Other treat"?' Now it was Jack's turn to be slightly confused.

'Don't you remember, Dad?' prompted Jo. 'That spin-off from the balloon launch when Tracy Goldman kindly gave you and Mum free tickets for her show next Thursday evening.'

'Oh, that,' remembered Jack, frowning. 'I'm sure your mum can find a friend to enjoy it with.'

'No, Jack, *we'll* enjoy it,' emphasised Audrey in a voice her husband knew left no margin for negotiation, 'so don't even *think* about opting out.'

'But modern music is just rubbish, Aud, and certainly not something I want to suffer for a whole evening.'

'In that case you'll probably enjoy Tracy Goldman's style then, Dad,' reassured Jo, 'because she sings mostly ballads and accompanies herself on guitar. So just look forward to having a nice evening out with Mum. She deserves it and, after all, you've got complementary tickets, so it's not costing you anything.'

'Okay, fair enough,' conceded Jack, 'although, actually, Aud, we do have something else to look forward to before even that.'

'Really?' Audrey, fixed her husband with suspicious eyes. 'Now what have you gone and arranged, Jack?'

'A canoe trip, love.'

'A what? Where?'

'The *Watercraft* Boatyard that Stuart Steadmore runs. I had a quick word just before we left this afternoon and booked one for tomorrow before the girls go home.'

Chapter Three

'Are you sure you don't want to go with Dad on this trip, Mum?' asked Amy as she lowered herself down onto the front seat of the sixteen-foot open canoe being held steady by a smiling young yard-hand.

'No thank you, dear.' It was next morning at the *Watercraft* yard and all the family were there for Jack's secretive expedition. Further down the quay, yard-hands were already sorting groups of cheery hirers onto their day-launches. Audrey however, with both girls returning home on the morrow, was pleased to have an excuse for a morning ashore. 'Your dad won't rest until he's checked whatever it is he saw yesterday, so you two go and have yourselves some fun while Jo and I take the little ones off into Norwich to do some shopping.'

'You don't know what you're missing, Aud,' declared Jack, easing himself down onto the rear seat and, with the alternative being a morning shopping with the grandchildren, all too well aware of what *he* was missing. Without wasting time, he picked up the paddle, turned to the young yard-hand holding the canoe steady and said, 'Right, we're all set, so let go.'

'Have a good trip, sir,' wished the lad, shoving them away from the quay and prompting Audrey's more cautionary instincts.

'Now, don't forget this is your first time in a canoe, Jack, so be careful.'

'Of course I will Aud. Enjoy your time with Jo and the children. We'll meet up here at midday and then it's lunch on me.'

'God willing,' muttered Audrey under her breath as her husband took his first tentative strokes, 'but good luck, the pair of you and take it steady,' she called after them.

'Thanks, Mum, we will,' shouted back Amy as they cleared the moorings and paddled away down the dyke towards the main river. Entranced by the silence of their passage and the clean way the canoe cut through the still water, she looked over her shoulder and smiled with contentment. 'This is lovely, Dad.'

'Yep, great isn't it.' Already settling into a steady rhythm, Jack too was thoroughly enjoying this sensation of being at one with nature. On his ranger patrols he'd often watched more experienced canoeists propelling themselves along with seemingly little effort, and now he was trying to do the same, helped by last night's instructions on YouTube.

There, he'd picked up tips on controlling direction from the back, either by hardening the power of the paddle-stroke one way or following it with a J-shaped exit to go the other. There was a bit of meandering at first as they progressed down the main river, but he was soon getting the hang of it.

'How about changing paddling side?' he suggested after a while, as one arm started to ache.

'Good idea, Dad.' They swapped over and immediately felt renewed energy. After another half-hour, Amy nodded ahead. 'Is that the entrance to the broad just coming up?'

'Yep. We've done well. Not much further.'

'And then where to, Dad?'

Where indeed? Much as he was enjoying this experience, even Jack was beginning to have doubts as to the rationality of this expedition, wondering if, aloft in the balloon yesterday, his own vivid imagination had perhaps got the better of him. Well, he would soon find out because, as they entered the broad itself, it was time to get out his handheld GPS.

The ability of being able to pinpoint position to within a few metres by means of orbiting satellites had always been a source of wonder to Jack, and to do it with an instrument no bigger than a mobile phone and powered by just two AA batteries, even more mystifying. What was undoubted, though, was the way it made his job so much easier in checking location, speed and distance as he patrolled the waterways. Up until now he'd never bothered to try the instrument's other gimmicks, but last night, for the first time, he'd programmed in some co-ordinates. They were the ones taken yesterday from the balloon's GPS and hastily scribbled down on Audrey's old receipt. Now they showed that position ninety degrees to his left. At least, he had a partial answer to Amy's question as he pointed to the edge of the broad and said, 'Somewhere in there.'

'What, in all those reeds? What on earth for, Dad?'

'Not sure, Amy. That's what we're here to find out.'

With some stronger paddle strokes, Jack turned the canoe's bow towards the encircling reedbeds while at the same time searching for a way in and an answer to what the GPS showed was just a hundred yards away.

*   *   *

At first glance, these marshes seemed an almost impenetrable barrier to further progress, the reedbed dense and seemingly towering over them. Plunging straight in with powerful strokes was an option, but protecting these habitats was one of Broadland's ways of combating climate change, and wanton damage was definitely something to be avoided. Instead, Jack turned the canoe southwards along the bed's slightly curving edge, searching for an opening that would allow them to enter its dense expanse.

Just when he was despairing of finding any such entry, he spotted the signs of what may have once been an old marshman's channel, obviously unused for years and easily overlooked due to the encroaching reeds. He pointed to it with his paddle. 'This could be a way in, Amy, so let's give it a try.'

As they nosed into the concealed entrance, Jack was pleased to see the tall reeds parting either side of their slow-moving bow without any apparent damage as the canoe moved on. Continuing with gentle strokes, they forged their way onward through this secluded, overgrown water-world with the GPS showing the waypoint getting ever closer and Jack feeling the excitement of discovering ... what?

Hopefully, they'd soon find out, but for now the surrounding reeds were eerily silent except for the constant song of reed warblers and buntings, until a sudden splash nearby caused them both to jump as the still water rippled slightly and a row of tiny bubbles went curving away into a secluded channel. Only one thing would leave such a trail and Jack smiled in mild embarrassment at his edginess. 'Only an otter, Amy ... probably swimming back to its holt ... but my GPS is showing only metres to go, so stop paddling.'

Adrenalin pumping, senses alert, both sat motionless as their slight way carried them slowly and silently on with the scene ahead limited to a few yards of dense reed. If there was anything there, Amy, up in the bow, would probably spot it first. 'Let me know if you see anything unusual,' whispered Jack, while inwardly wondering why he felt the need to keep his voice low. Once more he dipped his paddle for a few gentle strokes, hoping that the figures he'd copied down in that drifting balloon were accurate, while realising all too well that there was no other way to discover what he had spotted.

As they forced their way a little further, with the reeds thickening and his own doubts building, Amy suddenly pointed straight ahead and said in a hushed but excited voice, 'I think I can see something, Dad ... there ... something buried in the reeds.'

She ducked down, and looking over the canoe's bow, Jack saw for himself a darker shape materialising ahead. 'You're right, Amy. A few more strokes and we'll be there.'

Paddling those last few metres, Jack's feelings were ones of relief that his initial suspicions were proving correct. For there, lying deep in the water, were the remains of an old wooden motor-cruiser.

*　　*　　*

Coming alongside the deck sunk almost level with the water, Jack estimated the boat to be perhaps twenty-eight feet in length. Beneath accumulated vegetation and mud its once varnished cabin extended back to an open cockpit in the stern where a traditional spoked steering wheel and chromed engine controls were similarly showing signs of long-exposure to the elements.

'My goodness, Dad, it's a wreck. What boat do you think it is?'

'That's what I aim to find out,' said Jack, grabbing a metal stern-cleat, still with the rotted remains of a mooring line attached. It wasn't unknown for boats, deemed beyond economic repair, to be illegally abandoned in remote Broadland backwaters, but something about the way this derelict had been left without attempt to salvage useful fittings, hinted at a more sinister purpose. The next few minutes might disclose just what that was. Taking a firm grip of the cleat, Jack heaved himself out of the canoe and onto the near-level side-deck. 'Okay, Amy, you stay here and hang on to that gunwale while I go and check.'

Thankfully, with the derelict obviously sitting on the bottom, there was no heave of its hull as he paused to steady himself on the slime-covered deck. The cockpit below was awash, but he lowered himself down onto side-seats and then further down into the cockpit itself, taking care not to plunge his sandaled feet into some treacherous opening unseen beneath six inches of murky water. Stepping cautiously, and glad he'd worn shorts for this expedition, Jack then sloshed his way towards the pair of small doors that gave access into the cabin, pulling them open before gingerly venturing down a further two steps into even deeper flooding and the stygian gloom within. A minute to let his eyes adjust, another to take in all he could see and then he was back up in fresh air and clambering down again into the canoe.

'What did you find, Dad?' Amy had clearly seen the upset look on her father's face as he emerged from the cabin. 'Are you all right?'

31

'I'll explain later, Amy. Right now I need to make an urgent call.'

He pulled out his mobile and keyed a familiar listed number. 'Bailey ... Jack Fellows here ... sorry to disturb your day off, but I've just found something that'll probably disturb a few more.'

*   *   *

Close on an hour later, a rather subdued Jack and Amy were paddling back into the *Watercraft* yard, a police car parked close to the office block and a familiar plain-clothes officer and two uniformed constables standing beside it. To one side, looking both confused and concerned, was the figure of Stuart Steadmore. As Jack brought the canoe alongside, they all came over, Steadmore bending down to steady it while Amy and her father climbed out.

'Jack, what on earth's happening?' Clearly, Steadmore had been told nothing of what had brought the police to the yard.

'You'll know soon enough, Stuart,' said Jack, stretching cramped muscles, 'but first I need to talk to this officer here.'

'Hello, Jack.' Detective Inspector Bailey held out his hand. 'I should have known who'd be ringing me from some far-flung corner of Broadland on a fine Sunday morning.'

'Yeah, sorry, Bailey, but I knew you'd want the first heads-up.'

'Would I? I deal in serious crime, Jack, not boating accidents.' He turned to young Steadmore, still hovering close by. 'Any chance of some place Jack and I can have a private chat?'

'You're welcome to use my office.'

'That'll be great, thanks.'

'Okay, Jack, so you've found a boat abandoned in a reedbed just off the broad,' confirmed Bailey as they walked towards the office.

'More than that, Bailey, it contained two human skeletons.'

Bailey paused for just two seconds at the office door to let this revelation sink in. 'You're sure about this are you, Jack?'

'Absolutely. I didn't spend too long on any detailed examination, but I've seen enough human remains in my time to know these two are the real thing.'

'Right ...' Bailey ushered Jack into the boatyard office, '... first thing is to get Broads Beat securing the area and gearing up for a night-watch.' As the DI called in on his mobile and waited to be put through to ops, he turned back to the ranger. 'So, what's the scene, Jack?'

'A waterlogged cabin,' explained Jack, closing the office door behind them, 'and two skeletal figures lying opposite each other on the cabin couches.'

'No immediate signs of foul play?'

'Not that I could see, Bailey, but I have a sickly feeling that this will ultimately turn into a criminal investigation.'

'That old copper's instinct of yours again?'

'Has it ever let you down before, Bailey?'

'No.'

As the DI's call was answered, Jack left him to it and went back to Amy waiting patiently with Steadmore. 'Sorry love, but I'm going to be involved here for a while yet. Call Mum and tell her I'm sorry, but the family lunch I promised is off for today.'

*   *   *

When Jack returned to the yard office, the DI had made his arrangements and was keen to hear more specific details.

'So you reckon this boat and its occupants had been there some time, Jack.'

'Years by the look of it.'

'Any rough estimate of how many?'

'Going by the state of the boat and that the remains have been reduced to skeletons, I'm thinking a minimum of twenty ... perhaps more.'

'Very strange, but aren't you jumping the gun by suggesting this might be suspicious? Couldn't it just be a case of accidental death such as carbon-monoxide poisoning?'

'That's certainly happened before,' admitted Jack, 'but the big question is, why had this boat been driven a hundred yards into that reedbed as though it was never intended to be found.'

'Could it have originally been anchored on the edge of the broad and the reeds grew around it over the years?'

Jack shook his head. 'It would've been spotted and checked within days if it had been sitting there with no sign of life. I'm absolutely certain it was hidden there intentionally, decades ago.'

'Some sort of suicide pact then?'

'Unlikely, Bailey. In my experience, couples who top themselves usually die in each other's arms, whereas these two are lying feet apart either side of a table.'

'If they *are* a couple,' said Bailey. 'I don't suppose you found or noticed anything that gave a clue to their gender or identity?'

'I know enough about police procedure, Bailey, not to go poking around a crime-scene ... but no, nothing obvious and all their clothing had long since rotted away. They were just skeletons lying there in a flooded cabin.'

'Hmm.' Bailey stroked his chin. 'How about the boat then? Any name or number?'

'Possibly, but it's sitting on the bottom, so any markings, if they're still there, are hidden below water. But, from what I could see, it was a traditional wooden motor cruiser, very basically built and fitted out, but pretty typical of the boats that cruised these waters fifty years ago.'

'So, any chance whatever happened could date from as long ago as that?'

'No, because it would've probably rotted away completely if it'd been there that long ...' Feeling the need to inject some positivity into this discussion, Jack quickly added, '... but I'm hoping it won't be too difficult to trace her once we get her out.'

'How difficult will that be?'

Jack shrugged. 'Depends what state it's in below the waterline, but it looked solid enough. All wooden boats leak a bit and I expect that's what sank her over time. My guess is that simply pumping her out will get her floating again, but getting those human remains out and transferred to another boat won't be easy. My recommendation is that we leave them where they are until we have the boat towed to a yard and craned out. The remains have been there for years, so another few days won't make any difference. Then the SOCO boys can do their work in a secure area ...'

'... and, hopefully, get us a line on who these remains really are,' said Bailey. 'So the sooner the forensic boys get doing their stuff, the sooner we'll have something to go on. One thing we can be doing, though, is checking who was reported missing around that time.' Before the DI could continue, his mobile rang. 'Bailey ... right, understood ... later then.' He rang off and turned back to the ranger. 'That was Broads Beat. They're going to bring their RIB here by road to save time, but that'll still be another hour yet.' He raised questioning eyebrows. 'In the meantime, any chance you could take me back to this boat right now so I can see for myself?'

Jack shook his head. 'Not in the canoe unless you've got an afternoon to spare. But the yard here might have something suitable to lend us.'

'Okay, let's see.'

Jack found Stuart Steadmore hovering close by the office, his expression a mixture of curiosity and apprehension. 'What's happening, Jack?' He nodded towards the two constables still standing on the quay. 'This isn't exactly good for business.'

'Nothing to concern the yard, Stuart,' reassured Jack, 'but you might be able to help us sort things more quickly.' He briefly explained their need for a boat suitable for working in shallow water.

'We've got the dory we sometimes hire out to fishermen.'

'That would do perfectly. Any chance of us having it for a couple of hours?'

'No problem. Give us ten minutes to get it ready for you.'

'Thanks Stuart, and throw in a couple of extra life-jackets so we can take those two constables as well and get them out of your hair.'

'Will do, Jack.'

As Steadmore went off to sort the boat, Jack did wonder how *Watercraft* would cope with a derelict and its long-dead crew in its yard.

*　　*　　*

'I can see what you mean about it being well-hidden,' said Bailey as Jack helmed through clumps of floating weed to bring the dory alongside the half-sunk cruiser. 'Why would anyone go to the trouble of forcing a boat into this reedy jungle unless they never planned on coming out again?'

'Exactly my thoughts, which leaves me to believe a third party intended they never would.'

This transit back to the scene had certainly been a faster one than the morning's, the dory's eight horsepower outboard taking merely twenty-five minutes in spite of Jack insisting they keep to the four mph speed limit while on the river. Only on the broad did he increase to five before then quickly slowing to idle as he nosed the dory slowly into the reedbed.

It wasn't easy pushing a way in, but once alongside the derelict, the DI turned to the two constables. 'Right, lads, you get our lines on this wreck while we go and have a snoop, but try not to disturb anything more than you have to.' Seconds later, having pulled on disposable gloves, both Ranger and DI were stepping across the small gap between the two craft.

'I didn't plan on getting wet-feet,' grumbled Bailey as they climbed down into the cruiser's cockpit, awash in ankle-deep water.

'And it gets a bit deeper in here,' warned Jack as he led them down into the cabin with its grim tableau of the two skeletons lying there above the foot-deep water.

Bailey studied the scene and stroked his chin. 'Hmm, like you said ... an unlikely suicide scenario, Jack, but something ended their boating life for good. The question is what?'

'Probably this,' said Jack, examining the remains in greater detail for the first time and pointing to a small hole in the forehead of each skull. 'Tell me if they're what I think they are?'

'It'll need the pathologist to confirm,' said Bailey, examining the pencil-sized holes, 'but they look horribly like small calibre bullet-holes to me.' He straightened up and took out his mobile. 'Right, I'll take a couple of preliminary photos for the record, but how long do you reckon before we can get this thing up and moved for the forensic boys to get stuck in?'

'It depends on how soon we can get a workboat big enough for the job, Bailey. *Watercraft* is unlikely to have one up to it, but I'll straightway get phoning and see what I can drum up from the Broads Authority.'

'Great.' The DI scanned the cabin's bare wooden interior, the small portholes devoid of even the remains of curtains, the general air of decay and tragedy. 'I get the impression this wasn't exactly a luxury cruiser even in its day, Jack. It all looks very basic. You sure there's nothing here that gives us an I.D. on it?'

Jack shook his head. 'No nothing. I looked before.' He cast his eyes about again, checking to see if there was anything he had missed. There was nothing except for a small object floating nearby. 'Hmm, there's something I didn't spot before.... probably just dislodged by our movement here in the hull.' Jack reached across and fished out the small hard-wood object. 'Well, what do you know ... one of our victims here was probably a pipe-smoker. At least that tells us that one of them was male.'

'Which stood to reason anyway,' shrugged Bailey, 'but doesn't get us any further to identifying them or the boat.'

'No, but there is something else I can try.' Sloshing his way back up and into the cockpit, Jack spent a wet few minutes before hauling open two largish hatch covers. 'Engine compartment, Bailey, and the water here might just be clear enough for me to get a serial number.' Getting even wetter, he knelt down to one side of the exposed machinery space and peered into the putrid water and the submerged engine. 'This looks like a Perkins diesel to me, so let's see ...' Rolling up his sleeves and leaning even lower into the bottom of the cockpit, Jack started wiping away some of the thick, smelly slime coating the engine.

'Strewth, what's that stink?' exclaimed one of the constables, watching the whole procedure from the dryness of the RIB.

'Bottom mud, but I've wiped away enough to see ... yep, there's the manufacturer's plate right where it should be on left hand side of the block ... take this down, constable ...' Jack slowly read off the fifteen letters and figures of the engine's data and serial number.

'Your Audrey's going to love it when you get home like that,' grinned Bailey, emerging into the cockpit and seeing the clinging black mud caking Jack's arms, face and clothes.

'All in a good cause ...' Jack went to the boat's side and attempted to wash off the worst, '... especially if it gives a lead as to whose boat this was.'

'Yeah, well, we need to put a watch on it tonight,' said Bailey, 'but I reckon it'll be enough if we just anchor a surveillance boat at the broad's entrance to keep an eye on things. Broads Beat should be here any time, so once they arrive we can leave them to sort it.' He turned to Jack and the two constables. 'Right, let's get back and start this ball really rolling.'

*   *   *

'I just hope you're smelling sweeter after that shower, Jack,' said Audrey, wrinkling her nose as her dressing-gowned husband strolled back into the lounge. 'Even Spike gave you a wide berth.'

'And I don't blame him.' Still towelling his hair, Jack nodded towards the utility room from whence came the sound of the washing machine on full workload. 'And sorry about the clothes.'

'I should think so,' grumbled Audrey. 'It was bad enough hearing our family Sunday lunch had gone for a burton without having to collect you looking like The Creature from the Black Lagoon.'

'Yeah, not very nice.' Jack, slumped onto the sofa. 'I must say, it's not often I have to ride home sitting inside a bin-bag.' He glanced about. 'Where are the girls?'

'Packing. Jo's other half gets home on Tuesday and Amy has to be back teaching the following day, so they're all off first thing.'

'It'll be quiet here without them, but life and work goes on ...' Jack paused for just a second to check his wife's mood, '... including for me, because I'm back on early duty tomorrow.'

Audrey dropped the parish magazine she'd been reading. 'I don't believe it. You told me you were off until mid-week?'

'I *was* until I called Broads Control on the way back to the yard to give them an update on the mystery boat. Seeing as I was already deeply involved, they decided it best if I stick with it and be out there with the patrol launch first thing in the morning.'

'To which I'm sure you readily agreed.' Audrey knew her husband well enough to know he was always happiest at the centre of the action. 'So, just what *is* happening tomorrow?'

'Hopefully, getting that wreck pumped out and afloat again. We've sorted a large workboat and gear from one of the bigger yards, and that'll be on-scene soon after dawn. Then, once the derelict's afloat, we'll tow her up to *Watercraft* for lifting out.'

'How does Stuart Steadmore feel about that?'

Jack shrugged. 'A bit worried it might affect trade, but I promised we'd keep things discreet and away from his customers. And there'll be some money for craning and storage fees, which managed to pacify the yard owner when Stuart called him to clear things.'

'So, who is the owner?'

'Apparently, a chap called Alec Turnberry, who lives in London and is rarely here. He seems happy to leave Stuart to run the yard, but this business has prompted him to drive up tomorrow just to see what's going on.'

'I'm not surprised. It's all a bit disturbing finding out we've been living within a mile of two undiscovered bodies for all those years.'

'I know, but hopefully the boat will be moved tomorrow, Aud, so try not to think of it too much.' Fully aware he hadn't been scoring too many points with his wife of late, Jack suddenly had an idea. 'Look, love, I let you all down for Sunday lunch, it's been a funny old ending to our anniversary weekend, and the girls head home tomorrow ... so why don't I treat us all to dinner out tonight instead?'

'Well, that would certainly help take our minds of this other horrible business,' acknowledged a happier Audrey. 'We'll have to find someone to look after William and Mandy, but there's a young lass from the church who said she was always up for child-minding while the girls were here, so I'll give her a call.'

As Audrey checked with the girls and then headed for the phone, Jack knew that, once again, he'd just managed to skate clear of very thin ice.

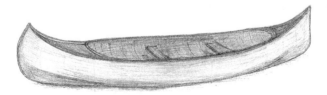

Chapter Four

That evening, at their local pub and savouring the candlelit contentment of a family gathering, Jack raised his glass for a toast. 'Well, cheers girls. It's been a real treat having you all with us ... and for our unforgettable balloon trip.'

Being centuries old, the pub's dining tables were separated by aged oak partitions with pillars joining the low solid beams above. Having arrived early, they had managed to secure a secluded alcove in the restaurant's far corner. Now, awaiting their ordered meals, Jo raised her glass in reply. 'And thank *you* Dad, for this lovely surprise and *you*, Mum, for sorting a babysitter at such short notice.'

'And we're just glad you both enjoyed the trip so much ...' affirmed Amy, before giving her mum a sympathetic smile and adding, '... but I suppose we should've guessed that, floating high over Broadland, Dad would've spotted something amiss on his patch below.' She took a sip of her wine. 'I did notice though, Dad, that you were very engrossed on your laptop while we were all getting ready, so no doubt you were Googling something to do with it all.'

'Only that long-ago balloon flight from Norwich that Kathy's re-enacting,' explained Jack. 'It really was an amazing feat, and yet so little is known about it, even here where it took place.'

'It's certainly new to me,' said Amy, 'so what was it all about?'

'Well, only if you're really interested ...' Jack hesitated, sensing varying degrees of enthusiasm for what could well be a long story, '... and ready for a bit of a local history.'

'Our meals will be a few minutes yet,' sighed Audrey, resignedly, 'so why not?'

Amy, though, sharing her father's love of all things adventurous and historical, was more receptive. 'I'd love to hear the story, Dad. It all sounds very intriguing.'

'Certainly audacious,' agreed Jack, 'and it all goes back to the late 18th century when a local chap called John Money decided to raise funds for the Norfolk and Norwich Hospital, founded just thirteen years before in 1772.'

To her surprise, Audrey found herself already warming to John Money. 'He sounds a very decent chap.'

'And a very gallant one too who'd fought with the 15th Light Dragoons in the American War of Independence but, by 1785, was a thirty-three year old half-pay major kicking his heels just south of Norwich on the family estate at Trowse Newton. Completely bored and hungry for adventure, he'd taken a trip from London in a very early British balloon. He was so enthralled that he then somehow talked the owner into loaning it for his own fund-raising scheme.'

'Which was ...?' asked an increasingly intrigued Jo.

'To lift off on his own from Norwich's Ranelagh Gardens and see just how far he could go. Pretty ambitious when you think it was only two years after the Montgolfier brothers had first got airborne in France, and here he was attempting the first long-distance balloon flight in history.'

'And was he successful?'

'Yes and no. He certainly flew a long distance, but not quite where he intended.' Jack used some cutlery to represent a very rough outline of the East Anglian coast. 'His plan was for the prevailing southerly winds to take him north over Lincolnshire, but soon after liftoff the wind veered unexpectedly north-west, which first brought him back over the city and then further south-east towards Lowestoft and the North Sea.'

'Oh gosh!' exclaimed Amy. 'What did he do?'

'Not a lot in the circumstances, seeing as his hydrogen vent valve had stuck and he couldn't get down. By the time it started to lose gas it was night and he was twenty miles offshore and splashing down into a choppy sea. Luckily, there was still enough gas to keep things afloat, but he faced a long night fighting to survive in the darkness.'

'Good job I'm hearing this story *after* my own flight,' declared Audrey. 'But what about poor Money ... did *he* survive?'

'Only just, Aud. He cut lose the basket and climbed up onto the balloon hoop, but was soon suffering from hypothermia. Boats were out looking for him, but by midnight most had given up and turned back. Thankfully, the Coastguard Cutter *Argus* stuck to it and finally spotted him in the moonlight. The poor chap had been up to his neck in water for five hours, and more dead than alive when they dragged him on board, but plenty of brandy poured down his throat had him gleefully recounting his experience by the time they reached Lowestoft.'

'Thank the Lord for that,' said Audrey. 'What a terrifying experience for the poor man. I just hope it was all worthwhile.'

'Very much so,' nodded Jack. 'Huge sums were raised for the N&N and Money went back into the army where he wrote a thesis on the use of balloons for the military and rose to the rank of general.'

'Quite a character then,' said Amy. 'And it's this flight that Kathy Caterall is intending to re-enact?'

'That's her plan,' affirmed Jack. 'The original flight launched on the 22nd of July, so she hopes to be lifting off as near that date as possible from the grounds of the new hospital to raise funds for them just like Money did all those years before.'

'Good for her,' praised Audrey, 'but before that, Jack, you have another little mystery of your own to sort.'

'Yes, this strange derelict boat business,' said Amy, lowering her voice so other diners wouldn't hear. 'What do you make of it, Dad?'

'It's all a bit early for any firm conclusions, Amy ...' but before Jack could continue, the waitress arrived with their orders, '... but let's now forget balloons and mysteries and enjoy our food.'

'Amen to that,' agreed Audrey with some relief as they all dug in to their chosen meals.

*   *   *

'So, Dad, do you really think it was murder, or is that just your wishful thinking.'

Not long past the starter and awaiting the main course, Amy, having also inherited her father's passion for crime, couldn't wait to resurrect the previous conversation.

'All indications point to it ...' Jack paused, '... but I never "wish" for murder, Amy, although I do seem to have a knack for smelling it out.'

'You're not kidding,' laughed Audrey, wrinkling her nose again at the memory. 'I think we all had the unwelcome pleasure of smelling this one out!'

Jack gave a guilty grin. 'Yes, sorry about that, girls, but I have a feeling that the repercussions from our macabre discovery won't be so easily washed away.'

'Crikey!' exclaimed Jo, frowning. 'I've just realised that if we hadn't treated you to the balloon trip, that old boat would never have been discovered and you'd all have been spared the trouble.'

'True,' agreed Audrey, 'but now at least those two poor souls will be getting a Christian burial.'

'Eventually, Aud,' pointed out Jack, 'but only after the coroner has held an inquest. And, before that, we need to find out just who those "poor souls" actually were.'

'That shouldn't be too difficult, should it?' chipped in Jo. 'Surely two people and their boat can't have gone missing without someone reporting it, however long ago it happened.'

'That's something I'll be checking, Jo. I was still in the Met back then, but I certainly don't recall ever hearing of any local boat missing without trace.'

'It's certainly all very mysterious,' pondered Amy, 'but now at least, DNA will quickly identify the remains.'

'Only once they have a genetic link to compare them to, and that won't be immediate because, with old bones like those, it could well come down to establishing the mitochondrial DNA. As far as we know, no-one seems to have taken the trouble to even report them missing, so finding a close relative after all this time won't be easy unless their DNA is already on the police data-base.'

'So, how will they do it, Dad?'

'Ah, that's where the salvaged boat might give us a lead,' explained Jack. 'One of my jobs tomorrow will be chasing down the serial number I got off the engine.'

'As well as trying to work out how and why that poor couple actually met their end,' added Jo, '... which you obviously suspect as foul play, Dad.'

'It's all very well for me to *suspect*, Jo, but what's needed is hard evidence.' Jack turned towards the next course just being brought to the table. 'Anyway, let's put mystery deaths and strange wrecks on the back-burner and enjoy the rest of our meal.'

With nods all round, the next half hour was spent on more cheerful banter as they all happily worked their way through two more courses. Finally, Jack dropped his spoon onto the scant remains of an apple pie and custard and sat back. 'Phew! That's me well and truly stuffed.'

'Me too,' admitted Audrey, joining the sighs of agreement from her daughters. 'I'm sure we're all ready for a coffee, but why don't we just head home and have it there?'

'Good idea.' Jack pushed back his chair and stood up. 'Give me five minutes and I'll go and settle the bill.'

As he made his way through the main dining area to the bar, Jack saw that one table, intimately set behind an old oak panel, was occupied by a couple he vaguely recognised. As so often happens in meeting people out of context, he took a second to actually place them.

Certainly the woman was looking very attractive in a light summer dress, the candlelight showing her auburn hair hanging long and loose around her tanned face and shoulders. Perhaps it was the fact that he had last seen that hair gathered in a ponytail beneath a baseball cap, that it took him a few seconds to recognise her as Kathy Caterall, their balloon pilot.

'Oh, hello, Kathy,' he greeted as their eyes met. It was an awkward moment, especially as he recognised her dining companion as Hans van Heiden.

It was the Dutchman who was the first to speak. 'It's Fellows isn't it ... Jack Fellows who it was I met yesterday at that farm?' He half rose in his seat in greeting.

'Yes, but please, don't get up.' Jack waved him back down. 'I'm sorry I've interrupted your meal.'

'No, that's all right,' replied Kathy without enthusiasm and looking slightly uncomfortable. 'Will you join us?'

Jack gave what he hoped was an understanding smile. 'Thanks anyway, but I'm with the family and we need to get home to relieve the babysitter ... and the dog. Enjoy the rest of your meal.'

Making a tactful retreat, he continued to the bar and had just finished settling up when he was surprised to find Kathy beside him, her expression a mixture of embarrassment and mild concern. 'Mr Fellows ...'

'Jack.'

'Err, Jack, I didn't expect to see *you* here tonight.'

Jack smiled, affably. 'I can well-imagine, but Stuart and I were with you when Van Heiden asked you out for a meal, so it's no secret is it?'

Kathy blushed slightly. 'Yes it *is*, because I know Stuart will be upset if he finds out.' She paused before fixing Jack with concerned eyes, 'Do you anticipate seeing him anytime soon?'

'Actually, I'll be seeing him tomorrow.'

'You will?' A brief flash of panic crossed Kathy's face. 'Oh damn!' She glanced furtively back to ensure she was out of sight and hearing of her escort. 'I'd hate Stuart to know I'm dating again so soon, Jack, so can you promise me you won't mention this.'

Jack put a reassuring hand on her shoulder. 'Don't worry, Kathy, it's none of my business. I'll be the sole of discretion and, anyway, we're all going to be too involved in other developments to have time for affairs of the heart.'

'Developments?' She obviously knew nothing of what else had been going on at the *Watercraft* yard regarding the mystery cruiser. 'What developments?'

'Something that's sprung up since I saw you last, but nothing that should concern you.' He cast his eyes towards her neglected date. 'Just go back and enjoy the rest of the evening and don't worry yourself.'

'Oh ... thank you so much ...' she paused to give Jack a peck on the cheek, '... I do so appreciate that.'

And then she was gone, leaving Jack to ponder the ways of life and the complications of young love.

*   *   *

'Well I never, Jack. Fancy bumping into those two dining here.'

Back at their own table, Audrey and the girls had been fascinated to hear Jack's report of the Kathy/Van Heiden encounter, so much so they decided to exit via a back door rather than cause the pair yet more embarrassment.

'Goodness, I wonder where this tangled web of romantic jealousies will eventually lead?' asked Audrey as they drove homeward, while pretty much summing up what they all were thinking.

'Who knows, Aud? And anyway, is it really any of our business?'

If Jack had thought these last words would end the discussion, they were doomed to failure as his wife and daughters spent the rest of the journey speculating about the relationships between Kathy and Stuart, Stuart and Tracy, Tracy and Kathy and now, the secretive dinner date between Kathy and Van Heiden.

Once Jack had pulled into their drive and switched off the engine, he gave a deep sigh. 'Let's go and have those coffees, girls, and check the children have behaved,' he said with weary acceptance.

*   *   *

A hot coffee was certainly something Walter Jarvis could have done with at this moment, as he stood outside a block of modern luxury flats overlooking the River Wensum and just a stone's throw from the Norwich city centre.

This was where Tracy had recently, on the strength of her burgeoning career, purchased the first home of her own. But not somewhere he had ever been invited, reflected Walter as he maintained his lonely vigil in the cold night air.

On first arriving, he'd been encouraged to see Tracy's Audi still parked in one of her two designated parking slots. Hoping this meant she was still at home and, perhaps, even now having second thoughts at his own suggestion, Walter steeled himself to press the buzzer of her apartment intercom. No reply. He tried again. Same result. So, she *was* out, but who with? That was something Walter now intended to discover before this miserable night was through.

Not that he had much doubt as to the name of tonight's companion. Having seen her flirting with Stuart Steadmore at the photo shoot, he felt sure it had to be him. Just that thought alone was enough to harden Walter's will to see his mission through and catch the two arriving back together.

However, with time dragging and the night getting colder, Walter's resolve began to falter and with it, the realization that his infatuation for Tracy was rapidly turning to unhealthy obsession. Perhaps, if his suspicions were correct, her humiliating rejection to his advances might well have to be just accepted as heartbreaking reality.

They say there is a fine line between love and hate, and one that Walter was soon crossing as he recalled Tracy's scorn and cruel words, leaving his bitter jealousy to slowly turn to thoughts of retribution.

But, how to achieve that? If he let the cat out of the bag, Tracy probably wouldn't be too bothered, but Kathy Caterall would be far from pleased and probably ditch Steadmore and his involvement in *Skyrides* in one foul swoop. And serve him right, thought Walter, before considering things more rationally and realising that jealousy between the two women would only intensify that bad feeling between them and be a professional disaster for Tracy ... and, in turn, for him.

Just as Jarvis was realising it might be best to keep this night's findings to himself, the flash of headlights entering the apartment complex and the purr of an engine, told him this vigil might just be coming to an end anyway. As the exterior security lights flashed on, he slunk further back into the shadows and watched as a Mercedes came gliding into Tracy's other dedicated slot.

Heart beating faster, Jarvis held his breath as he recognised Tracy in the passenger seat. Within seconds of the car stopping, the driver was out and chivalrously opening her door. In the brightness of the security lights, Jarvis could see the car's personalised number plate as clearly as the identity of the man now escorting Tracy into her apartment block, the two doubtless destined for a night of togetherness that he could only dream of.

Jarvis slowly left his place of concealment, his distracted brain trying to assess the ramifications of what he had just seen and learned. He had indeed established that Tracy was seeing someone but, far from being that cool buck Steadmore, it was someone else he clearly recognised, and someone even more deserving of a good dose of retribution.

Scheming how that could be achieved now filled Jarvis's thoughts as he trod a weary way homeward to his own small flat on the city's southern outskirts. It was a long walk, but one absorbed by the ever-more malicious plans darkening his way.

Chapter Five

'Great, she's finally breaking free. I thought for a moment she was stuck in the mud for good.' It was eleven-thirty the next morning and the lead hand of the salvage team was breathing a sigh of relief and turning to Jack. 'Okay, shall we try towing her out?'

Four hours earlier, the tug had arrived with three crew and two engine-driven pumps, the latter running continuously to churn out muddy water until the hull finally broke free to float once more among the reeds that had concealed it for all those years. The police RIB and Jack's launch had ensured it stayed that way, but now it was time to haul the mystery cruiser along the rather choked channel and back onto the broad.

Jack started his own engine in preparation. 'Yep, let's give it a try. Presumably you'll get the RIB to run a long towing cable to it?'

'Too true ... no way we could get in there.' The tug skipper fished out his hand-held VHF and made a brief call to his men who immediately manoeuvred closer stern-in while the RIB trailed its thick towing cable into the reedbed. Soon there came a tumble of prop wash from the tug's stern, the cable tightened and Jack prayed it held as it took the strain. After what seemed an eternity, there came just the merest hint of movement that increased only slightly over the next ten minutes as the derelict slowly emerged, wraith-like from its reedy prison. The hull was still low in the water, encrusted with weed and molluscs, but now afloat and back in open water for the first time in decades. Jack slowly brought his own launch alongside. 'Great job. Well done.'

'Yeah, glad it worked.' The skipper hopped across to the tug. 'We'll leave the pumps running and my mate still onboard just in case.'

'Good idea.' Jack indicated back upriver. 'You know where to take her?'

'The *Watercraft* yard?'

'Correct.'

'Right, we'll shorten the cable and be on our way.'

Already, passing cruisers were slowing to stare at this strange flotilla which, with the Broads Beat RIB leading, was now cautiously getting underway again. Following astern, Jack couldn't help thinking of Amy's words last night as she pointed out how all this could have been spared if he'd never spotted that scene of long-abandonment. "Let sleeping dogs lie" was the old saying, and perhaps that applied to sunken boats as well. Then he thought of the two skeletons onboard whose story needed to be unravelled and told. How many years since they had last sailed these waters?

That was just one of many questions yet to be answered, but for now they were free of their muddy grave as the wreck progressed slowly up river, the pumps continually expelling water still entering through her long-rotted planks. Only after a tense hour was the *Watercraft* yard eventually in sight.

As the tug slowed, Jack could see a large mobile crane standing ready with two figures beside it, one recognised as Stuart Steadmore, probably curious to see what junk was being inflicted on the yard. Jack couldn't place the somewhat older man beside him wearing a large peaked cap and aviator sunglasses but, further down the quay, several police officers stood watching and waiting. He could imagine them wondering what this ramshackle boat and its long-dead crew would reveal.

Not as much as I am though, thought Jack as he brought his own launch alongside.

*   *   *

By the time Jack had moored, the tug was already easing in its charge as a belch of exhaust smoke and burst of power from the hired crane showed it ready for the lift. As the derelict was brought alongside, yard-hands took its lines, the crane boom swung over and two canvas strops were passed under the old hull. More power then as the crane took up the strain and, by the time Jack made his way along the quay, a foot more freeboard was showing between the old cruiser's gunwale and waterline.

'A sorry sight you've brought us there,' said Stuart, as Jack paused beside the crane.

'Yes, and perhaps with an even sorrier story behind it.'

'What sort of story?' It was the stranger standing just apart from Stuart, in his early sixties, clean-shaven and with a far-from happy expression. 'And how long is that thing going to be in my yard?'

'Ah, you must be *Watercraft*'s owner,' said Jack holding out his hand. 'I'm Jack Fellows.'

'Turnberry ...' he didn't offer a hand in return, but only a scowl, '... and you still haven't answered my question.'

'That's because the police aren't sure yet how long the investigation will take.'

'Well, the shorter the better, because crime scenes aren't going to help our business here.'

'Who said it was a crime investigation, Mr Turnberry?'

'I just ... assumed ... with all this police presence.'

'Fair enough, and I do realise using your yard isn't ideal,' sympathised Jack, 'but the police will be paying you for the storage and if you can give us a corner of the yard away from public eyes, I'm sure we'll be able to keep things discreet.'

By now the crane had lifted the cruiser out completely, water pouring from several open seams in the lower hull thick with black slime and fresh-water mussels. The yard-owner turned to his manager and nodded to a large shed standing at the far end of the yard. 'Get them to hide it behind there.' Then he stomped off, obviously far from happy at the prospect of this decrepit boat being craned into his yard.

Steadmore turned back to Jack. 'Sorry about that, but he's just worried about how it might hurt our trade.' He nodded towards the main shed. 'It'll be well out of sight behind there, but I can't guarantee our customers won't go nosing, especially when word gets out.'

'Don't worry, Stuart, there'll be a uniformed officer on duty making sure they don't,' assured Jack. 'Hopefully that'll keep your boss happy.'

'If anything can,' said the young manager with a shrug. 'Thankfully, he'll be returning to London later today. He's not here very often, which suits us all just fine.'

'Pain in the neck then, is he?' said Jack. 'You say he bought the yard about thirty years ago?'

'Yeah, I think so, but that was long before I came here – in fact, just before I was born.'

'In that case, you probably don't know who the previous owners were?'

'No idea,' replied Steadmore, 'and I don't even think Mr Turnberry knows. I asked him once and he explained he'd bought the place through London solicitors acting on the owner's behalf.' He shrugged. 'It's not something that ever came up again.'

'Hmm, that's strange.' Jack nodded towards the line of dayboats moored up to the quay. 'Certainly, the yard changed hands long before Audrey and I moved down here from London, but I do recall hearing mention that it was originally *Cecilian Cruisers*.'

'Yep, but some of the old hands told me that Turnberry got rid of the fleet soon after taking on the yard.' Stuart shrugged. 'Seems he could see that cruiser hire in small yards had had its day and that it would take too much investment to expand and compete. So he changed the name to *Watercraft*, rented out the moorings and just concentrated on hiring out day-boats and canoes.'

'So, what happened to the old cruisers he no longer wanted?'

'Sold off to private owners, apparently, which worked out well because most of them stayed here, so the yard still got income from their mooring fees and maintenance.'

'Something a lot of Broadland yards did back then,' said Jack, pausing to watch the crane trundle the derelict further into the yard, men holding its lines to prevent swing and sway. 'Do you know if *Cecilian*'s cruisers were wooden, Stuart?'

'Yes, most of them, and lovely boats they were, judging by old photos. You still see some restored and cruising the Broads to this day.' The young manager nodded towards the old boat now being cautiously eased into its new resting place. 'But I'm pretty sure that old wreck wasn't one of them.'

Jack shrugged. 'Just a thought, but that boat came from some place and our next job will be to find out just where.'

'Good luck on that,' wished Steadmore as the derelict was swung into the space behind the shed where the crane then gently lowered it down onto supporting blocks. 'Let me go and check that it's all secure, Jack.' He gave a half-humorous grin. 'I'd hate it to get damaged.'

Jack smiled at his irony. 'I'll come with you for a closer look myself.'

While young Steadmore checked all was secure, Jack examined the boat's bow and stern, hoping to discover some form of identifying marks but, in the event, finding none.

'Name and numbers all seem to have disappeared along with most of the paintwork.'

'Only to be expected after all that time half-submerged, Jack.'

'I guess so, Stuart, but, one way or another, we'll eventually get this old boat to give up its secrets ... and here's a team well-equipped to do just that,' he added as a police mini-bus entered the yard and parked nearby.

Even as its occupants climbed out to don white hooded coveralls, another car arrived bringing DI Bailey. He straightway joined Jack. 'Right, here she is then. If these SOCO boys can't get us a few clues, no-one will.'

'Any forensics will help,' acknowledged Jack, 'but I'm hoping I'll soon get a lead of my own as to the boat's identity. When we know that, you'll at least have a time frame on which to base your investigation.'

Bailey nodded. 'Agreed Jack, but any thoughts on how you'll do that?'

'Mainly by using chaps hereabouts who know the Broads and its boating history. Some of them have an encyclopaedic knowledge of every boat that ever floated here, so I aim to tap into their resources and come up with something soon.' Jack shook the DI's hand. 'In the meantime, good luck with your side, Bailey, and I'll appreciate any updates in developments.'

'And you likewise,' said the DI before going off to talk to his SOCO team.

*   *   *

Jack was just about to make his way back to the launch when the *Skyrides* Land Rover came swinging into the yard and parked close by. Kathy and a young woman he didn't recognise, climbed out and, after a brief curious glance towards all the police activity around the wrecked cruiser, made their way into the shed.

Assuming Kathy had come to check her balloon and as the main door of the shed had been left half-open, Jack walked inside to join them without knocking.

'Ah, so this is where you keep it,' he said by way of announcing his arrival.

There was enough natural light inside the shed for him to see it was half-filled by the *Skyrides* recovery trailer with the whole balloon rig still stashed on board, but with the tarpaulin cover part-removed from the basket and burner. The two young women were examining these closely, the stranger intent on writing in a notebook. Both swung around in surprise at Jack's unexpected entry.

'Oh, hello, Jack.' Kathy stood up and beamed a smile of welcome. 'What brings you here ... or need I ask,' she quipped before nodding to the side of the shed, beyond which the unseen derelict was now lying, 'seeing as you seem to have discovered your own *Mary Rose* out there?'

'If only it were that innocent, Kathy. The *Mary Celeste* would be more like it.'

'Yes, we couldn't help noticing lots of police. Nothing too sinister, I hope.'

'Actually, I spotted that boat during our balloon trip last Saturday,' explained Jack by way of avoiding a direct answer. 'It was half-sunk in the reed-bed just off the main broad. Have you ever noticed it yourself when you've flown over?'

51

Kathy shook her head. 'Can't say I have but, of course, we're usually on a different flight-path each trip.'

'But you did say you'd landed at Wildmarsh Farm before,' pointed out Jack, 'so, presumably, that wasn't the first time you'd crossed the broad.'

'No, but usually by that stage I'm too intent on looking ahead for a good landing area to give anything other than a cursory scan of the scene below.'

'Of course.' Jack pointed to the balloon. 'Giving her a check over?'

'Not really, just doing a bit of business with Phillipa.' She glanced towards the other young woman standing silently by and realised that she'd made no introductions. 'Oh, sorry both of you ... Jack, this is Phillipa Keyworth ... Phillipa, Jack Fellows.'

'Good to meet you, Phillipa,' said Jack, shaking the hand of this young woman who was, perhaps, slightly older than Kathy. 'Are you booking a flight?'

'Not for myself,' she said with a grin, 'but I'm here today to do some preliminaries for a special balloon flight Kathy hopes to make later this summer.'

'Ah yes, the John Money epic flight re-enactment.' Jack turned back to Kathy. 'I heard you telling Hans van Heiden about it last Saturday.'

'Oh right.' Kathy recollected the conversation and smiled. 'Well, Phillipa got to hear of it too, called me this morning to see if she could help in any way, and here we are.'

'Are you a balloonist yourself then, Phillipa?'

'No, but they do fascinate me and I *am* an events-organiser, so I thought perhaps Kathy might need a bit of expertise on that front.'

'Too true I do,' agreed *Skyrides'* owner. 'So Phillipa is going to start sorting the pre-event publicity. We just popped in today for her to have a look at the basket and check how that compares with the one dear John Money would have had.'

'And how does it?'

'Not much difference, actually. Back then it would have been the same old wicker job we still use today, though mine is reinforced with alloy tubing.' She nodded towards the folded fabric of the balloon itself. 'Of course, that's modern Dacron instead of the silk Money's would have been made from, and lifted by hot air instead of the gas he used.'

'It'll still look pretty authentic to me,' assured Jack, 'and the added attraction is that you'll also be raising funds for the same cause John Money supported all those years ago.'

'Yes, and that's where I come in,' said Phillipa. 'It's going to attract a lot of public interest when Kathy lifts off from the hospital grounds during their annual fete, especially if I manage to drum up some good media publicity.' She shrugged. 'I've already been in touch with a number of TV contacts and they're well up for giving us plenty of coverage. The only problem is that they also want to be there for the landing ...'

'... which is something you can never predict with balloons,' added Kathy.

'As poor old Money found out the hard way,' said Jack, smiling. 'So, let's hope the winds are more favourable on your day.'

'Absolutely, because I certainly don't intend to re-enact *that* ...' Kathy held up crossed fingers, '... but there are other logistical issues I need to sort, seeing as the hospital executive is naturally anxious that we plan it meticulously and have every safeguard in place before we go launching from their site.'

'Which means even more paperwork to sort out and funds needed,' said Phillipa.

Jack smiled sympathetically. 'It seems that money is what this is all about in more ways than one.'

'What's all this about "money"?' It was Alec Turnberry, suddenly appearing in the shed doorway and taking off his sunglasses. He turned to Kathy. 'I saw your Land Rover and guessed you must be in here checking your flying machine.' Sidling up to her, he put his arm around her shoulders. 'And how is my favourite aeronaut?'

'Trying to work out how to raise money for a good cause ...' Kathy gave a little twist to shrug off Turnberry's clearly-unwelcome arm, '... so, if you really want to help, a donation would be nice.'

'You're joking,' scoffed Turnberry, sliding his evicted arm down to Kathy's waist. 'What with a full-blown police enquiry going on in the yard and the public wondering what other horrors we've got tucked away here ...' he paused to give Jack a meaningful look, '... I'll be lucky to stay in business at all. And anyway, I don't believe in giving money to worthless bloody charities. Never have, so don't intend to start now.'

'No charity is worthless, Mr Turnberry.' Phillipa Keyworth was making no effort to disguise her dislike of these abhorrent sentiments and the man who had made them. 'I just hope you don't need some charity yourself one day.'

The yard-owner gave a dismissive snort. 'Yeah, well charity begins at home.' He turned to Kathy. 'Like the way I let you use my shed.'

'For which I pay,' reminded Kathy, 'but for which I'm still very grateful.'

'And so you should be.' Turnberry gave Kathy's waist a squeeze.

Unfortunately for the yard-owner, Stuart Steadmore chose this very moment to walk into the shed. It at least prompted Turnberry to immediately let go of his hold on Kathy and turn his frown on his manager. 'What do you want?'

Steadmore paused, fixing his employer with a contemptuous glare. 'Just checking how you want me to invoice for the boat storage.'

'How would I know? Go and check with the police.' He turned to Jack. 'What's the most we can claim for putting up with that heap of wreckage?'

'Your standard boat-storage rate for the yard would seem the fairest, Mr Turnberry.' Jack was also finding this man's charms very easy to resist.

'What, with all the harm this must be doing to my trade?' He came closer to Jack and held a warning finger in his face. 'So be prepared to get a hefty bill, and don't be too long in paying it.'

Jack took the finger and slowly moved it away from his face. 'That's something between you and the police, Turnberry, so I suggest you do the civil thing and introduce yourself to DI Bailey.'

But Alec Turnberry shook his head. 'No way. I employ a manager to deal with the running of the yard.'

'Have it your own way,' grunted Jack before turning back to young Steadmore. 'Go and have a chat with DI Bailey, Stuart. He'll give you the address to send the bill.'

'Thanks, Jack,' said Steadmore with a smile to the ranger and a threatening glance to his boss before leaving the shed with clenched fists.

'And I need to be on my way as well.' Jack turned to the two young women. 'Nice to meet you, Phillipa, and good luck with your fund-raising.' Then, completely ignoring Turnberry, he walked out of the shed and within ten minutes was back afloat in his launch, heading downriver and already tapping a well-used number into his mobile.

*   *   *

Also using her mobile, was Phillipa Keyworth.

After Jack's departure, she'd made up an excuse to leave the shed herself, found a quiet spot well away from all other activity and called a familiar number of her own. It was answered immediately and after the briefest of exchanges she got straightway to business.

'Hi, I'm at the boatyard with Kathy and I'm calling to tell you this place

54

is a hive of police activity ... no, I'm not entirely sure why, but it's something to do with an old boat they've found somewhere downriver.' With the person on the other end clearly less than happy with this situation, Phillipa hastened to reassure. 'Don't worry, it's got nothing to do with us except it'll complicate things a bit. Anyway, I think Kathy trusts me, so I'll report back as soon as I have something more to tell. But just stay away from this yard if you don't want to be answering awkward questions.'

After assurances to meet up soon, she clicked off and went to rejoin Kathy in the shed.

*　　*　　*

'Ted ... Jack Fellows.'

'Jack ... and what can I do for you?' Ted Finchley had spent a lifetime building wooden boats, and these beautiful creations of oak and cedar remained his great love. Now retired from full-time employment, he spent three days a week volunteering at the Museum of the Broads where his exhaustive knowledge of Broadland boats and their histories were a constant asset.

'This mystery boat we found at the weekend, Ted ... have you heard about it?'

'I heard rumours, Jack. Any clues yet as to its identity?'

'No, and that's what I'm hoping you can help me with. For starters, have you any recollection of a boat going missing two or three decades ago.'

'Nothing I can recall.' Even over the rumble of his engine, Jack could almost hear Ted's brain ticking over. 'Surely there's still some clue on it somewhere, Jack ... a name or number on the hull at least?'

'None that I could see. But it is a wooden boat that's been submerged to almost deck-level for probably decades, so it's lost most of its paint and varnish, along with any name or number it might have had.' Jack paused. 'The thing is, Ted, I'm sure you, with all your knowledge of old wooden boats, might even recognise it or, failing that, come up with something that would give us a clue as to its identity or the fleet it might once have belonged to.'

'I could try, Jack, but, of course, I'd need to see the boat itself, inside and out.'

'Which will be a problem until the forensic boys have done their stuff,' explained Jack. 'What I will do though is email you a photo and see if that rings any bells.'

'Sure, send it straight to me and I'll do what I can. And then let me know when it's ok to see it. I'm working at the museum for the next few days, but I'll be able to nip off to *Watercraft* once you give me the nod.'

'Thanks, Ted, and perhaps, by then, I might have a bit of extra info myself, because my next job is to talk to someone about Perkins engines.'

*   *   *

'Right, here's your whisky and ginger,' said Audrey, putting down the tumbler next to her own as, late that same day, she and Jack settled down in the conservatory with Spike to enjoy the last of the afternoon sun. 'So, how is solving the great boat mystery progressing?'

'Okay as regards getting it ashore, but no luck identifying it yet,' admitted Jack, picking up his drink and giving Spike a loving scratch on the head. 'I've just emailed a photo of the wreck to Ted Finchley in the hope he might find a match in his photo archive of cruisers past and present.'

'And if he doesn't?'

'Then I'll get clearance from Bailey for him to go through the boat with a fine-toothed comb in the hope he'll find a clue the rest of us have missed.'

'Didn't you say you thought the engine might throw some light on its identity?'

'That *was* my hope, Aud, and I did ring the local agents for Perkins engines on the off-chance they could match that serial number to a name.'

'And ...'

'And they said they'd look into it. The trouble is their records only go back five years. Old invoices might just bring up the number if they supplied the engine, but that would entail more man-hours than we could expect them to give at this stage. They did promise to check with Perkins, though, and perhaps get them to have a quick scan of their own files. But, in reality, I'm not holding out for much success on the engine front.'

'Oh dear, probably another dead end then. But you say you met the owner of *Watercraft* when the boat was being craned out. What was *he* like?'

'Alec Turnberry ...' Jack wrinkled his nose, '... I can't say I took to the man.'

'Why's that?'

'Just that he seems a surly blighter, and something of a letch too, seeing the way he couldn't keep his hands off poor Kathy when I was there. He only dropped them when young Steadmore walked in.'

56

'That must have been a bit tense if Stuart noticed.'

'He certainly had the measure of the man and I think it would have been more than tense if I hadn't been there. Otherwise I think Stuart would've decked him one.'

'Which would have lost him his job as well as his girl.'

'Too true,' agreed Jack, taking a sip of his whisky. 'Seeing the way his fists were clenching, I got the feeling our Stuart might have more temper than is good for him.'

'Then thank goodness his boss shows up so rarely. Did you say Turnberry lives in London?'

'That's right, and Stuart made it quite clear that's where he prefers him to be. And I can't blame him, because there's just something about Turnberry that gets my back itching. Apart from his obnoxious and belligerent nature, I did notice one thing that seemed a bit strange.'

'What?'

'Oh, just the smallest of details that just didn't quite ring true.' Jack shook his head and gave Spike another stroke. 'Probably nothing, but what *is* strange to me is why the man owns a boat business like *Watercraft* when his heart's obviously not in it.'

'You did say he bought it about thirty years ago, Jack. Perhaps his interest has just dwindled after all that time.'

'Yeah, but my experience of men tells me he's something of a bad lot anyway and someone the previous owners of *Cecilian Cruisers* would've been reluctant to sell to if they'd met him face-to-face.'

Audrey looked puzzled. 'So, didn't they?'

'No. According to Stuart, all the legal side of the transaction was done purely through London solicitors.'

'Is that normal?'

'Not generally, but not impossible. I thought at first it was the sellers wanting to stay anonymous, but now I'm not sure. Anyway, it's curious enough for me to want to find out more about the whole deal, so I might just have a word with my old chums in the Met and see what they can dig up.'

Audrey sighed. 'Oh, Jack, don't you have enough on right now with this mystery cruiser business?'

'Probably, but something in my water tells me this could somehow be connected.'

'How?'

'Ah, that's what I need to find out, Aud, and, hopefully, a bit of searching on the internet might drum up something.'

'Well, supper won't be for half an hour yet, love, so you can get started now if you want to.'

Jack knocked back the rest of his whisky and was about to follow his wife's advice when the telephone rang.

*　　*　　*

'Hi Jack ...Bailey ... just calling to update you on progress.'

'Thanks, mate, I appreciate you keeping me in the loop. So, what's happening?'

'Well, the SOCO team gave the whole boat their full treatment before the coroner's men finally came and took the remains back to the lab.'

'Not the nicest of jobs,' said Jack, remembering his own days in Thames Division and the many grim scenes he'd witnessed there.

'Ah well, it's what they're paid for,' said the DI, whose increasing years of service had given him a more jaundiced view of procedures. 'Anyway, an hour ago I got the preliminary report from the pathologist.'

'Good. So, what's the verdict?'

'That they're the remains of a male in his late thirties and a female possibly two years younger.'

'A couple then, but not in the first flush of youth?'

'That's right, but of average height with no distinguishing abnormalities other than their cause of death.'

'Which is ...?'

'What we first suspected. In each case, a twenty-two calibre bullet straight into the skull.'

'Any exit wounds?'

'No, the bullets were still lodged in the brain of each victim.'

'Not unusual for small calibre shootings, even at close range, but how about the weapon?'

'The CSI team didn't find one, which at least confirms it wasn't suicide.'

'... but cold-blooded murder.' Jack gave a little sigh. 'How about any clue to their ID though?'

'Nothing as yet. No record of any such couple reported missing in that time frame and the pathologist reckons the only way we'll get DNA is the mitochondrial route.'

'Which isn't going to happen tomorrow.'

'Nope ... more like a week, and even then it won't be much use unless we have a potential match.'

'That's going to hold things up then. You still happy for me to see what I can come up with in the meantime?'

'Absolutely. You'll probably have more luck than us with your knowledge of Broadland and all your dealings with the boating fraternity.'

'I'll do what I can, Bailey. Actually, I'm already following up a couple of lines of enquiry in the hope of identifying the boat.'

'Why doesn't that surprise me? Any luck so far?'

'Not yet, and it might need another good going-over by a boat expert. Will that be okay now the SOCO team have done their stuff?'

'I don't see why not. It's still a crime-scene, of course, but let me know when you want to go ahead, and I'll warn the security lads.'

'Will do, Bailey, and thanks. Good night.'

As Jack rang off and went back to pour another whisky, he knew he was committed now to bringing this investigation to a successful conclusion and deliver the peace and justice an unknown man and woman deserved.

Chapter Six

'Well, love, it seems you've got a day to yourself after all.' Audrey placed a rack of toast on the kitchen table and sighed. 'I must say, it does seem very quiet without the family about, so any plans?'

'Actually, I have.' Jack helped himself to a slice and got buttering. 'Knowing you'd be feeling a bit lost, I thought we might enjoy a nice little ride out together.'

'Sound's lovely. Where to?'

'Wildmarsh Farm.'

'The place we landed in the balloon on Saturday?' Audrey sat down, poured herself a coffee and leant across the table. 'I presume this has to be something to do with your latest investigation, Jack, but what on earth do you think you'll find there to help?'

'Probably nothing, but I won't know until it's checked out.'

'But surely an abandoned farm can't have anything to do with an abandoned boat, can it?'

'Well, there's the clue for a start, Aud ... they're both abandoned. And I'm still curious as to why that chap Hans van Heiden was hanging around the place,' continued Jack, reaching for the marmalade, 'because I'd stake my pension that his story about following the balloon on his bike, was a load of old poppycock.'

'But, love, even if the place is no longer in use, surely *someone* still owns it, which means we can't just trespass on private land.'

'Why not? If there's no-one there, who's going to challenge us?'

'But if there is?'

'We'll just have to plead innocent nosiness, but at least we might get to find out who it *does* belong to.'

'Oh well, I suppose it would be quiet here in the house on my own so I may as well come along,' conceded Audrey, 'and Spike will enjoy a run in the countryside.' She gulped down her coffee and sighed. 'Okay, Jack, finish your breakfast while I get changed and then let's see where this next crazy journey takes us.'

*   *   *

Certainly, the appalling state of the track leading to Wildmarsh Farm was doing nothing to ease the apprehension Audrey was feeling as they lurched slowly towards the distant house and barn.

'Hard to think of anyone still owning this. It's so isolated and desolate,' she muttered, gripping the handhold as Jack eased them around yet another deep rut.

On either side the fields still showed some signs of cultivation but, though the main road was just behind them and familiar local landmarks lay just a few miles distant, the strange stillness of the place, coupled with the ominous squawk of rooks in the surrounding trees, produced an unsettling, even sinister, atmosphere of neglect.

'You're right there,' agreed Jack as he finally brought them to a halt on the overgrown, potholed driveway in front of the house and paused to scan the surrounding dereliction. 'It's certainly easy to imagine dark deeds happening here.'

Deriving little encouragement from Jack's words, Audrey climbed out of the car, clipped on Spike's lead and joined her husband in studying the old farmhouse.

It stood there, ramshackle and dilapidated, as though itself mourning happier times. Now, with missing roof-tiles, rotting window frames devoid of paint, and the front door in a state of collapse, Audrey could see it was many years since it had been lived in. Two pigeons suddenly flapping their noisy way out of a gaping hole in the gables caused her to jump and Spike's hackles to rise.

'At least there's some life left in the old place,' joked Jack as his alarmed wife took a firm grip of his arm.

'Yes, but what a shame it's been allowed to get into this state,' said Audrey, pulling herself together and her fleece a little closer around her. 'This must have been a lovely house once.'

'Very much so, and I'd like to know *why* it's been allowed to get like this.' Jack took his wife's hand and squeezed it reassuringly. 'Nothing to be afraid of, so let's take a closer look at the barn.'

As they made their way around the house and across a farmyard strewn with piles of rubbish and the rusting remains of abandoned machinery, Spike was pulling at his lead, happy to be sniffing out unfamiliar smells. However, it wasn't until they had worked their way around to the other side of the barn that they realised they were not alone. For there, standing in stark contrast to all the dilapidation around it, was an open-topped sports car, while from inside the barn itself came the sound of light hammering on wood. Audrey's grip on her husband's hand tightened as she whispered, 'Jack, we shouldn't be here ... come on, let's go now before we're seen.'

'What, and miss this chance of finding out what's going on? No way. Come on, but keep Spike on a short lead.'

Without further ado, Audrey felt herself being led through a leaning wooden access door and into the dark and gloomy interior of a building, its earthen floor strewn with the remains of rotting plant-life and rat infestation. What she wasn't expecting was the sole occupant to be a slim young woman in wax jacket and smart jeans, tapping the sides of the barn with a small hammer.

Audrey's first reaction was that this female was legitimately carrying out some sort of structural survey on the old building. Heaven knows, it needed it, she thought. But then that assumption was just as quickly dispelled as, on hearing the Fellows' footfall, the woman sprang around, her reactions so guilty that she dropped the hammer while her face went visibly white with shock. It was, however, a face that Jack immediately recognised.

'Hello, Phillipa. What brings you here?'

She breathed a sigh of relief. 'Oh my goodness, Jack, you scared me stiff.'

'So I can see, and sorry for that.' Jack turned back to his wife. 'Audrey, this is Phillipa Keyworth who's looking after publicity for Kathy's balloon re-enactment.'

'Oh right ...' Audrey smiled and offered her hand, '... Jack told me all about your project.'

'It's Kathy's project really,' said Phillipa, taking Audrey's hand, but still deep-breathing as she got her emotions back under control. 'I'm handling the publicity while encouraging some big businesses to get out their wallets.' She seemed to suddenly realise that she hadn't actually answered Jack's initial question. 'Oh, yes ... why am I here?' She knelt down to give Spike a fuss, but possibly herself time to collect her thoughts. 'Well, you remember me explaining how the media were keen to be at the actual balloon landing site ... so I thought I'd check out this farm as a possibility, seeing as this is where you landed on *your* flight.'

'And your conclusion ...?'

'It could be ideal.'

'Assuming the balloon ever actually gets here,' said a puzzled Jack. 'Surely, as Kathy said, the landing spot will depend on the wind on the day.'

'Generally speaking, yes,' acknowledged Phillipa, 'but the prevailing wind in this country is south-west and the balloon pilot does have some control on direction by varying the height ...'

'... because the wind veers and strengthens with altitude,' added Jack.

'Exactly. And this place would be perfect for the media crews ... plenty of parking and somewhere in the dry if the day's iffy.'

'As long as they can take the stink of decaying farm rubbish,' replied Jack, wrinkling his nose. He nodded to the hammer lying on the earthen floor. 'So, what's with the poking around?'

'Oh, this?' She picked up the tool with an unconvincing expression of nonchalance. 'Just checking for any power cables that the TV teams could plug into.'

'This place doesn't look like it's been touched by too much technology to me, but surely the best way to get all the info you need would be to talk to the owner.' Jack gave a questioning frown. 'You don't happen to know who that is, by any chance?'

'Sorry, not a clue. I just assumed Kathy knew, seeing as she often lands here.' Phillipa took a quick glance at her watch. 'Oh gosh ... running late ... must go.'

'Yes, and we need to get moving ourselves.'

As they all walked outside, Phillipa paused by her car. 'Good to see you again, Jack...' she shook the ranger's hand with a slightly dubious look of her own, '... for whatever reason *you* are here.'

'Oh, just a bit of nostalgia to remind us of Saturday's exciting trip and to give Spike a walk.'

'Yes, that must have been thrilling.' She jumped into her car and started up. 'Good to meet you too, Audrey, and you, Spike. Hopefully I'll see you all again very soon.'

'Quite a dynamic young woman, but she'd be better driving a four-by-four,' observed Audrey as they watched Phillipa Keyworth weaving her way speedily down the Wildmarsh farm-track while attempting to avoid the worst of the ruts, dirt and loose stones. She turned back to Jack. 'So, has our visit here made anything any clearer for you?'

'Not really,' admitted Jack. 'If anything, it's made everything just that much more mystifying ... but it has at least confirmed that something's going on here, and probably far more significant than I'd previously imagined.'

*   *   *

'I don't know about your suspicions, Jack, but Phillipa Keyworth seemed a very pleasant young woman to me. And she's obviously very keen to ensure that all goes well for Kathy's re-enactment.'

'What, you mean you believed all that baloney about checking out Wildmarsh Farm for the media?' Back on the main road, Jack shook his head in disbelief, never quite able to decide whether he found his wife's naivety frustrating or endearing. 'A total load of rubbish, if I ever heard it.'

'Really? Why do you think that?'

'For the simple reason that she knows as well as I do that there would be no way you could predict where a balloon will land with that much certainty. And I can't think of a less-enticing place to host the media than in that run-down farm and its filthy, smelly barn.' Jack shook his head again. 'Believe me, I know human nature well enough to be certain Ms Keyworth was thinking on her feet to hide the *real* reason she was there.'

'Which was ...?'

'Ah, that I'd dearly like to know ... and which I aim to find out.'

'So you think all that tapping the wood was for some other reason?'

'Of course it was. Whoever heard of searching for electrics with a hammer? You know I don't believe in coincidences, Aud, and I reckon that both she and Van Heiden were snooping about there at different times for the same reason.'

'And that is ...?'

'The reason anyone goes furtively poking around someone else's property ... to look for something hidden there.' Jack banged the steering wheel. 'I'd love to know what, but one thing I'm sure of is that the answer to all this lies back there at that run-down farm.' He turned to Audrey. 'Didn't Kathy mention that it used to be an RAF airstrip?'

'Yes, during the war, apparently.'

'Well, I know someone who can probably confirm all that and perhaps give me a lead to what's transpired since. I'll give him a call tonight.'

'But surely whatever this strange business is, it can't be connected to the abandoned boat you found.'

'Difficult to see how, I grant you,' admitted Jack as he swung left off the main road back towards the waterways. 'We do seem to have found ourselves two different mysteries to solve here, but my instinct still tells me they might yet come together as one. Anyway, we're close by so let's call in at *Watercraft* and see how that end of the investigation's going.'

'I'll leave you to your enquiries then, Jack, while I take Spike to feed these to the ducks,' said Audrey, exiting the car clutching some slightly-mouldy grapes from the picnic they had never touched.

'Fine.' Jack left wife and Border Collie by the quay and made his way to the yard office where he found Stuart Steadmore on the phone.

'Right, boss, if that's how you feel, I'll make sure she never does. No, I've got your message loud and clear. Okay. Goodbye.' He slammed down the phone. 'What's got his back up now, I wonder?'

'More problems, Stuart?'

Steadmore shrugged. 'That was my bloody boss with another sudden bee in his bonnet. Apparently, he's somehow heard I arranged Tracy's photo shoot with the balloon. It's got damn-all to do with him, but he seems to think I have plans to invite her here next to pose on one of our dayboats.'

'And do you plan to?'

'Not at all, so I don't know where he got that idea. Mind you, now he's put the thought into my head, it would be good publicity for *Water-craft.*' Steadmore mulled over the possibility, but then shook his head and shrugged. 'Not that Tracy would be up for the idea anyway. A tatty old yard like this wouldn't be glamorous enough for her these days, so he doesn't need to worry.'

'Why would he anyway, Stuart?'

'Oh, according to him, he doesn't want to see Broadland tainted by an influx of brash celebrities and the popular press. He got quite snarky about it.'

'Hmm, he doesn't seem the type to worry unduly about that sort of thing,' mused Jack, 'but he may have a point, and anyway ...' he nodded outside to where another car had just driven into the yard, '... you seem to have got enough publicity and a steady flow of customers queuing for boats.'

The yard manager raised his brows. 'Yeah, it's been non-stop bookings since word of the mystery boat got out on last-night's local TV news.'

'I can imagine. A bit of mystery and intrigue is always guaranteed to trigger public interest.'

Steadmore frowned. 'More like morbid curiosity if you ask me, Jack. They can't actually see a lot behind all the police barriers, but loads of them seem satisfied simply hanging around the yard taking selfies while others just want a dayboat to see where the abandoned cruiser was hidden.'

'Ah well, it's an ill wind … and all that,' said Jack while, at the same time, sensing that even an increased trade hadn't lightened the mood of the yard's young manager. 'How about Kathy, though? Any luck with bridge-building between you two?'

Steadmore looked crestfallen and shook his head. 'Not so far, Jack. She was here yesterday, as you know, but too busy with that event-organiser woman to even say "hello".'

'Don't give up, though,' encouraged Jack. 'Give it time. She and Phillipa seem to have a lot on their plate at the moment.'

'You mean that crazy re-enactment idea of Kathy's,' responded Stuart. 'Raising money for the Norfolk and Norwich Hospital was a great idea of hers, but it's Phillipa Keyworth who's taken over publicity.'

'How did those two get to know each other in the first place?'

'They didn't, as far as I know. From what I gather, Phillipa just got wind of the project and contacted Kathy to offer her PR services for free. Kathy jumped at the idea of having someone else handling promotion because that isn't her scene at all.'

'Surely good news all round then?'

'I suppose,' conceded Steadmore, 'and I just wish Phillipa was the *only* new person in Kathy's life. But she seems infatuated with this Dutchman now as well, and he's way too old for her.'

'He'll be going back to Holland soon though Stuart,' reassured Jack, 'so hopefully that little romance will only be short-lived.'

'Let's hope so, but what worries me, Jack, is that if Kathy's unattached again, Turnberry may try his luck, thinking she likes older men.'

'Yes, I saw the way he behaved the other day,' sympathised Jack. 'Not nice, but I can assure you Kathy was having none of it. How long has he acted like that?'

'Ever since Kathy first came here looking for storage. I'm sure the only reason he let her rent the shed so cheaply was because he fancied her. The only saving grace is that he's hardly ever here.'

Jack nodded. 'Thinking of that, Stuart, what does he actually do when he *is* here?'

'Nothing much,' shrugged Steadmore. 'Just keeps his head down and mooches around the place picking fault with everything.'

'So, he doesn't help with the maintenance … working on the boat's engines or the like?'

'Good Lord no! Turnberry's not the sort to ever get his hands dirty.' It was Steadmore's turn to give the ranger a perplexed frown. 'Why do you ask anyway, Jack?'

'Oh, nothing really,' hedged Jack. 'Just a very small point I was trying to make sense of.'

'Yeah, well I'm not saying he wouldn't get his hands dirty in other ways,' said Steadmore with a knowing look. 'Between you and me, I reckon he's a bit dodgy and the only reason I've stuck it this long is to watch out for Kathy ... though a fat lot of good that did me in the end.'

'I wouldn't worry too much about her and Van Heiden,' said Jack. 'I'm sure it's just her way of getting back at you over Tracy.'

'She's got nothing to "get back" about, Jack, and nothing to worry about on that score. It's me that has to worry about her and Van Whatishisname.' He gave a heartfelt groan and clenched his fists. 'I tell you, Jack, he might only be here for a few days, but he's another man I'm not sure of.'

'You could be right, but try not to worry. And anyway, Stuart ...' Jack glanced outside to where another party of hopeful boaters were heading for the office, '... I can see you've got your hands full here right now, so I'll leave you to it and go and see how things are progressing behind the shed.'

'Not a lot going on there, actually,' said Steadmore, heading out of the door to meet his latest customers. 'All the forensic people have gone and there's just a security bloke left in charge.'

'Right, I'll not bother now then.'

Jack left and found Spike asleep in the shade and Audrey sitting on a tree stump enjoying watching a moorhen, cute with its yellow-tipped red beak and pale green legs, running over the rough grass looking for food.

'Nothing for me here, Aud, so let's head home for a welcome cuppa.'

As they walked to the car, Audrey could tell something was still niggling Jack and wasn't at all surprised when he handed her the keys and said, 'Here, you get Spike settled in the car while I just pop back to ask Stuart a quick question.'

When he returned, a matter of minutes later, she knew better than to enquire as to what that question had been, but instead asked how Stuart was.

'Despite booming business, pretty down, actually. Turnberry's obviously giving him a hard time and he's still very cut up at the thought of Kathy involved with Van Heiden.'

'Poor chap. But what about Tracy Goldman? She was making eyes at him, wasn't she, so why doesn't he ask her out and just move on?'

'Because he probably realises that she's way out of his league now and, anyway, it's Kathy he loves. What worries me is that he does have a bit of a temper which, coupled with jealousy, might drive him to do something he'll later regret.'

'What a mess all this is,' sighed Audrey as Jack backed the car and slowly drove out of the yard. 'And now you also have Phillipa Keyworth's unexpected appearance and suspicious behaviour at Wildmarsh Farm to think about. How do you plan to sort that one out?'

'For starters, by making another phone call just as soon as we get home.'

'Who to now?'

'Charlie Hedborough.'

Audrey vaguely recognised the name, but decided not to even ask for clarification. As they turned on to the main road and headed for home, her thoughts now were more on that promised cup of tea.

*   *   *

'Charlie ... Jack Fellows.' Back home, and while Audrey brewed tea, Jack had taken the opportunity to make his call.

Charlie Hedborough was an old acquaintance, now a retired local government officer who, back in his National Service days, had flown early jets in the RAF. He made no secret of the fact that those few years were the highlight of his life and now kept the memories alive and his own brain active by researching and writing the history of local wartime airfields.

'Jack ... good to hear from you.'

'Sorry it's been so long, Charlie, but I'm hoping you can help me with a bit of aeronautical gen.'

'If I can, but aviation's changed a lot since my day, Jack, so don't expect too much.'

'I won't, Charlie, because what I need is right in your area of expertise ... a local airfield.'

'Ah, now you're talking. Which one?'

'Wildmarsh Farm.'

'Wildmarsh ... crikey now you are delving into obscure areas, Jack. Wildmarsh was never an air*field* as such ... just an air*strip* that operated as a satellite to the main station at Ludham.'

'Okay, but for what purpose?'

'A very special one, from what I gather, but one still cloaked in a certain amount of secrecy.'

'I'm intrigued already, Charlie. Go on,'

'Well, the farm itself was commandeered by the government midway through the war. For what reason, they never disclosed, and I can under-stand why if all the local rumours were halfway true.'

68

'Which were?' asked an increasingly fascinated Jack.

'Ah, now you're really getting into shady business.' The old pilot paused. 'Look, why don't we meet up in a few days and have a chat about it. That'll give me some time to dig into more detail with a local old boy I know who grew up around the place at that time.'

'Sounds good, Charlie, but while you're talking to this local source, can you ask him if he knew of any particularly significant happening at Wildmarsh back then.'

'In what way?'

'I don't really know ... just some odd occurrence that could be the basis of an investigation.'

'Investigating what?'

'I'll explain that when we meet.'

'Fair enough, Jack. In the meantime, I'll get delving into all I can find at my end. As soon as I have something for you, I'll call to arrange an r/v for the debrief.'

'Thanks, Charlie, I really appreciate it,' said Jack while giving an inward chuckle at the ex-servicemen's love of the old vernacular. 'I'll look forward to your call and we'll make the rendezvous somewhere I can buy you a drink for your trouble.'

*　　　*　　　*

Back in the kitchen, Audrey listened to this latest development with limited enthusiasm.

'Oh, Jack, can't you just concentrate on solving the mystery of the skeletons without going off on a tangent.' She gave a long-suffering sigh. 'Are you sure, love, you aren't just becoming ... well, just a tad obsessive?'

Jack poured them each a cup of tea and sat down. 'Could be, but you know full well that I can sense when things aren't what they seem and I'm like a dog with a bone until I find out why.'

'Yes, well talking of dogs, there's a poor one here desperate for his evening walk,' said Audrey as Spike made another attempt to get his master's attention. So, drink your tea and let's all enjoy a stroll by the river to take your mind off investigations for just a short while at least.'

Ten minutes had them strolling beside the river, peaceful now with most boats moored for the night and only the sudden splash of a fish turning over or the wash of a landing swan to disturb its placid surface. With

Spike off his lead and eagerly chasing some indefinable scents, Jack was already relishing the closeness of nature and the sense of calm it brought. He smiled and took Audrey's hand. 'Good idea of yours to come here ... a whole world away from the darker side of life.'

'I'd have thought, after all those years at Scotland Yard, you would've seen enough of that to last you a lifetime.' Audrey gave his hand an extra squeeze. 'But here you are, back on a case, when you should be just enjoying retirement and leaving crime-fighting to those whose job it is.'

'I know, but sussing wrongdoing and bringing those responsible to justice *was* my life and just because I'm out of it now doesn't mean I can shake it off like an old coat.' Jack paused to throw a stick for Spike. 'But, you're right ...' he swept his hand over their tranquil surroundings, '... this is what life's really about and I need to start making the most of it ... once I've seen this latest mystery through.'

'You're right, Jack, and I realise it's going to be hard for you to stop,' accepted Audrey with an affectionate smile, 'and, I suppose, it has at least kept those old grey cells of yours ticking over.'

'While I've still got some,' added Jack with a chuckle. 'And it's good keeping in touch with characters I've met along the way ... like that old aviator Charlie Hedborough. I'm looking forward to seeing him again and finding out what he's come up with.'

'Yes, well as long as you don't make it this Thursday.'

'Thursday?'

Audrey tutted, in exasperation. 'Surely you haven't forgotten already ... our evening in Norwich, Jack ... to see Tracy Goldman?'

'Oh, crikey, yes ... slipped my mind. Yes, it'll certainly be an experience,' he managed to say through slightly gritted teeth.

Audrey squeezed his hand. 'It'll do you good to have a night out and something to take your mind off other things.'

'I guess so,' he muttered, pausing to throw Spike another stick back down the riverbank as a sign it was time to head homeward.

As they retraced their steps, with the collie now zigzagging ahead, nose to the ground from one smell to another, Jack's thoughts were on how shared times such as this brought life back into perspective. This was one of those evenings he wished could go on forever and, as they neared the small staithe where they would leave the river, he saw the perfect place to prolong it just a little while longer. 'Ah good, the bench-seat's free, so let's just have a sit and soak up the last of the sunshine.'

With the church behind them, the dreamy river in front, and only birdsong to disturb the peace and tranquillity of it all, nowhere could be more idyllic. Sitting there, hand-in-hand, Spike flat out beside them, Jack was feeling the contentment that only moments like this could bring. As he looked up to feel those last rays of sun warming his face, he smiled as a Marsh Harrier circled overhead, marvelling at how little effort it took to soar effortlessly on the evening thermals. Pointing it out to Audrey, he couldn't help feeling slightly sentimental. 'Well, love, we've had a taste of what that's like. To think we were floating over here ourselves just a few days ago on our wonderful balloon trip.'

'... celebrating our Ruby Anniversary. Where have those years gone, Jack?'

'Too quickly, but goodness knows how you've put up with me for all forty of them, what with my unsociable hours, my fixation for sniffing out trouble and chasing the wrong-doer.'

'And neither do I,' laughed Audrey, 'because you've certainly tested my patience at times with one thing or another. But, please, will you promise me that this is the last investigation you get yourself involved with?'

But, instead of replying, Jack had leapt to his feet to take the mooring lines of a hire-cruiser idling in towards the quay, its skipper delighted to have found such a perfect place for their night-stop.

With the boat secure, Jack put Spike on his lead and held out a caring hand to his wife. 'Come on, love, time for a toddy before bed.'

As they walked home, Jack was realising all too well how lucky he'd been to side-step his wife's plea, but Audrey had been a constant support through all their life together and perhaps it wasn't fair to continue avoiding this issue. Perhaps, like the river beside them, it was best to sometimes just go with the flow.

Chapter Seven

'How's this, Aud?' It was Thursday and a far-from-enthusiastic Jack was checking that his light-coloured chinos, shirt, tie and sports jacket were okay for Tracy Goldman's evening gig.

'I'm sure that'll be just fine, love ...' Audrey paused at a thought, 'but perhaps leave the tie. Everyone seems to have open necks these days.'

'Good idea,' agreed Jack, gladly whipping it off and undoing the top button of his shirt. 'It's years since I've ventured into a night club, and then we had to be suited and booted or we weren't allowed in.'

'I didn't know you were ever a clubber.'

'I wasn't. I'm talking of back in my Met days, when any time I went into a night club, it was to make myself unpopular.'

'Ah yes ... well just ensure you don't make yourself unpopular tonight at *Fidel's.*'

'Is that where we're going?' Jack was feeling less keen than ever. 'Sounds like it should be in Havana rather than Norwich.'

'I hear it's a lovely place,' encouraged Audrey, 'and it's a redeveloped old warehouse right by the river, so you won't feel totally out of your comfort zone.'

'Right, well let's go get it done with,' said Jack ungraciously as, casting an envious eye at Spike asleep in his basket, he followed his wife out to the car.

*   *   *

As is so often the case when you dread something, Jack was finding *Fidel's* nowhere near as daunting as he'd feared. In reality, the nightclub was turning out to be a moderately-sized venue lit, not by revolving disco-lights as he had imagined, but by shaded lamps on intimate tables surrounding a small dance area.

'Well, isn't this lovely?' enthused Audrey as they threaded their way through the few tables already occupied, to one close to the dance-floor.

'I hope you're not expecting me to dance,' warned Jack as they sat down.

'No, don't panic. I just wanted to be close to the stage,' explained Audrey, indicating the small raised area where a small backing group on guitars, keyboard and drums were already treating the audience to a pleasing selection of country-and-western melodies, 'but you can go and get me a glass of white wine instead.'

Drinks in hand and back at their table, Jack felt himself relaxing and actually enjoying what, he had to admit, was a warm and congenial atmosphere.

'Now, aren't you glad you came?' asked Audrey.

'So far, so good,' he confessed, offering his own glass of lager as a toast to what now promised to be a pleasurable evening ahead.

Over the next forty-five minutes, as they sat chatting in pleasant anticipation of entertainment yet to come, the remaining empty tables of the club gradually filled.

'It certainly seems our home-grown star has a strong following of all ages,' observed Jack glancing back into the subdued light of the club. 'It's a full house back there.' With just table lamps, it wasn't easy to make out individual faces, but now all eyes turned towards the stage as one person he recognised walked on. It was Walter Jarvis, Tracy's self-styled manager.

'Good evening, ladies and gentlemen, good to see so many of you here tonight. But I know it's not me you've come to see so, without further ado, please give a big hand to Norwich's own Tracy Goldman.'

The audience certainly reacted enthusiastically, breaking into spontaneous applause as the rising star walked onto the stage, smiling broadly, looking at ease in the spotlight in her black tight-fitting jeans tucked into white cowboy boots, checked shirt tied at the waist, and carrying a guitar.

Clapping along with the rest, Jack whispered to Audrey, 'I'd forgotten she played the guitar.'

Tracy thanked the audience for their support before going straight into a lively country-and-western number that got everyone's feet tapping – even Jack's. What followed was a repertoire of country music interspersed with quiet, melodic ballads and even some pop arrangements. Her voice was wide-ranging with a unique tone, her guitar playing amazing, and each number met with rapturous applause. The first half was nearing its end as Tracy, in her lilting voice with just a trace of its Norfolk accent, announced, 'Almost time for our break, but I'll end with a number from my new album that I know you'll recognise. *Dream Along* is a song I wrote early in my career, but which has been such a big part of my success.'

From the heartfelt cheer that went up, it was clearly a favourite with the audience, but even as Tracy strummed the first chords, a voice shouted, 'Oh no you didn't.'

Tracy stopped mid-chord and the spotlight swivelled to the back of the club, illuminating the figure of a young woman, standing with hands on hips, her mouth trembling with anger as she shouted, 'We *co*-wrote that number, and you know it.'

Everyone turned to face this heckler, stunned that anyone would choose this moment to make such a public accusation. None more stunned than Jack, though, as he recognised the owner of the voice. For it was none other than Kathy Caterall.

*   *   *

For a few seconds everyone was speechless, before there came calls from the fans of 'shame on you' and 'sit down and shut up.'

On stage, the staring Tracy was soon joined by the ever-attentive Walter Jarvis while an officious-looking man in a dark suit was already making his way to where the now-silent Kathy still stood. 'Okay, miss, that's enough. Let's go,' he said before leading her, unceremoniously, out of the club.

It was Jarvis who handled things on the stage. 'I'm sorry for that ladies and gentlemen. Tracy's going to take a quick break now and then the show will continue in twenty minutes for the second half of the programme.' And with that, the star of the evening left the stage with her manager's arm around her, her audience slightly bewildered and Jack already on his feet.

'Come on, Aud ... get your coat on ... we're off.'

'And miss the second half?' Audrey frowned. 'It's not fair on Tracy to just walk out because of what happened.'

'It's Kathy who probably needs our support right now.' Jack helped his wife into her coat. 'So come on and let's find out just what all that was about.'

On the way to the door they met the security guard just returning and, outside, Kathy standing in the darkness sobbing her heart out. Jack straightway put a reassuring hand on her shoulder. 'Good grief, girl, what came over you?'

She shook her head in confusion. 'I'm so sorry ... I've messed up every-one's evening haven't I? ... but I just saw red.'

Jack glanced about them. Already a few passers-by were pausing to see the cause of this upset. 'Look, things are a bit too public here. Let's all go and find ourselves a pleasant pub where we can have a drink and chat.'

*   *   *

With Audrey in the back of their car with a motherly arm around Kathy's shaking shoulders, Jack soon had them out of the city to where a traditional pub sat overlooking the River Yare.

Two cruisers were moored alongside, their crews in the saloon bar enjoying an evening ashore. Jack ushered Audrey and Kathy to a quiet corner table before heading for the bar and returning with two large brandies for the ladies and a half of lager shandy for himself.

'Here, I think you both need these. Come on, Kathy, take a good sup to calm your nerves.'

'Oh gosh, thanks, Jack.' She took a gulp and closed her eyes, recovering her composure as the liquor did its work. 'So sorry again for that scene.'

'It certainly came out of the blue, I must say. But what you said back there ... that you helped write *Dream Along* ... is that correct?'

'Absolutely.' Kathy studied her glass as she swirled her brandy. Finally, she looked up. 'It's a long story, Jack, but I guess you ... both of you ... deserve an explanation.'

'If we're to understand and help you, we certainly do,' said Jack, sitting back and folding his arms, 'because, even back at our balloon launch, I sensed there was friction between you and Tracy and that you must have known each other before.'

'I more than *knew* her, Jack,' said Kathy, 'seeing as we're actually half-sisters.'

'Half-sisters!' Jack's eyes widened. 'Now, that's something I would never have guessed. The pair of you are so different.'

'In many ways,' agreed Kathy, 'but we share the same mum ... called Sandra Caterall.'

'I'm thinking you are the older of the two,' judged Audrey.

'That's right, but only by eighteen months. From what little my mum told me, I was the result of a loving but doomed relationship she had when living and working in London. Being pregnant and alone wasn't easy and so she up sticked and moved here to Norwich away from judgemental friends and expensive living.'

'So you were actually born here, Kathy?'

'Yes, at the N&N.'

'But you never knew who your father was?'

'No, and Mum refused to discuss it other than to say he never even knew she'd become pregnant. As I got older, I got to realise that was a subject best avoided and gave up asking.'

'Okay, but then, after settling in Norwich, your mum become pregnant again ... in another relationship?'

'Yes, but being not much more than a baby myself, I have no recollection of there ever being a man around ... but of course, there must've been someone.'

'Could it have been *your* dad who was still involved with your mum?'

'No, I'm pretty sure it wasn't. Mum was always insistent that we were *half*-sisters.'

'So, once again, the identity of the father remained a secret,' surmised an increasingly intrigued Audrey. 'Do you think Tracy has any idea who he was?'

But, once again, Kathy shook her head. 'I'm pretty sure she doesn't. Growing up together, we naturally talked about it, but neither of us could work out who our fathers could be. Certainly on our birth certificates we've both got "Father unknown" and just our mother's surname.'

'Which is why I didn't make the family connection,' realised Jack, 'because Tracy is now Goldman.'

'Which is her stage-name,' explained Kathy. She gave a wry smile. 'Tracy Caterall doesn't quite have the right ring to it, does it?'

'I suppose not,' laughed Jack, 'but back then you both at least had a half-sibling to grow up with. How *was* your relationship when you were youngsters?'

'Absolutely fine. I loved having a kid sister and someone to play with and spoil rotten, even though Mum always took Tracy's side and I could never seem to do anything right.'

'You mean she was the favourite?'

'By miles, Jack.' Kathy took another good sip of her brandy. 'Not only was she the baby of the family, but was much prettier than me with her blonde hair and lovely blue eyes. It didn't really bother me at first but, as I got older, I found the injustice of it harder to accept.'

'And obviously still do,' sympathised Audrey. 'But how did the pair of you get on as teenagers?'

'Oh, really well, more like good friends than sisters, even though we were obviously in different year groups at school and our characters were very different. You see, I was always the quiet, studious one, whereas Tracy was always bubbly and gregarious. The one thing we did have in common though was a love of singing.' Kathy paused, smiling to herself as she remembered those happy days. 'One Christmas, Mum bought us a karaoke machine and we spent hours messing around on it, pretending to be Kylie.'

'Sounds just like our two,' reminisced Audrey, 'only they used hairbrushes and the CD player ...'

'... and couldn't sing in tune,' added Jack, grimacing, 'but where did *your* love of music lead you next?'

'To us both taking up the guitar at school. We used to share lunch-time sessions and then practiced together again most evenings when we should probably have been doing our homework. Eventually we started making up songs of our own and became pretty good. Our music teacher recognised we had talent and encouraged us to take part in school concerts, which seemed to go down well. So well, in fact, that word got around and we were soon being asked to perform in public, and even getting paid for some gigs.'

'You must have been good,' acknowledged Audrey.

'I guess so, though it was Tracy who had the better voice, whereas it was me who had a talent for writing our numbers.' Kathy shrugged. 'I suppose that's where the rot started to set in with our relationship.'

'That's a shame.' Audrey looked concerned. 'How come?'

'Oh, Tracy getting all the adulation and always in the spotlight, while it was me writing most of the material, grafting behind the scenes and getting very little thanks or recognition. But it was after she employed Jarvis behind my back and made me feel I was just a spare part, that I decided I'd had enough and chucked it all in. By then I'd developed a love for ballooning anyway, so I cut my losses and applied myself to that, determined to prove myself better than Tracy in at least one activity.'

'Which you certainly seem to have achieved,' said Jack, 'even managing to set up *Skyrides* as a successful operation, whereas Tracy went on to win *Stars* ...'

'... partly by taking full credit for her lead numbers,' completed Kathy, 'when in fact, they were ones *I'd* written in our old gig days ... or at least the music, though we often collaborated on the lyrics.'

'And is that what you did in *Dream Along*?'

'Definitely, but since it's become such a hit, Tracy's conveniently forgotten that fact. And, to make matters worse, she's now gone and signed up with a top musical agency to manage her career. I just know I won't stand a chance of recognition now, with them fighting her corner, so I've already told her that I'll keep quiet if she's prepared to be fair and share the royalties with me.'

'And ...?'

'And, all I get are replies from Walter Jarvis saying there was nothing in writing and that I must have profited from it when we performed it together.'

'And did you?'

'Hardly, Jack. In those days we were lucky to even get our travelling expenses. Then, long after we'd split up and Tracy went on to win *Stars*, I actually felt proud of her ... that is until she claimed she was the sole writer of *Dream Along*. Now, tonight, I've gone and made a fool of myself and people will just think it's sour grapes and jealousy. But it's more the injustice of the thing that rankles me. Here I am, struggling to raise the money for this re-enactment while Tracy rakes it in without giving me a penny.'

'But you never took out a copyright for the song or anything?' asked Audrey.

'No, back then, that would have cost more than we ever earned.'

'I'm not sure you would have needed to,' pointed out Jack. 'I think you'd have a claim as long as someone could vouch that the number had been written by both of you. Is there some old programme or something with the song listed and your names as credits?'

'*I* certainly don't have one, but possibly one of our old gig venues might still have copies.'

'Or perhaps your mum does,' suggested Audrey, knowing how she treasured every little memento of their own daughters. 'And where does your mother Sandra actually stand in all this, because surely it upsets her to see you both at loggerheads?'

'Perhaps, but I've seen less and less of her over the past years, so I certainly won't make contact again now just to ask a favour. And, anyway, she'd still take Tracy's side, especially as she's doubtless glorifying in her blue-eyed daughter's new-found fame.'

'So, does your mum still live in Norwich?' asked Jack

'Yes, but on her own now since Tracy had the money to move out into her own flat.'

'Well, can't you at least try and appeal to Tracy's good nature then?' said Audrey. 'She's your half-sister after all and you do seem to have got on really well when you were younger.'

'Little chance of that now after making a complete fool of myself in front of all her fans,' sighed a sniffing Kathy. 'No, Audrey, I've gone and completely blown it. Her new agents won't want anything to do with me once they hear of my outburst, because the last thing they'll want for their new prodigy is bad publicity like that.'

'I can't see them wanting Jarvis hanging around either,' added Jack, 'so I should think poor old Walter's days are well-and-truly numbered too.'

'Poor lad,' sympathized Audrey. 'He won't take that easily, especially as he seems to be a bit smitten with her.'

'Not a *bit* smitten, Audrey,' scoffed Kathy, 'the fool's totally besotted.'

'You're right there,' agreed Jack, 'but how did he get the job in the first place?'

'As I said, that was Tracy's doing. As we got more gigs, she reckoned we needed someone to look after sound and lighting and that sort of stuff. Jarvis was a jobbing electrician who'd done some work for Mum, so Tracy got him onboard. He did a good enough job at first, but when Tracy went solo and began making a name for herself, she started treating him like a skivvy. But the poor chap became so infatuated with her that he put up with it and now spends his whole life trying to please her, which is why he won't support my claim to share any royalties rightly mine.'

'I can see you're up against it,' conceded Jack, 'and it's obviously been a contentious issue for quite a time now, so what prompted you to make such a public remonstration tonight?'

'Good question,' acknowledged Kathy, despairingly. 'I guess I was upset anyway, because I never intended going to *Fidel's* to start with, but was looking forward to an evening with Hans.'

'Van Heiden ... the Dutch art expert?'

'That's right.' She wiped the corner of her eye with the back of her hand. 'But he rang to say he couldn't make it and that it was probably best if we didn't see each other again.'

'Oh dear,' tutted Audrey. 'I can see why you were a bit uptight ... but he did seem rather old for you anyway, and long-distance romances aren't ideal. I really do think you're better off anyway with someone younger and more local.'

'Like Stuart Steadmore, you mean?'

'Well ... yes. He seems such a perfect match for you.'

'You're right, he is,' agreed Kathy, 'but there's no way I'm going to play second-fiddle to Tracy. Did you see the way she flirted with him? I admit I only first agreed to go out with Hans to make Stu jealous, but then I found myself enjoying his company. I thought we got on well, and it was a novelty being dated by an older man who seemed so much more worldly than people my age.'

'Not *your* world, though, Kathy,' said Jack, 'but none of this helps your current problem of lost royalties ... which could be worth a considerable amount if *Dream Along* becomes a hit. What about me having a word with either Jarvis or your mum?'

'Thanks for offering, Jack, but I doubt anything would help now. Jarvis will *always* take Tracy's side whether she's right or wrong, and so will Mother.'

'It does all seem very unfair,' said Audrey, sighing deeply.

Kathy shrugged. 'Yeah, well that's life, so I'd better just accept things as they are and get on with it.'

'Probably be best as things stand,' agreed Jack, 'but try not to be too despondent. Money might be tight at present, but you still have your balloon business, which gives a lot of people a lot of pleasure.'

'Ballooning is quite an unusual way to earn a living,' remarked Audrey. 'What got you interested in such a pursuit in the first place?'

For the first time that evening, Kathy smiled. 'I don't know why, but since I was little I'd always had a fascination for flying, and as we lived near the site in Norwich where they launched the balloons from, I'd pester mum to let me stand by the fence and watch them take off. I suppose our family circumstances had something to do with it, but to me that balloon was like a magic carpet that could take me up into a world I could only dream of. So, as soon as Tracy and me started making a bit of money from our gigs, I saved up enough to take my first flight and it was the most wonderful day of my life and all I'd ever imagined. And since then I've never looked back. It was as if I had flying in my blood.'

'And now you've got an exciting project ahead of you,' encouraged Jack while mentally mulling over what Kathy had just said.

'Or I did have.' Kathy finished off the dregs of her brandy. 'I'm not sure anyone will want anything to do with me after tonight.'

'Who knows what the morrow will bring.' Jack glanced at his watch. 'Right now, Kathy, I think the best thing for you is a good night's sleep, so let's get you home. How did you get to *Fidel's*?'

'I walked.'

'So you live in Norwich?'

'Not exactly, Jack. I live on a boat and just brought her into the city for this week.'

Kathy Caterall was certainly a young woman blessed with idiosyncrasy as well as nerve, thought Jack as they left the pub and headed back to Norwich.

*　　　*　　　*

Twenty-five minutes had them back in the city and drawing to a halt on Riverside Road with the adjacent River Wensum ebbing slowly in the pale moonlight. As they all climbed out of the car, Jack cast a questioning glance towards the several boats lining its banks. 'Where's yours, Kathy?'

'Just a little further down towards Foundry Bridge. There weren't too many boats when I arrived, so I tucked in there close to the Yacht Station offices.'

'Well, it's a pleasant evening, so we'll walk you to it. Besides, I'd like to see your boat.'

All three set off along the city moorings, on one side, trees separating them from the still-busy road above and, on the other, shaded lamps glowing cosily behind the curtained cabin windows of moored cruisers. 'Have you been here long?' asked Audrey.

'Just a few days, but I'm heading back to my permanent moorings tomorrow.'

'Where are they?' asked Jack.

'Up the River Ant at Wayford Bridge Marina.'

'So, quite close to the *Watercraft* yard, but a long trip back.'

'Yes, about ten hours in my slow old bus, but I'll probably night-stop somewhere along the way.' She indicated ahead to where a narrow-beamed boat lay close to the Yacht Station. 'Well, there she is, my other pride-and-joy.'

'And very nice too,' said Jack as they stopped beside this long narrow-boat's black-painted hull and light-green topsides. 'Not too many canal boats on the Broads, but a steel hull is certainly an advantage when you're dodging inexperienced hirers.' He nodded to the name embellished amidships on the cabin. '*Balloonatic*. I can see the connection, but I hope it's only by name and not nature.'

'Well, a lot of people do think I'm mad, spending my working life aloft with fire and fabric,' smiled Kathy before giving a grimace, 'and probably more so after the scene tonight.' She nodded towards her boat. 'You're both very welcome to come aboard for a nightcap.'

'Thanks anyway, but I'm back patrolling tomorrow and you've got a long

81

trip ahead to Wayford ... which is a pleasant place to be,' added Jack, 'but I'd have thought it would have been more convenient for you to have had a mooring in the *Watercraft* yard, right there with your balloon?'

'It might have been,' she agreed, 'but there was no way I wanted to be even more beholden to Alec Turnberry. It's bad enough having to fight off advances on his occasional visits, but actually *living* in his yard would be too much.'

'I can appreciate that, seeing how over-familiar he was with you in the shed. And anyway, having the freedom to go off cruising between your balloon flights must be an ideal way to live your life.'

'It is as long as I can keep the money rolling in, Jack. In fact, that was one of the reasons I brought *Balloonatic* to Norwich this week ... to find sponsorship for the John Money re-enactment.'

'Coming by road or rail would have been a lot quicker for that,' said Jack, 'so I'm guessing there was a more enticing motive for taking the river route.'

'Ah, yes, I was forgetting you were so perceptive,' smiled Kathy. 'And, of course, you're correct.' She glanced wistfully through the bridge to where, on the opposite bank, the lights of the *Hotel Nelson* shone enticingly. 'Hans van Heiden is staying there, so the thought of being close by did appeal ... that is until tonight when he stood me up.'

'So instead, you walked to *Fidel's* and ...'

'... made a complete ass of myself,' completed Kathy with a shake of her head. She pointed to the cabin of her floating home. 'Are you positive you won't have that coffee?'

'Not tonight, Kathy, but I'm sure our paths will cross soon on the northern rivers, and then I'll very thankfully take you up on your offer.'

'I'll look forward to that, Jack, and thanks so much again for sorting me out tonight. I know I've been irrational, but just talking to you both has brought everything once more into perspective.'

'Glad we've helped, Kathy.'

'And we're always around if you need an ear,' added Audrey.

There were big hugs all round and then, as Kathy boarded her floating home and lights appeared in its cabin, the Fellows made their way back along the quay and then up the next steps to the road. At the top, Jack paused to glance back to *Balloonatic*. 'Good, Kathy seems to have snugged down for the night.'

'Why wouldn't she have?' asked a puzzled Audrey.

'Just that she might have decided to make one more desperate visit to the hotel for a last try with Van Heiden ... which would have been awkward, Aud, seeing as I want us to take a quick nose there ourselves.'

'What, in the *Nelson*? What on earth for?'

'I just want to check for myself that Van Heiden really is staying there.'

'Why, for goodness' sake?'

'Because some old instinct tells me there's more to all this than meets the eye ... so come on, it won't take long.'

Minutes later they were crossing Foundry Bridge with the River Wensum flowing seawards beneath. 'I'm not cut out for this sleuthing business, Jack,' complained Audrey as her husband ushered her into the hotel. 'I just can't imagine what you hope to achieve?'

'Just a glance at the visitors' book, if nothing else,' said Jack as they entered the reception area and a young man behind the desk looked up enquiringly.

'Can I help you, sir?'

'Err ... just meeting friends in the dining room,' replied Jack as he just as immediately hustled Audrey away from the desk and into the adjoining corridor. 'Shush ... this way ... quick.'

'What's going on ...' protested Audrey before her husband placed a finger over his lips and pointed towards the main door.

For there, just entering, was Hans van Heiden himself, very much the man-about-town and clearly happy after a night out.

Jack and Audrey remained out of sight as the Dutchman collected his room-key from reception. More intriguing, though, was the woman on his arm, vivacious, elegant and someone they both recognised.

It was Phillipa Keyworth.

*   *   *

'Well, that's enough revelations for one night,' sighed Audrey as they drove homeward. 'To think that Van Heiden raised poor Kathy's hopes of a relationship when, all along, he was just two-timing with the woman supposedly helping her.'

It was twenty minutes now since Jack and Audrey had assured themselves the coast was clear and beat a hasty retreat from hotel to car.

'I think this all goes a lot further than mere amorous adventure,' said Jack, 'and that there's more to Van Heiden and Phillipa Keyworth's relationship than meets the eye. For starters, it's too coincidental that both of them seem to have a particular interest in Wildmarsh Farm.'

'Yes, we've certainly seen both of them there at one time or another,' recalled Audrey, 'but why do they seem drawn to such an isolated, ramshackled old place as that?'

'I'm still not sure,' admitted Jack, 'but it has to be something pretty significant for an outwardly respectable art expert and an equally professional young woman to get so involved.'

'In more ways than one, going by what we saw tonight,' added Audrey, tutting. 'Such goings on.'

'We don't know what Van Heiden's domestic situation is in Holland, Aud, but assuming he's single, then I guess he's as entitled to ask Phillipa Keyworth out as he did Kathy.'

'True, and as it happens, I think Kathy's had a lucky escape before getting too involved. The man's obviously totally unscrupulous and I wouldn't believe a word he says but, that aside, tell me how you plan to solve the mystery of what's going on at Wildmarsh Farm.'

'By delving into its history, which must be where the answer lies,' explained Jack, glad to be off the subject of personal relationships, 'and which I'm hoping Charlie Hedborough is already investigating for me.'

'Doubtless it'll throw up even more revelations for you to worry about,' groaned Audrey as they turned off the main road for the last two miles to home. 'And, talking of revelations, there's that other bolt from the blue ... of Kathy and Tracy being half-sisters.'

'Yeah, that was just as much an eye-opener for me,' admitted Jack, 'but it certainly gives us a better understanding of the tensions at play between those two, even if it does raise some interesting questions as well.'

'Which are?'

'Well, how did their mum Sandra earn a living? There's been no mention of her having a job, and yet she still managed to support and raise two girls.'

'Perhaps one or both fathers paid maintenance ... or is there just the *one* same father for both girls?'

'Another good question, Aud, which has given me even more food for thought.'

'Such as?'

'Something I need to check on the internet first,' said Jack. 'In the meantime, we need to ponder where Phillipa Keyworth sits in this whole conundrum.'

'On Van Heiden's lap by the look of it,' said Audrey with a snigger, 'but *he's* not to be trusted and I bet that Phillipa's no saint either.' She looked across to her husband who'd obviously gone into one of his deep-thought zones even as he swung into their drive. Giving him a gentle nudge, she brought him back to the present. 'Jack, now what's started buzzing around that devious mind of yours?'

'What? ... Oh ...' Jack switched off the engine, '... something you just said, Aud.'

'What did I just say?'

'Something that triggered a possible solution to one side of this mystery.'

Undoing her seatbelt, Audrey gave a heartfelt sigh. 'Quite honestly, I'm losing track of just which mystery we're even talking about. Is this about the derelict boat, the *Watercraft* yard, Wildmarsh Farm or this new Kathy/ Tracy business?'

'Even I'm not sure,' admitted Jack as he climbed out and followed his wife to the front door. 'Right now, first priority is a hot drink and unwind before we hit the sack, so you put the kettle on while I just check for any phone messages.'

There was just one, but it was the one Jack had hoped for.

'Hi, Jack ... Ted Finchley ... sorry for taking so long to get back ... not a lot to tell you yet about your mystery boat, I'm afraid. Truth is, it's a pretty standard design for that period of build, which I reckon is 1920s. I know lots of the yards put their own little mods on the ones they built, but to check that I need to have a real close inspection inside and out. So, can you arrange that and let me know? Cheers for now.'

Jack tuned off the answering machine. That was another job he'd need to do on the morrow after a good night's sleep. It had been quite an evening, but he was pleased Audrey hadn't let him off the *Fidel's* treat. Perhaps it really was time to stop trying to control life and, instead, let it control you.

Chapter Eight

'Right, Aud, a quick breakfast and then I'm off.'

'Just glad you're back on the river,' replied Audrey, thankful at seeing some things returning to as near normal as life could ever be with her husband. She paused to pour him a coffee in his favourite cup. 'So, relax with this for at least a few more minutes while I pack your lunch.'

'Thanks, love.' Jack sat down at the kitchen table. 'Sorry if things seem a bit rushed this morning, but I've been busy on the laptop.'

'Googling what this time, Jack?'

'Something I got thinking about last night after our chat with Kathy, and then the clue you gave me on the way home.'

'I'm still trying to work out how an evening of supposed pleasure and relaxation, turned out to be one of such disruption and angst,' said Audrey, buttering some bread before loading it with slices of Edam topped with pickle. 'And to find out that all along, those two are actually half-sisters.'

'Which makes the situation all the more painful for both of them. Kathy was certainly daft to do what she did, and I'm wondering how poor Tracy feels this morning after having her performance so badly disrupted.'

'Probably not as bad as Kathy when she reads this.' Audrey tossed across the local paper just delivered.

'NORWICH STAR'S HOMETOWN DEBUT BLIGHTED BY PROTESTOR,' read Jack with dismay. 'Oh crikey, that will have shoved a spanner in the works for Kathy's project hopes.'

'Yes, well she's only got herself to blame.' Audrey fished out Jack's lunch-box from the cupboard. 'Thankfully, with different surnames, the papers still haven't cottoned on that they're sisters, but I guess it's only time before they do. That really was such a stupid thing for a supposedly-sensible girl to do.'

'That's the problem when you see red and lose your cool, Aud. The result is usually the three Rs.'

'The three Rs?'

'Ranting, Raving and Remorse, and I'm guessing Kathy is experiencing the latter even as we speak.'

'I'm sure she is ... but what were these clues she and I gave you last night?'

'Just her mention of Tracy having an agent to manage her affairs and you saying Phillipa was obviously no saint.'

'Just a casual observation, Jack, so how did that help?'

'By giving me a lead to something I've been puzzling over, which is the name the old boatyard used to have.'

'What, *Cecilian*?'

'Yep. It's been bugging me ever since Stuart told me the sale of the yard was done anonymously. It seemed a somewhat un-nautical name for a boatyard, but one that rang a bell at the back of my mind. And then you mentioned saints and it clicked, so I googled *Saint* Cecilia and, what-do-you-know, she's the patron saint of music.'

'Well, that's a new saint to me. Mind you, there seems to be a saint for everything these days,' said an underwhelmed Audrey, 'but what's that got to do with anything?'

'Because I've been trying to work out who the original owners of the yard were ... this London outfit who wanted the place sold through a third party. I reckoned that if they called their subsidiary hire-boat business *Cecilian*, then that could also be the name of the parent company, in which case ...'

'... *Cecilian* could well be something to do with music,' said Audrey, following her husband's reasoning 'And ...?'

'... *Cecilian Promotions* actually exists, Aud, not in London, but in the Fens, and it's a musical agency.'

'The Fens! That seems an out of the way place to run a music business.' Lunch packed and flask filled, Audrey sat herself down. 'Would it be pushing our luck too far to think that it's this *Cecilian* agency that Tracy's signed up with?'

'You can never "push too far" in an investigation, and when lines of enquiry start gelling it usually means you're on to something. Anyway, apparently this outfit is owned and run by a chap called ...' Jack paused to glance at a hand-written note, '... Frazer Dunbar, so I'll give him a ring later to feel him out. Before that, though, I need to give Bailey a call and confirm clearance for Ted Finchley to inspect the boat. Blimey, Aud, look at the time!' he suddenly exclaimed, grabbing his bag, flask and lunch box, 'I need to be off.' A quick kiss for his wife and then he was out of the door and on his way.

Ex-policeman, River Ranger, Private investigator, supposed art lover and now he's delving into the world of music, thought Audrey as she heard their car speed hastily up the road. What next, she wondered as she sat back and poured herself a coffee.

*   *   *

At this same time, seventy miles west in the Cambridgeshire Fens, another couple had just had their breakfast interrupted by an unexpected telephone call.

'Who was that, Frazer?' asked Margo Dunbar, pausing from peeling an orange as her husband came back into the kitchen wiping his glasses.

'Would you believe, Tracy Goldman.' Frazer popped his specs back on before sitting down once more to his neglected bacon and eggs and his wife's look of astonishment. 'Yeah, I know, I was as shocked myself that she'd managed to get out of bed before midday.'

'Quite. What momentous happening triggered that?'

'A bit of an upset actually.' Frazer pushed aside the congealed fry-up and instead poured himself another coffee. 'Seems that her debut performance in Norwich last night was blighted by a protestor.'

'Protesting about what?'

'Tracy taking all the credit for writing *Dream Along*, her signature number.'

'Oh well I don't have to ask who it was doing the protesting then. It had to be that aggrieved half sister of hers ...'

'... Kathy Caterall,' completed Frazer in confirmation. 'It seems that she's now more determined than ever to get a cut of Tracy's royalties.'

'Perhaps we need to think seriously about paying her off then, if only to avoid the bad PR this could bring.' Margo paused to separate the slices of her orange before wiping her hands. Nearly a decade younger than Frazer, she still had the looks that had attracted him all those years ago and the satisfaction of people thinking their age gap was even greater. Along with an already-bossy nature, she had developed indifference to the feelings of others along with a reputation for straight-talking. 'So, how much are we talking about, Frazer?'

Her husband paused to spoon in a couple of sugars. 'A few months ago, virtually nothing, but now, with Tracy all set for the big time, probably thousands.'

'More like a hundred grand,' speculated Margo, frowning. 'But Tracy's

88

not quite there yet, so we're still only talking damage limitation and some derisory sum. We can't leave it much longer, though.'

'True.' Frazer shook his head despondently. 'I tell you, Margo, this was one complication we could have done without.'

'Yes, well, we have to take the rough with the smooth and this won't go away, Frazer,' said the ever-pragmatic Margo. 'Tracy Goldman could well be our cash-cow for the future and we certainly don't want anything jeopardising that.'

'No, of course not, but thank God I handed all that side over to you.'

'Especially as you still enjoy a generous slice of the income,' reminded Margo, 'and that I thankfully revel in the cut and thrust of the music scene while you just content yourself messing about on that blessed boat of yours on the Norfolk Broads.'

'Better than upping my blood-pressure by endlessly trying to do deals between aspiring pop stars with inflated egos and venue owners always wanting something for nothing.'

'Yes, well, someone has to keep this agency going, Frazer. Meanwhile, what vital project do you have planned next for your beloved *Fenland Raider*?'

Ignoring his wife's sarcasm, Frazer poured himself another coffee. 'Seeing as you're so interested, fixing the electrics, because they're still tripping out whenever I go onto shore power.'

'Yes, well, it would have been our own finances "tripping out" by now if I hadn't taken the helm of *Cecilian Promotions* and kept that afloat,' sniped Margo, who had no idea what shore power was and certainly had no interest in finding out. 'If you'd put as much energy into the agency as you have on that damn boat, we'd be quids-in by now.'

'We wouldn't if I'd had to pay a marine engineer instead of doing it myself,' argued Frazer.

'You'd have had your own engineer, Frazer, if you hadn't gone and sold your boatyard all those years ago. If you'd kept that you could've had *Raider* maintained for nothing while you made income from the hire fleet.'

'I know, but I've told you before, Margo, the small cruiser fleets had had their day and it was time to offload.'

'But you say the chap who bought it has done okay?'

'Yes, by downsizing to just day-boats and canoes. Perhaps I should have tried that … but at least I kept Wildmarsh Farm, which still turns a buck by renting the fields to farmers.'

'While that lovely old farmhouse gradually falls into dereliction,' grumbled Margo, raising again a contentious subject in the Dunbar household. 'Why on earth don't we renovate the place before it falls down completely and live there ourselves. Broadland is a beautiful area compared to the desolation of the Fens, and you wouldn't have to keep travelling backwards and forwards to go on *Fenland Raider*.'

'Oh God, Margo, how many times have we had this conversation?' groaned Frazer. 'You know full well why it suits us living in the isolation of The Fens. You said yourself it's best running the agency where demanding clients can't just drop in.'

'... and where we go from week-to-week in the same old routine,' moaned Margo bitterly. 'But if you've no intention of ever living at Wildmarsh, then why don't you just sell the place before it falls down completely?'

'Just sentiment really. Don't forget, it's where I grew up and where all my earliest memories were created.'

Margo scoffed. 'More than memories if you ask me.'

'What do you mean by that?'

'I mean there's something else about that tumbledown old pile that stops you ever getting rid of it ... some dark secret that one day might come back to bite you.'

'Rubbish.' Frazer had had enough of his wife's conjecturing. 'You don't know what you're talking about, Margo. Just stick to running the agency and leave the Norfolk side to me.'

'Yes, you'd like that wouldn't you?' Margo nodded vaguely eastwards. 'So you can have some fun playing away while I'm stuck here keeping the business going.'

'Well, if you're that suspicious, why don't you join me on *Raider* for a bit of cruising one weekend and then you'll see for yourself what I get up to.'

'I'm not *that* desperate, Frazer, and you know you're on safe ground there with my hatred of both boats and water ...' Margo tipped the remains of her orange into the bin, '... which is exactly why you know darned well I'll refuse.'

'You're forgetting we do have a client in Norwich, remember, who I can see while I'm up there sorting the boat,' defended Frazer. 'Right now Tracy Goldman's our *only* lucrative money-spinner, so we need to look after her.'

'Exactly, so perhaps you need to get there straightaway and solve this song-rights debacle before the national press get their teeth into it. It could ruin her before she ever makes the big time if it's not sorted quickly.'

'Leaving all the time and money we've invested to go down with her,' agreed Frazer while snatching back the coffee cup his wife was about to clear with the rest of the breakfast things. Knowing it would annoy her even more, he reached for his pipe and began pressing fresh tobacco into its bowl. 'At least it saves accommodation expenses if I stay on *Raider*.'

'As long as that's the only place you stay,' retorted Margo with the clatter of crockery being almost thrown into the sink. 'Perhaps you're right and one day I should join you there just to check what you really get up to.' Seeing her husband about to strike a match, she quickly added, '... and don't even think of lighting up that revolting thing in the kitchen.'

*   *   *

Back in Broadland, Jack was by now well into his morning's patrol in weather that could only be termed bracing.

Crossing the broad with a moderate north-north-easterly breeze blowing against the flood tide, the resultant curling wavelets glinted enticingly in the sunshine as four sailing boats healed to the gusts as they tacked to windward. Managing to avoid those same conditions was a group of canoeists, stroking down the eastern edge in the slight lee of the reedbed, oblivious to the mystery that had lain hidden there for decades.

How quickly human nature seemed to accept transgression and tragedy these days, thought Jack as he upped the revs of his launch slightly and headed for the broad's northern exit. With each day's news reporting some form of violence in the country, it now seemed to be virtually accepted as a feature of everyday life and forgotten just as quickly. 'Ah well,' he muttered to himself before picking up his mobile and calling Ted Finchley.

'Ted ... Jack Fellows ... I've got clearance from the SIO for us to check over the boat. Would you be available today?'

'No problem. What time?'

'I'm heading upriver to the boatyard now. Shall we say in an hour?'

'Sounds good. I'll see you there.'

*   *   *

The *Watercraft* yard seemed to have returned to almost-normal operation when, forty minutes later, Jack nosed his launch into the moorings.

'Looks like things have calmed down again, Stuart,' he said with a smile, as the yard manager came out to meet him.

'Yep, thanks to a keen breeze and the boat mystery already yesterday's news.' Steadmore stood up after securing Jack's lines. 'Back to our old level of business now, which makes life a bit less hectic.'

'Not so good financially though.'

Steadmore shrugged. 'The yard does okay anyway, Jack. At least it ticks over enough to keep the boss reasonably happy.'

'Is Mr Turnberry here today?' asked Jack, stepping ashore.

'You're joking?' Steadmore gave a humourless laugh. 'No way he'll spend any more time here than he has to. Just as soon as he was sure he'd be getting storage money for your wreck, he hot-footed home.'

'Has he always been that hands-off?'

'Certainly as long as I've been here. Not that I complain, Jack ... I prefer running my own show without the likes of him looking over my shoulder.' He raised his brows enquiringly. 'So, anything immediate I can help you with?'

'Not really, Stuart. I just wanted to check the yard was happy storing the derelict for a while yet. I'm actually meeting Ted Finchley here in fifteen minutes so we can give it a once-over.'

'Time for a quick coffee then,' offered Steadmore, indicating towards the office. 'Let's go inside out of this wind.'

As they walked across the yard, that wind seemed to be strengthening, shifting the boats at their moorings and causing the boatyard pennant on the small mast atop the main shed to snap and crack in the gusts. 'Certainly not the weather for ballooning,' commented Jack as they passed Kathy's rig store.

'Not that she'll be getting many bookings anyway after last night's fiasco at *Fidel's*,' said Steadmore, frowning. 'I read about it in this morning's EDP. Stupid girl, losing it like that. It's Tracy I now feel sorry for.'

'Did you know of their relationship?' probed Jack, not wishing to give too much away.

'What, that they were half-sisters? Oh, yeah, Kathy told me when Trace first won *Stars*, though even then she was a bit worked up about the whole thing. Sisterly jealousy I guess, and last night it just boiled over.'

'I'm sure they'll make up in time,' said Jack as they entered the office block. 'Certainly neither of them will benefit from public fallouts.'

'Too true they won't,' agreed Steadmore, ushering Jack into a good-sized room beyond reception. 'This is the boss's office actually, but as he's rarely here, I use it for day-to-day stuff. Take a seat.'

With Steadmore off to sort coffees, Jack settled down on a wooden chair and scanned an office much the same as many found in Broadland boatyards. There was the somewhat shabby second-hand furniture covered in a miscellany of un-touched paperwork, boat models, discarded tools and oily engine parts, while hanging on the wooden walls were the usual old Broadland prints in their cobwebbed frames ... but also something else, enough out of place as to catch Jack's attention.

Mounted on a varnished wooden plaque was a length of tubular alloy, one end sealed and the other, a circular hand-grip. Set in its base was a tarnished brass plaque. Jack wiped away a layer of dust and read, *Flt Lt J B Dunbar DFC – 06/09/1943*

'Hmm, what's the story behind this, Stuart?' he asked as the manager returned with two mugs of coffee.

'Never been quite sure myself,' he admitted, handing Jack his drink. 'The boss reckons it was there when he bought the yard, so it must've been put there by the previous owner.'

'Who remains something of an enigma,' recalled Jack. 'But if this was his, then he, or perhaps his father, was probably an RAF pilot.'

'How'd you figure that out?' asked Steadmore, settling behind the desk.

'Because *Flt Lt* is an abbreviation for Flight Lieutenant, an Air Force rank, and J B Dunbar had clearly served during World War Two and been awarded the Distinguished Flying Cross for bravery in, or before, 1943.'

'I'll take your word for that, Jack,' conceded the young manager, taking a sip of his coffee, 'but how'd you work out he was a pilot?'

'Only because that looks to me like the control-column of an aircraft.'

'What ... you mean a joystick?'

'That's right. And I'm concluding Dunbar flew fighters or some other single-pilot aircraft, because larger ones like bombers and transports were invariably controlled with a half-wheel or yoke.'

'Well, I've always wondered what it was,' said Steadmore, finishing his coffee, 'and something I can tell Kathy about ... if she ever speaks to me again.'

'Why, did she ever show an interest in it?'

'Only a casual one, but she always thought it must be off some old aircraft, wanted to find out the story behind the name, but never got around to it.' He shrugged. 'I guess now we'll never know.'

'Possibly,' said Jack, pulling out his mobile. 'But would you mind if I took a photo of it?'

'Sure, go ahead, though I can't imagine what for.'

'Oh, just an interest of mine in aviation history,' replied Jack with crossed fingers before glancing out of the window to see an elderly figure just cycling into the yard. 'But here's Ted, so thanks for the coffee, Stuart, and we'll talk again later ...' he paused for just another second, '... and don't think too badly of Kathy. If my instincts are true, then it won't be too long before you two are back together again.'

'Ah, I hope so,' affirmed Steadmore as Jack disappeared out of the door.

*   *   *

Just entering another area of Broadland, but by a completely different mode of transport, was the girl herself.

At the helm of *Balloonatic*, hair blowing in the brisk north-easterly, Kathy was just leaving the comparatively sheltered waters of the River Yare and nosing into the widening approaches of Breydon Water. Today, with the tide in its last stages of ebb, but running against a wind all the stronger for blowing over this large expanse of water and mudflats close to the North Sea, Breydon this morning appeared decidedly hostile. On the inland broads, wind-against-tide invariably produced short-spaced wavelets but here, on what had once been an open estuary, were actual white-topped rollers.

One thing Breydon didn't have, though, was a speed restriction and Kathy leant forward into the open doorway of the cabin and eased the throttle forward slightly. Narrowboats were designed for canals, not open water, but their rugged steel construction meant they could take plenty of hammering and she had little compunction in plunging onward, hitting each wave with a resounding smack and ducking as another sheet of spray came flying over the narrow roof of *Balloonatic*'s cabin.

Pulling up the hood of her oilskin, she gave her full attention to helming a course along the marked channel. Tough as narrowboats were, they had the disadvantage of shallow draft and, in a lively breeze like this, were susceptible to leeway enough to have them crabbing downwind and out of the channel. And on Breydon that would inevitably mean instant grounding on the mudflats stretching for miles on either side. So Kathy took a firmer grip of the tiller, put in some drift angle to have *Balloonatic* tracking nicely along the fairway, and sat herself down on the wooden seat across the stern.

This also gave her a little more shelter from the showers of chilly salt-water coming over the cabin roof to hit her face. In a way it was invigorating and she was actually enjoying these challenging conditions with nature at its most raw, feeling a million miles from last night's embarrassing fiasco, all the problems that lay behind it and the ramifications it might yet bring. Here, life came down to simply steering your own course through whatever trials and tribulations it threw at you. She breathed a sigh of contentment that was instantly neutralised by the ringing of her mobile phone.

'Kathy Caterall.' She tried not to show her irritation in case it was someone enquiring about flights or even wanting to book a group charter. On the other hand, it could well be a call from the media wanting her comments on last night.

In the event, it was neither. 'Oh, hello, Kathy,' said the assured female voice at the other end, 'my name's Margo Dunbar from *Cecilian Promotions*. Is now a good time to talk?'

'Actually, I'm having trouble hearing you as I'm on a boat just crossing a pretty wild stretch of water ...' this woman's name meant nothing to Kathy, nor the organisation she represented, but it sounded intriguing enough to divide her attention for a few minutes for the result it might bring, '... but go ahead.'

'Oh, right, I'll keep it short. You're probably aware, Kathy, that we *now* manage your sister Tracy.'

'*Half*-sister, actually,' corrected Kathy, raising her voice above the constant buffeting of wind and water, 'but, yes, I heard that she'd recently signed on with a professional agency, but didn't know which. No doubt you'll be watching her back from now on,' she added sourly.

'I prefer to think that we give good advice to our clients, steer them along the right path to success and solve any problems along the way,' replied Margo Dunbar, 'and right now Tracy's only problem is your demand for royalties you feel you're entitled to.'

'For *Dream Along* ... that's correct, Ms Dunbar, but it's more than a "feeling". I composed the music to that song and wrote the lyrics together with Tracy so, by rights, I'm surely entitled to three-quarters of the royalties.'

'Yes, well so far we've seen no evidence to support your claim, Kathy, so legally we owe you nothing.' There was just a slight pause for that to sink in and another sheet of spray to come flying over the cabin roof. 'But to avoid any more public outbursts like the one last night, we're prepared to offer you an immediate settlement.'

'How much?'

'Two thousand pounds ... but that's a one-off, once only payment on condition you make no further claim.'

'Knowing full well that I could lose out on a fortune if Tracy makes the big time,' seethed Kathy.

'There's no guarantee at all that your half-sister's career is assured,' said the increasingly rattled voice at the other end, 'whereas what we're offering *you* now could be in your bank this afternoon.'

The channel was curving slightly more easterly as Kathy neared the wide expanse of Breydon Bridge. In the lee of Great Yarmouth, the apparent wind was easing slightly, but not her resolve. 'Sorry, Ms Dunbar, but you can keep your measly two grand and I'll hang out for what's rightfully mine.'

'You're making a big mistake, young lady.' There was another pause at the other end. 'Okay, let me talk with Frazer and I'll see if we can raise the stakes.'

'I'm assuming "Frazer" is a partner in *Cecilian Promotions?*'

'Yes, and also my husband. Frazer founded the agency, but he's semi-retired now, leaving me to manage it.'

'Lucky for you,' retorted Kathy, sarcastically. 'Well, let's hope you eventually "manage" to see some sense.'

With that final quip she rang off just as the mighty spans of Breydon Bridge went gliding overhead, the road traffic crossing a symbol of the everyday life to which she was now reluctantly returning. Very soon she'd be turning left into the River Bure on the second half of this passage, but with a good hour before the tide turned fully in her favour.

Having entered the calmer waters of the Bure and cleared the two low bridges close to its entrance, she was nearing the yacht station, a good place to wait for the flood tide onwards and where she could take advantage of the onshore facilities to have a warm shower and a change into dry clothes.

With *Balloonatic's* lines taken and secured by the ever-helpful station rangers, ten minutes saw Kathy luxuriating under a comforting hot spray, but her mind still mulling over the conversation she'd just had on Breydon. It was still puzzling her, because something about it was strangely familiar. She couldn't think what until the penny dropped twenty minutes later when she was stepping back aboard *Balloonatic*.

Of course, it was the agent's surname – Dunbar – probably a common enough name in Scotland, but one she'd seen before and somewhere much nearer to her home mooring.

Chapter Nine

'So, Ted, what do you reckon?'

Well north-west of Kathy's present position, onboard the mystery cruiser in the *Watercraft* yard, Jack bent down to where Ted Finchley was kneeling to examine a section of the internal structure.

'Bit of a rum'n all round, if you ask me. I'm puttin' her age at not less than fifty years and probably built on the broads, seein' as her scantlings are more for inland waters than the sea.' The old boatbuilder paused to scratch his head. 'Wouldn't like to say who by though, but whoever he was, he weren't try'n to impress by his standard of work.'

'How'd you mean, Ted?'

'Well, take the way he's nailed the hull-planks to the ribs ...' Ted aimed his torch at the section of boat framing he'd just been examining, '... see the way he's just bent the end of the nails over the rib to fasten them. If he'd been doin' a quality job, he'd have clenched the copper nails into a rove with a cup-shaped washer on the inside, and then spread the end over it like a rivet.'

'So, we can assume the boat wasn't built for any discerning wealthy customer.' Jack took a look around the gloomy interior of the cabin. 'I got the impression from the start that the finish on this boat was pretty basic. I know it's been abandoned for at least thirty years, but there's no sign of it being kitted out for any extended stay on board. Almost a bare hull, in fact.'

'That's roit,' agreed Ted, 'but I did notice these.' He shone his torch up onto the cabin deckhead. 'What d'you reckon them's for?'

Jack studied the two large hooks fixed to the roof beams, one for'ard and the other closer to the aft end of the cabin. 'Fishing rods?'

'My thoughts exactly.' Ted switched off his torch. 'My guess is that this 'ere boat was built for a fisherman, which is why he weren't too fussy.'

'But no rods now,' said Jack, casting his eye about the cabin's sparse interior, 'which means the couple we found here either weren't anglers themselves or, at least, they didn't intend fishing on their last trip.' He gave Ted a questioning look. 'But you've found nothing that could lead us back to where this boat was built?'

'Certainly nothing in 'ere,' said Ted, pulling himself to his feet. 'And you say you couldn't find no trace of name or number on the 'ull, Jack?'

'No, nothing.'

'Mind if I have a look though.'

'Be my guest.'

Both men climbed out of the cabin, down the ladder placed near the cockpit and back to ground level. Immediately, Ted started examining the boat's transom. 'One place we should find 'em if they's 'ere.'

'I've already looked, Ted.'

'Yeah, but I can see this old tub had more than one coat of paint in her long life ...' he pointed to where some white paint still clung to the rotting woodwork, '... and this bit 'ere is where the registration number would 'ave been.'

'But long-since faded away, Ted.'

'Or painted over. Seein' how the owner weren't too particular on cosmetics, I'm reckoning they didn't do too fussy a rub-down between coats. So's, what I'm hopin' is that under this last coat there could be the original numbers that got painted over.' Ted pulled out his large pocket-knife and began carefully scraping away at the remaining paint layer. After a few minutes, to Jack's amazement, the outline of some numbers began to appear.

'By gosh, Ted, I believe you've found something.'

'Or at least the remains of ...' Ted began wiping away at the outline of a letter and three numbers, '... B ... 2 ... 6 ... 4, they looks to me.'

'Brilliant!' Jack pulled out his notebook and wrote down this welcome result. 'I'll get straight onto Henry Mayhew back at registrations and see what magic he can work.'

'Yeah, Henry'll sort that for yer,' agreed Ted, wiping the blade of his knife before returning it to his pocket and pausing to look around the yard. 'Ah, the old *Cecilian* yard. Seems a long time now since they had a cruiser fleet 'ere.'

'Did you know much about the old set-up, Ted?'

The old boatbuilder shook his head. 'Not much really. They was a bit of a newcomer to the Broads when they set up ... what? ... forty-odd years ago. What was new for them times, though, was that they had a girl runnin' the place.'

'Really?' This was news to Jack. 'Who was she?'

'Can't really remember 'cept she had the reputation of bein' a bit of a looker.' Ted stroked his chin. 'Now what was her name? ... Alice ... that's right, it were Alice.'

'Any idea what became of her, Ted?'

'Nope ... so long ago, Jack, and they really only ran the yard for about ten years before they sold up an' it became *Watercraft*. Sorry I can't be more 'elp.'

'Ted, you've been a mountain of help,' assured Jack, giving the old boatbuilder a grateful slap on the back. 'In fact, finding that number this morning could well crack this whole case.'

Back at his launch, Jack met Stuart Steadmore just seeing a young couple off in a dayboat. The yard manager nodded towards the old cruiser. 'Find anything helpful, Jack?'

'We certainly did,' answered Jack without going into detail. 'I'm letting DI Bailey know, so expect his forensic team back again tomorrow.'

'Okay.' Steadmore grinned. 'Hopefully that means we might soon be shot of you for good.'

'Perhaps so,' agreed Jack as he slipped his lines and motored away back on patrol.

*   *   *

At the same time as Jack was making his call to Broads Authority registrations, in her riverside penthouse, Tracy Goldman was pouring out her woes to her mum.

Lounging back on the luxurious sofa, Sandra Caterall ran ringless fingers through once- auburn hair now prematurely streaked with grey. As a single mum, her own life until now had been a constant struggle as she gave her daughters the best start she could. Now at least, Tracy's blossoming career promised, perhaps, the dawn of better times for them both. Until, that was, she'd received Tracy's sobbing call earlier that morning. Like any good mum, she'd rushed over to spend the next ninety minutes listening to an increasingly-anguished account of the night-club debacle and the unwelcome media frenzy it had triggered. She was about to offer her own conciliatory take on the situation when the chime of Tracy's mobile interrupted them.

Slightly annoyed, Tracy put down her coffee and frowned as she saw the caller's name. Moving to the window seat, she sat with mounting despondency as she listened to the voice at the other end.

'Not another of those damn newspapers was it?' asked Sandra when the call had ended and noticing yet more tears welling in her daughter's eyes.

'No, but I almost wish it had been,' sniffed Tracy, throwing her mobile into a corner and slumping into the chair opposite. 'It was Margo Dunbar calling to say she'd made Kathy a reasonable offer to back off.'

'And ...?'

'.. my dear sister just flatly rejected it.' Blinking back yet more tears from bloodshot eyes dark-circled from a lost night's sleep, Tracy put her head in her hands, her tangled hair hanging lankly around it. In skinny jeans and tee-shirt, she was well aware of being far from the glamorous image so carefully choreographed over the last few weeks. 'Bloody agents ... they're creaming off a big enough cut of my earnings to have had this sorted by now.'

'Now, try and calm down, love. Getting upset won't help,' urged Sandra, cradling her luke-warm mug of coffee while wondering how else to help resolve this acrimonious falling-out between her two daughters. Growing up, they'd got on well despite their different characters and she'd tried hard not to favour one above the other. But Kathy had always been headstrong with a determined streak of independence, whereas Tracy, eighteen months younger, had been more laid-back and content to let life take its course. Even so, it had been a shock listening to Tracy's account of her sister's uncalled-for outburst regarding the rights to *Dream Along*. Angered at seeing her youngest so upset, she hadn't hesitated to take her side. 'And don't go blaming *Cecilian* for this mess, love. It's that sister of yours who needs sorting out, not your agent.'

'I'm not so sure, Mum.' Tracy valued her mum's support and affection but, just the same, felt some guilt at this on-going conflict with kith-and-kin. 'To be honest, Kathy did write the music and most of the lyrics to *Dream Along*, and I just made a few suggestions.'

'Which probably made it the hit it is ...' persisted Sandra, '... that and the way you sing it.'

Tracy shook her head. 'No, it was appearing on *Stars* that made it a hit, Mum. I've been very lucky and, perhaps, it's only fair that Kath shares that luck ... or at least some of it.'

'Rubbish, Kathy played no part at all in you making the big time,' persisted Sandra, 'and just you remember that it was *me* introducing you to *Cecilian Promotions* that made *all* this possible.'

'I certainly won't with you reminding me all the time,' retorted Tracy, somewhat sick and tired of this repeating theme. 'And of how Frazer Dunbar owed you a favour from your London days. But Kathy *is* my sister, Mum, and blood's thicker than water, isn't it?'

'Maybe, but it wasn't blood that got you all this,' reminded Sandra, sweeping her hand across her daughter's sumptuous new abode. 'It was all the work Frazer put in to get you that *Stars* audition, all the publicity he wangled to win public support and votes, and now more gig-bookings than you can handle.'

'Actually, it was his wife, Margo, who did most of all that,' corrected Tracy, beginning to see her mother in a different light. 'To be frank, it beats me how Frazer keeps *Cecilian Promotions* going, seeing as he's seldom at home. If you ask me, it's Margo who's the mainspring in that agency while he just goes off enjoying his boat.'

'Only because she knows what she wants and doesn't give up until she gets it ...' Sandra thumped her mug down so hard on the side-table, that some of the cold coffee spilled over, '... which is how she got her claws into Frazer in the first place. She was a second-rate singer performing in third-rate clubs until he saw her and fancied her looks. By the time he realised *that* was her *only* asset, she'd already wormed her way into his bed *and* agency.'

'Well, perhaps she was a crap singer,' conceded Tracy, 'but as an agent, she gets things done ... like you had to do bringing up me and Kathy without our fathers being part of our lives.'

'You're right, it was hard having to be both mother and father, but my own fault, seeing as I'd been fool enough to make the same mistake twice!' Sandra paused to wipe away a tear. 'Not that I've ever regretted any of it. I couldn't imagine life without you and Kathy.'

'Which is why I've come to realise you should treat us both the same, Mum, and help Kathy get her share of the royalties.'

'She's got her head too much up in the clouds to want any help from me,' sniffled Sandra.

'Perhaps that's better than stars in her eyes,' countered Tracy. 'As it is, we've both had to follow our own lights wherever they lead us.'

'Yes, well make sure yours don't lead *you* into the wrong bloke's arms ...' Sandra took out another tissue and wiped up her spilt coffee, '... talking of which, has that road-manager of yours, Jarvis, still got the hots for you?'

Tracy rolled her eyes. 'Unfortunately, yes, and I still can't seem to get it across that I wouldn't fancy him if he was the last man on earth.'

'In which case, you might just have to get shot of him completely,' advised Sandra. 'You're way above his league in every way now, Trace, but watch out, because there'll be plenty of others trying to cash in on your fortunes.'

Including my own mother, thought Tracy cynically as she went off to brew some fresh coffee.

*　　*　　*

Also pouring himself a coffee was Jack Fellows, having just moored up in the pleasant setting of How Hill. Before he could even take a sip, however, his mobile rang. It was Henry Mayhew at Broads Authority registrations.

'Hi Jack. I'm probably interrupting your break, but I thought you'd want the information I've managed to dig up on that derelict boat of yours.'

'Crikey, that was fast work, Henry ...' Jack screwed the top back on his thermos, pushed aside the cup and pulled a notepad from his bag, '... but go ahead, I'm all ears.'

Henry quickly relayed his findings. 'Not a lot, Jack, but I hope it helps.'

'It's certainly another step forward, and thanks for tracking down the info so quickly.'

Call ended, Jack thoughtfully scanned the meagre details he'd written down, absent-mindedly retrieving his lukewarm coffee and about to dunk one of Audrey's shortbreads when his mobile rang again. This time it was Charlie Hedborough.

'Charlie ...,' once again Jack abandoned his snack, '... how's the Wild-marsh Farm investigation going?'

'Very interestingly, actually.' The ex-pilot sounded quite enthusiastic. 'I made contact again with that local chap who was living near the old strip when he was a boy during the war.'

'You say "a boy", Charlie?'

'Yep, just eight years old at the time, but one who was dead keen on aircraft and everything about them. He still has clear memories of some of the happenings at the strip back then, including one that was certainly out of the ordinary even for those wartime days.'

'This does sound interesting, Charlie.' Jack had even forgotten his short-bread. 'So, what happened?'

'Something even I've not heard of before, and a bit too involved to relate right now on the phone, but are you busy tomorrow?'

'No, a day off actually. Why?'

'Because I'm planning on taking my boat out, so how about you join me at Brundall Marina for a trip upriver and lunch at a pub where I can tell you all I've got.'

'Can't wait to hear it, Charlie. Give me a time and I'll be there.'

Jack had just rung off and was contemplating pouring himself a fresh coffee when he saw a familiar canal narrowboat just sliding into a spare mooring further down-quay.

Emptying his now-cold coffee over the side and throwing the shortbread to some ducks, he went to help with its ropes, happy a more comfortable break awaited him onboard *Balloonatic* with Kathy Caterall.

* * *

'You've certainly stamped your mark on this boat,' said Jack, sitting back on a comfortable side-berth in *Balloonatic*'s cosy saloon with a mug of fresh-brewed coffee in his hand.

The interior of Kathy's floating home was certainly everything he would have expected of someone with a sense of romantic bygones. Although warm enough now to not need the wood-burning stove in the aft corner, he could imagine the cosiness it would bring to this snug den with its brass lamps, velvet curtains and wood panelling. On that panelling were hanging numerous framed sepia black-and-white pictures of period balloon ascents together with colour prints of her own airborne adventures.

'Yes, it's the perfect bolt-hole,' said Kathy, sitting down beside him. 'A solid place to lay my head, and one I can shift to any other location that takes my fancy.'

'Except I hope you're not planning on *re*-locating out of Broadland, Kathy.'

'Not immediately, no, but the way things are shaping with both family and relationships, who knows what the future holds.' She sighed. 'The song-rights dispute took another turn this morning, which makes me think there'll be no quick solution.' Kathy related the call from Margo Dunbar and how she'd rejected the agent's first offer.

'You really think it's best holding out for more?' queried Jack. 'Is it worth all the stress and hassle that might bring?'

She gave a little shrug. 'It's more a question of principle with me, Jack, and we *could* be talking serious money if *Dream Along* climbs up the charts.'

'In my experience, the only ones who make big money out of this sort of action are the lawyers,' warned Jack, taking a sip of his coffee. 'I can see you wanting what's rightfully yours, Kathy, but both you and your sister would do better sorting this whole thing out of court.'

'Yes, I know you're right, Jack,' she acknowledged. 'The last thing I want is to drive a wedge between us. After all, she and Mum are the only family I've got.'

'So, you have no contact with your father or any idea who he is?'

'No, none.'

'And what about Tracy? Are you sure she doesn't know who her father is either?'

'Absolutely.'

'But both you and Tracy must have been curious to find out, especially as you got older?'

'Yes, we were, and we often discussed it together but, as I told you and Audrey in the pub, Mum got so upset if we ever mentioned it, that we gave up asking. In fact, I sometimes wonder if Mum herself is a hundred percent sure who they were.'

'Whatever, she seems to have done a good job of bringing the two of you up and, despite this latest falling out, she's seen you both make a success of your lives.' Jack paused for just a second to return to their original discussion. 'But, going back to your telephone conversation with Margo Dunbar this morning ... have *you* had any previous dealings with that agency before?'

'None at all before this morning ...' Kathy raised an eyebrow, '... but why do you ask?'

'Because the name of the agency is the same as the old *Watercraft* yard.'

'*Cecilian Promotions* and *Cecilian Cruisers*, you mean?' Kathy nodded. 'Yes, and surely that must be more than a coincidence, Jack ... as is the name of "Dunbar", because that rang a bell with me when Margo introduced herself. I couldn't think why at first, and it was only later when I was about to leave Yarmouth that I remembered.'

'Because that's the name on a plaque attached to an old aircraft joystick in the yard office?'

'That's right,' confirmed Kathy, '"J B Dunbar DFC", whoever he was.'

'Definitely someone I'd like to find out more about,' said Jack. 'And you say this Margo Dunbar mentioned her husband's name was Frazer?'

'Yes. Apparently he founded the agency but, being quite a bit older than his wife, has now more or less retired.'

'Nevertheless, he'd know if their agency had any connection with the old yard and who this decorated pilot was. He might at least be able to join up a few loose ends in the other mystery I'm trying to solve.'

'You mean the identity of that derelict boat and its skeleton crew,' recalled Kathy with a shudder. 'And you think they might be linked in some way? How?'

'Who knows, but I also remember you telling Van Heiden back at Wildmarsh Farm, that the place always gave you the shivers. Any idea why?'

Kathy shook her head. 'No, none, except I often get the feeling that someone's just walked over my grave when I'm there. But I'm also strangely drawn towards that aircraft control-column in the yard office ... a sort of weird feeling that it's trying to tell me something.'

'Yes, Stuart Steadmore told me it held a fascination for you,' said Jack.

'You've been talking to Stuart?' There was a momentary flash of concern in Kathy's blue eyes. 'How is he?'

'Oh, okay and coping, but he obviously still holds a flame for you, Kathy.' Jack leaned a little closer and lowered his voice. 'I know it's none of my business, but I really feel you two should bury the hatchet and give it another try.'

'Well, my attempts at sowing a few wild oats certainly haven't been too fertile,' she confessed with a sheepish smile and shrug. 'I guess we all need to swallow our pride sometimes and admit we were wrong. Anyway, let me get this commemorative balloon flight out of the way and then I can start thinking of getting my personal life back on track again.'

'Ah yes, the John Money re-enactment ... how's that going?'

'Lots to do and arrange, but Phillipa's being an absolute God-send. As you know, like Money's epic, all donations are going to the N&N, and she's finding lots of willing sponsors.'

'Well done Phillipa ... obviously a very competent young lady. What's her background?'

'All in PR, from what I gather, though I believe she did do a bit of antique dealing at some time.'

'Really. What sort of antiques exactly?'

'Oh, I don't know specifics, Jack. She just casually mentioned one day that she'd spent time attending antique auctions.' Kathy frowned. 'Any reason you're so interested?'

'No, just a fascination of mine for old things,' fibbed Jack, knocking back the remains of his coffee. 'Anyway, don't leave it too long before offering an olive branch to poor Stuart.' He stood up. 'Right, back to patrolling for me, but with plenty to think about.'

'Well, I hope some of the things we've talked about this morning help a bit,' said Kathy as she followed Jack through the for'ard well door.

'It'll at least be another angle to follow, because that joystick back at the yard seemed to be telling *me* something too,' confessed Jack as he stepped ashore, 'and perhaps tomorrow it might find a voice.'

And with that, Jack headed back to his launch, leaving Kathy Caterall strangely curious, but as bemused as ever.

*   *   *

Also bemused, or at least caught off guard, was Stuart Steadmore. Having just seen a young couple off in a dayboat, he was making his way back to the office when his mobile rang. Presuming it was another customer calling to make a booking, he'd instead been surprised to find out who the caller was, and even more surprised at the direction the conversation had straightway taken.

'So, what's happening with the old boat? Are the police still sniffing around it?'

'Not until today,' he answered, 'but Jack Fellows and some old boat-builder were having a good rummage around it this morning.'

'Really. What did they want?'

'I'm not sure, but from what I gathered, I think they were trying to identify it.'

'And did they?'

'I don't know, but I got the impression they'd discovered some crucial clue that the forensic lot are following up tomorrow.'

'Tomorrow, you say. So, have the police still got a night-watch on the boat?'

'Not anymore. The last chap here gave the impression that security was winding down.'

'So, the yard's empty tonight. Wouldn't it be a pity if some arsonist got in and torched the thing.'

'What are you talking about?' Stuart couldn't believe the way this conversation seemed to be going. 'No-one's likely to do that! We've never had anything worse than a few local hooligans breaking the odd window before.'

'Until tonight, maybe?'

With those few meaningful words, it began to dawn on Stuart just what he was being asked to do. 'You mean you want *me* to burn the boat?'

'Let's say I'd be more than grateful if it was found a charred wreck by tomorrow morning.'

There had been further discussion that had only deepened the dilemma that Stuart faced after ending the call. He'd never done anything illegal in his life, but the reward would possibly be life-changing. Did he have the nerve?

He remained seated at his desk for a long time mulling the options and realising that, one way or another, the decision he now took could well be the making or breaking of him.

*   *   *

Someone else questioning their nerve this afternoon was Walter Jarvis as he nervously tapped a number into his mobile.

'*Cecilian Promotions,*' came the abrupt reply.

'Oh, hello, is Frazer Dunbar there, please?' asked Walter.

'No, I'm afraid not. He's away in Norwich for a few days.' The female voice at the other end sounded very businesslike. 'This is his wife, Margo Dunbar. Can I help you?'

'Err ... possibly ...' stammered Walter. 'We haven't actually met, Mrs Dunbar, but my name's Walter Jarvis, Tracy Goldman's road manager.'

'Oh yes, Tracy has mentioned you.' Mrs Dunbar gave the impression that whatever mention Tracy *had* made, hadn't been that favourable as regards her roady. 'I am rather busy right now, but if you keep this short I can spare you five minutes. So, how can I help you, Jarvis?'

Margo Dunbar's condescending tone and the offhand way she used only his surname was already grating on Walter, so he made an effort to sound a little more forthright himself. 'Well ... actually ... it's me calling to help you ... Margo.'

'I beg your pardon.'

'I'm calling to tell you something you may want to know.'

'I can't think what,' replied an irritated voice, 'so please stop wasting my time and come to the point.'

'The *point*,' said Walter with emphasis, 'is that your husband is having an affair with Tracy Goldman.'

'An affair ...?' Margo's voice faltered, '... with our client?' An inward gasp was quickly followed by a hiss of scorn. 'What rubbish. How dare you come calling me with such ridiculous accusations?'

'Because it's a fact, *Mrs* Dunbar. I've seen them together.'

'Of course you have.' Margo Dunbar was regaining some of her old frostiness. 'Frazer's Tracy Goldman's agent, for goodness' sake. They're going to meet from time to time to discuss the course of her career.'

'At night ... in her flat ... and until the early hours?'

There was a pregnant pause at the other end before Margo Dunbar asked, 'You have proof of this?'

'No, I don't, but I can get it if you want.'

'And what's in this for you? Blackmail?'

'I don't want money, if that's what you think,' answered an increasingly-confident Walter. 'All I want is for Tracy not to go making a fool of herself with a man old enough to be her father.'

'Well, I know for a fact my husband is staying on his boat while he's in Norwich,' stated Margo, 'and he'll only be visiting Tracy to discuss future promotions.'

'And you know that for *sure*, do you?' countered Walter. Not receiving an immediate reply, he pressed on. 'Well, how's about I just keep an eye on him for the next couple of nights to put your mind at rest.'

'Why not, if it will disprove your ridiculous accusations,' agreed Margo, deriding the very idea while, at the same time, realising this was an opportunity to check what Frazer really did get up to while he was away. 'My husband's boat is called *Fenland Raider* and moored in Brundall Marina.'

'Right, no charge for my services, Mrs Dunbar, and I'll give you a call if I have any news,' promised Walter before ringing off.

In her Fenland office, Margo Dunbar switched off her phone and sat back, wondering if this shock revelation might actually be true. She had to admit she'd had her own suspicions, which now began turning to downright fury as she thought of all the ways she'd helped her husband turn failing *Cecilian Promotions* into a lucrative, money-making agency while he swanned off on his boat. Thanks to her, it was now a successful concern and Frazer, a man of considerable assets. Well, if there *was* any truth in what Jarvis had told her, she would surely take her philandering husband well-and-truly to the cleaners and get her legal half.

Margo Dunbar went into her bespoke kitchen, made herself a coffee, and sat down to work out the actual sum. It was while resentfully indulging in this exercise that it occurred to her there may be a way to get it all.

Chapter Ten

Ten minutes before the agreed meet-up time of 10:30, Jack parked his car at Brundall Marina and made his way to Charlie Hedborough's mooring.

Over the years, Jack had met Charlie several times in his boat, *Flyboy*, a twenty-five foot aft-steering cruiser, probably a good four decades old, but always immaculate. Knowing his background, Jack suspected Charlie probably maintained the boat more on aeronautical principles than marine. And there she was, halfway down the jetty, cockpit cover down, engine warming, an RAF ensign flying from her staff and Charlie giving a final polish to the windscreen.

'Morning, Jack,' he greeted, jumping ashore with outstretched hand, 'good to see you again.'

'And you, Charlie ...' Jack pointed towards the flapping ensign, '... even if it is under unauthorised colours.'

'Yeah, I know, not strictly by the book,' acknowledged Hedborough, 'but I'm proud of my service time and like to give the old flag a flutter.'

'Why not, Charlie?' Jack moved to the boat's mooring lines. 'Like me to handle the ropes for you?'

'That would be great, so let go aft, please.'

Five more minutes and they were under way and, shortly after that, nosing out of the marina and into the River Yare.

A few hire-boats were already cruising this widest of the Broadland rivers and, sitting on his seat at the wheel, Charlie gave a satisfied sigh. 'Ah, this is the life, Jack. Sunshine, fresh air and, dare I say it, no Air Traffic Control telling me where to go.'

'No, the boating world is still regulated by a good dose of common sense,' agreed Jack, standing beside the old aviator while enjoying the experience of being on the river with no obligation other than relaxation and pleasant companionship. 'But, talking of aviation matters, Charlie, tell me what you found out about Wildmarsh Farm.'

*   *   *

'It wasn't easy,' explained Charlie, upping the revs slightly as they cleared the Brundall area and cruised into more pastoral waters. 'In fact, the most enigmatic research I've ever done. The breakthrough, though, was finding someone who actually remembered the place when it was an active airstrip.'

'You mean this young plane-spotter you found who'd lived near the place.'

'That's right, Ernie Burrows, who still lives there as an eighty-nine-year-old.'

'... but, as you said, was only eight at the time?'

'Yes, but even at that young age, like many lads during World War Two, he was mad about flying and aircraft and kept a record of any air-activity he could spot.'

'And was there much to "spot" at Wildmarsh Farm?'

'No, very little actually,' said Charlie as he eased *Flyboy* around another of the Yare's lazy meanders. 'Ludham was the main airfield just down the road with squadrons of Spitfire and, later, Typhoon fighters, but Wildmarsh was only a grass strip too short for those fast birds.'

'So, what did the young Ernie actually see at Wildmarsh?'

'Virtually nothing during daylight hours, seeing as the rare times it was used were pretty hush-hush. The Air Ministry had bought the place early in the war, by compulsory purchase from the old couple who farmed it.'

'For what purpose?'

'That was never disclosed and it's still not something you'll ever find in public archives, but thanks to Ernie and the good chat I had with him over a glass or two of ale, I've formed a pretty good suspicion.'

Jack raised his brows. 'Go on.'

'Well, the best clue is the type of aircraft young Ernie saw taking off and landing there on moonlit nights. Luckily, his bedroom overlooked the strip and so he could watch what were obviously training sessions in a large, high wing, single-engine aircraft.'

'Could he say what type?'

'Absolutely. He was an enthusiastic expert on the subject and had no trouble identifying the aircraft practising night take-off and landings at Wildmarsh as Westland Lysanders.'

'Lysanders! Weren't they the planes they used for dropping spies in occupied France?'

'The very ones,' agreed Charlie. 'And bringing agents out as well. And, I'm sure, that was what the training was all about at Wildmarsh, seeing as Ernie said that those night flying sessions were all done with just the aid of a few hand-held torches.'

'... simulating the resistance workers meeting the drops at the other end,' twigged Jack.

'Exactly,' nodded Charlie. 'They managed that with just three torches ... one to mark the landing spot and the other two at the far end of the LZ. That's all they had.'

'LZ?'

'Landing Zone.'

'Ah, right, but whatever they called it, it doesn't sound like it was a job for the faint-hearted.' Jack frowned. 'But Norfolk's a long way from occupied France ... unless ...'

'... they were launching missions into the Low Countries,' said Charlie, completing Jack's train of thought, 'and that's what I'm sure it was all about. Both the Dutch and Belgians had very active resistance movements that needed support by our Special Operations Executive, so I'm pretty certain Wildmarsh was where the pilots trained and the aircraft flew from to reach there.'

'Which explains why the whole place was operating under such a strict blanket of secrecy. I guess there are many tales of bravery and tragedy originating from there that will never be told.'

'I'm sure there are,' agreed Charlie, 'but there's one particular incident that did stand out in Ernie's memory and that might be of interest to you.'

'Really? Tell me more, Charlie.'

But the old aviator was indicating ahead to the next bend, around which a traditional pub was just coming into view. 'There's the *Woods End*, Jack. I'll let you buy me a pint in exchange for the full story over lunch.'

*　　*　　*

Much further upriver, in her home on the city outskirts, Sandra Caterall quickly dried her hands from washing up to answer her mobile. She was pleased to see it was from Tracy, but that quickly turned to renewed concern when she heard yet more sobs at the other end.

'Trace, love, pull yourself together and tell me what's the matter now.'

'Oh, Mum, I've just had a call from Margo Dunbar.'

'What, with more bad news about this song-rights business?'

'No, worse than that,' blubbed Tracy between sobs. 'She was ringing this time to accuse me of having an affair with her husband.'

'What, Frazer? Surely not. Where on earth did she get that idea?'

'I haven't a clue, but someone seems to have convinced Margo enough for her to warn me that she'd put an immediate stop to my singing career if it turned out to be true.'

'Has she ... she any grounds for that suspicion?' asked Sandra, nervous at further inflaming her already distraught daughter.

'No, of course not, Mum.'

Sandra was pleased that at least her daughter's immediate denial carried with it enough of her old spirit to stop the blubbering.

'How about Frazer then? Has he been in any way ... er ... inappropriate?'

'Not really, Mum. Oh, I suppose he has been a little bit over-familiar at times when we've been alone, but I just put that down to the world of show-business.' Tracy gave a half-crying giggle. 'They're all such a kissy lot, that I guess some of it rubs off.'

'But not with you, Trace?'

'Certainly not.'

'So you promise me Margo Dunbar is completely barking up the wrong tree?'

'Absolutely.'

'I don't particularly like the woman, but would it help if I spoke to her?' asked Sandra, who had met this other half of *Cecilian Promotions*, a couple of times before.

'I don't think so, Mum, seeing as she seemed determined to think I was lying, even when I swore there was definitely nothing going on between us.'

'So, how do you plan to handle it?'

'The only other way that might just get the truth across to her. By talking to Frazer and getting *him* to convince his neurotic wife.'

Sandra closed her eyes in apprehension. 'I really don't think that would be a good idea, Trace. In fact, you'd be best just giving him a wide berth so you don't add fuel to this malicious rumour, especially as we don't know who's spreading it.'

But her daughter was not to be deterred. 'No, I need to snap this in the bud right now, Mum. I'm not going to stand by and be accused of something so ludicrous. My singing career depends on that woman's support and she needs to know the truth.'

'Just don't do anything foolish,' pleaded Sandra, before realising she was talking to an-already dead line.

She switched off her mobile and sat down at the kitchen table. Where would this desperate situation lead? There were already enough troubles coming home to roost without the prospect of this confrontation and the truths it might bring out.

Sandra picked up her phone again and tapped a listed number. She needed to talk, and the sooner the better.

*   *   *

In the dining room of the *Woods End* pub there was already talk. With meals ordered and glasses of best ale being enjoyed, Jack and Charlie sat back in pleasant anticipation of a good lunch. They could have been any two retired gents savouring a get-together except, in Jack's case, he was more than anxious to hear the conclusion of Charlie's research.

'So, what was this incident that young Ernie Burrows watched unfold, presumably, from his bedroom window? I thought everything that went on at Wildmarsh during the war was supposed to be top secret.'

'And so it was,' agreed Charlie, 'but the best security in the world would be hard-pushed to keep everything from gossiping Norfolk villagers.'

'So, is this account based on fact or tittle-tattle?'

'A bit of both, I suspect.' Before Charlie could explain further, their meals arrived and they were nearly half-way through the course before the old aviator could continue his story. 'The thing to remember, Jack, is that young Ernie was a lad who kept his eyes and ears open, and had a good idea of all that was going on, including one significant incident.'

'Which was ...?'

'A Lysander crash at the field in late 1943. He actually remembers hearing the aircraft returning in the early hours. Being full-moonlight, he knew there would be no bomber ops that night and so the roar of a lone aircraft, with what sounded like a failing engine, was enough to have him out of bed to see what was happening.'

'So, what did he see?' asked Jack, pausing from buttering a roll.

'Not the aircraft at first, as it was showing no lights. But he could still hear the engine before it suddenly stopped. Ernie had listened to a lot of aero engines during the war and the way this one cut abruptly told him it wasn't the pilot simply throttling back for landing, but one completely failing. Then he saw the aircraft itself in the moonlight, easily recognisable as a Lysander gliding down onto Wildmarsh.'

'Did it land safely?'

'Apparently so, but the pilot had to have been pretty skilled to get it down, because the old kite must've been badly damaged.'

'How did Ernie know that?' queried Jack.

'Because he didn't hear it take off again and then, three days later, he saw what looked like a Lysander hidden under covers and with its wings off, being taken away by low-loader along the back lanes.' Charlie paused to push away his plate. 'Doubtless off to a repair depot for a rebuild.'

'Presumably as a result of damage sustained by enemy action on a mission,' said Jack, 'but surely that wasn't an unusual happening during those wartime years.'

'Not at all,' agreed Charlie, 'but it was the rumours that began circulating around the village in the next few days that set it apart in young Ernie's memory.'

'Rumours?'

'That the pilot had brought the aircraft in with one dead occupant on board.'

'How did that story take root?'

'Just the way everything was hushed up after locals spotted an RAF ambulance arrive at the farm and then depart a short time later. When they questioned an airman from Ludham about it later in the pub, he let on that it had been collecting a body. I believe the village vicar then even asked the Ludham station commander why they couldn't have buried the casualty in the parish churchyard, but received a terse reply that "other arrangements had been made". Such secrecy was only guaranteed to increase local suspicion of clandestine operations.'

'Which I'm sure they were,' said Jack, 'but what's your take on the story, Charlie?'

'Probably the same as yours, Jack ... that the Lysander had been sent to Holland to collect an agent or other important personage, and then caught a packet from enemy ground-fire or night fighter on return.'

'... when the unfortunate passenger was fatally wounded,' presumed Jack. 'But why Holland, Charlie?'

'Because Norfolk would allow the shortest route to a pickup there. If the r/v had been in Belgium, then, for the same reason, a field down in Essex would have been used. So Holland had to be the destination, and we know that the identities of all our foreign operatives was kept secret to prevent repercussions by the Gestapo on their families back home.'

'That certainly all makes sense,' granted Jack, 'but what happened to Wildmarsh after the war, because it looks like it hasn't been lived in for years?'

'Yes, I did make enquiries about that, Jack. Sadly, it seems the old previous owners had both died before war's end with no traceable relations.

Consequently, the government put the place up for auction and it was bought by a chap called ...' Charlie paused to extract a handwritten note from his pocket, '... John Dunbar.'

Jack stiffened in his seat. 'I know that name ... or at least a "J Dunbar".'

'Really?' It was Charlie Hedborough's turn to be surprised. 'How?'

'I'll explain later, Charlie. Do you know any more about this Dunbar chap?'

'Only what Ernie could relate, because his own dad worked on the farm for years. Apparently Dunbar had been an RAF pilot during the war, but then settled down to farming with a new wife and to raise a family. Ernie said he sometimes played with the kids ... a boy called Frazer and his sister Alice.'

'Alice?'

'That's right. Do you know her?'

'No, except it's a name I heard just a day or so ago.'

'Oh, okay. Anyway, neither Frazer or Alice was interested in farming and, when their father John died in the 1980s, they put the farmland out to rent.'

'Hmm, all very interesting,' admitted Jack. 'And how lucky we are that your Ernie Burrows could remember all these details.'

'Yes, he's still pretty sharp,' acknowledged Charlie. 'In fact, most of it was still pretty fresh in his memory.'

Jack frowned. 'How come?'

'Because he'd had to relate this whole story only a few weeks before, apparently to a young woman doing some research of her own.'

Jack pushed away his plate and leaned a little closer across the table. 'He didn't happen to mention the name of this "young woman" did he?'

'He did actually,' said Charlie with a satisfied grin, 'seeing as she made such an impression on the old boy by being both attractive and so keen to hear his story. Her name was Phillipa Keyworth.'

*   *   *

'A lovely lunch, thanks, Jack,' said Charlie as they cruised back to Brundall on the ebb tide, 'though I didn't intend you to pick up the tab.'

'My pleasure, Charlie, and you certainly earned it for finding out such invaluable information.' Beside the skipper, Jack turned to face him for confirmation of something else they'd discussed. 'And you reckon that mounted joystick I showed you on my phone could well be out of a Lysander?'

'I reckon it could,' agreed the old aviator as they slowed on entering Brundall waters. 'Of course those great old aircraft were well before my time, but I'm pretty sure the Lysander had a spade-grip control column the same as that. Just to be sure, though, I'll get the RAF Museum to confirm it and let you know.'

'That would be great,' thanked Jack as they turned into the entrance to the marina. 'Okay, harbour stations for me.'

Minutes later and they were nudging into *Flyboy*'s berth and Jack was jumping ashore with the lines, making fast and then joining his skipper back onboard as the engine was shut down. After receiving assurance that there was nothing more he could do to help, he made his way back to his car and headed for home.

To get from the marina back to Brundall's main street, however, involved crossing the railway line at the village station. Here there were level-crossing gates and, at this hour, they were just closing for the 5:15 train from Norwich to Yarmouth.

Trains were another love of Jack's, and this delay was of no consequence as he sat back with contented interest as this local one drew in.

Being late afternoon, most of the passengers getting off were commuters, arriving home from work in Norwich. As Jack watched them spill out of the carriages, he recalled memories of his own commuting days when he was based at Scotland Yard, spending each morning and evening squashed like a sardine in rattling tube trains. It served to remind him how grateful he was to be enjoying a job in idyllic surroundings where he could almost walk to work.

Most of these disembarking passengers obviously lived in the residential part of Brundall and were heading straight up the road from the station. Only a few were crossing the footbridge over the line to waterside homes beside the River Yare or, perhaps, staying aboard boats in the marina. For his own amusement, Jack studied their faces to see if he could work out which.

It was then he noticed one slightly-built young man, pausing as though uncertain of where to go, and whose face was vaguely familiar. Jack cast his mind back as he struggled to think where he'd seen him before. Then he remembered it was not only at the launch of their balloon trip, but also at *Fidel's* night club in Norwich.

It was Tracy Goldman's put-upon roady, Walter Jarvis.

In *Balloonatic* moored at Wayford Bridge, Kathy Caterall was doing some hard thinking of her own. Uppermost in her mind were Jack Fellows' wise words and how he'd advised her to heal the rift with Stuart before it was too late.

She'd certainly missed spending time with Stuart and the fun times they'd shared together. She also knew she'd over-reacted to Tracy's harmless flirtations and been a fool to attempt to even the score by going out with Hans van Heiden. Realising now how strong her feelings had always been for Stuart, the time had surely come to make amends.

Kathy glanced at the bulkhead clock. It was almost six o'clock. After supper, she'd planned to do her weekly shop at the local supermarket followed by a drink at the village pub, if only to share some company. How much nicer if that drink could be with Stuart, talking over past differences and making up again.

An obvious first move would be to give him a call. She knew that he'd be working late at the yard until the last day-boat returned and then spend an hour or so checking they were shipshape for the morrow. After that he'd be spending more time scanning his mails for bookings and closing the day's paperwork. Perhaps telephoning might just get a response she didn't want and that simply turning up might be the best way to avoid unnecessary misunderstandings.

Already feeling better at having a plan, Kathy set too preparing her light meal while hoping it might be the last alone for the foreseeable future.

*　　*　　*

'Mmm, do I detect the welcoming aroma of baking, Aud?' One man already assured of loving companionship was Jack Fellows, sticking his head around the kitchen door and sniffing like a bloodhound on the trail. 'Your delicious scones, if I'm not mistaken.'

'Yes, well, keep your fingers off,' warned Audrey, waving a spatula in mock threat, 'because we'll be eating supper in just fifteen minutes.'

'Time for a quick cuppa though,' said Jack, sitting down at the kitchen table, pouring himself some tea and patting Spike, who had just emerged from beneath to demand his master's homecoming fuss. 'Then I need to make a phone call after ...' he was still eyeing Audrey's scones, '... just one of those to stave off imminent starvation?'

'Just one then,' relented Audrey, pushing across the cooling rack and butter dish, 'though goodness knows where you put it all, seeing as how you had a full lunch today with Charlie Hedborough.' She wiped her hands and sat down opposite with her own cuppa. 'Anyway, how did that go?'

'Very interestingly, actually.' Jack broke open his scone and buttered it generously while explaining all that the day's meeting had revealed.

'What a very sad story. So many brave people risking their lives and for that Dutch resistance worker, escaping the Germans, only for it to end in his death,' lamented Audrey after listening to the account of the Lysander incident, 'but how does a shot-up plane help solve the mystery of those skeletons on the cruiser?'

'I'm not sure if it will,' confessed Jack while checking the kitchen clock, 'but time to make that quick call which might just provide a link.'

Ten minutes had Audrey all set to dish up and her husband back at the table. 'Well, Jack, any revelations?'

'Sadly, no. I rang *Cecilian Promotions* but Frazer Dunbar wasn't there. According to his wife, he's on his boat at Brundall Marina for a few days.' Jack sighed. 'A pity I hadn't known that earlier when I was there as I could've looked him up then.'

'Ah well, something to do tomorrow,' placated Audrey.

'Yep. Wife Margo gave me the name of his boat and the berth number and said I should find him alone ...' Jack stroked his chin, '... although she said that with a slight edge to her voice.'

'How do you mean?'

'Oh, just that she gave the impression of being a bit uptight at his being there.'

'Probably just another boating widow fed up with the amount of time her husband spends away from home.' Audrey dished some meat and veg onto Jack's plate. 'Anyway, why is finding a connection between the yard and agency so important?'

'Because there's a good chance the pilot flying that Lysander was the "J B Dunbar" named on that mounted joystick at the *Watercraft* yard,' said Jack, liberally salting his meal. 'Charlie Hedborough rang me on the way home to confirm that Lysanders were fitted with that type of stick, so there's another link to Wildmarsh Farm.'

'Which you say was purchased by Dunbar when it was auctioned off after the war,' recalled Audrey, gently taking the salt cellar from her husband's hands. 'You'd think that if he'd had a bad experience there, it would be the last place he'd want to own.'

'Yes, very strange,' agreed Jack, 'and even stranger that he'd have the sort of money to pay for it.'

'Unless he came from a wealthy family. But I can see how you're connecting him and *Cecilian Cruisers* to the Frazer Dunbar who runs *Cecilian Promotions*.'

'Exactly, Aud. Frazer Dunbar can't be that common a name, so I'm assuming he has to be Flight Lieutenant Dunbar's so who, according to Charlie's informant, had a sister called Alice. It all fits into place, as Ted Finchley reckoned that back then, a young woman called Alice actually ran the old cruiser fleet.'

'My goodness, all these names and connections,' sighed Audrey, sitting down with her own supper. 'So let me get this straight, Jack ... that after the war, this RAF pilot, John Dunbar, came up with enough money to purchase Wildmarsh and raised two children there, Frazer and Alice.'

'That's right.'

'But did Charlie's informant ... this Ernie Burrows ... know what happened to his wife?'

'Died tragically of cancer when the children were in their late teens,' explained Jack. 'Apparently son Frazer had no interest in farming, but was well into the music scene, so he left home soon after and set up *Cecilian Promotions* down in London.'

'So, what happened to Alice?'

'Being a devoted daughter, she stayed with her father until he died in the early eighties, leaving quite a wealthy estate, including a generous legacy to Ernie's dad. Being the only son, Frazer would have been the main beneficiary, but I'm sure Alice was also well provided for.'

'She certainly deserved to be, having looked after her father all those years,' declared Audrey.

'Undoubtedly,' agreed Jack. 'Like I said, Frazer had no interest in farming and instead had founded his own promotions agency in London. According to Ernie, after his dad's death he rented out the land to surrounding farmers, kept the house and outbuildings for Alice to live in and eventually used his share of the inheritance to set up *Cecilian Cruisers* with his sister as manager.'

'Well, at least Alice remained in the family home and was able to work in a family business, but what a coincidence that, all these years later, Tracy Goldman has signed on with Frazer's *Cecilian Promotions*.' Audrey shook her head. 'It's a small world.'

'Isn't it just,' agreed Jack sceptically, 'and more than a coincidence, if my instincts serve me right. Finding those skeletons on that boat has injected a whole new aspect into a story I'm just starting to unravel. Oh, and just to add to odd happenings, who should I see arriving at Brundall Station just an hour ago, but young Walter Jarvis.'

'Tracy's roady? What was he was doing there?'

'I've no idea, and he seemed a bit uncertain himself, as though he was in unfamiliar territory.' Jack paused, thoughtfully. 'I wonder if he was off to see Frazer himself?'

'Possibly, seeing as they're both involved in Tracy's career,' agreed Audrey.

'Yeah, but not without friction, according to Kathy.'

'Well, perhaps they've found some common ground,' said Audrey, frowning as her husband helped himself to extra mash. 'And thinking of common ground, love, it must've been a shock hearing Phillipa Keyworth had also tracked down Ernie and been delving into the history of Wildmarsh as well as you.'

'It certainly was, though perhaps it shouldn't have been, seeing as we'd already found her there looking suspicious when we went for our own poke around.'

Audrey shook her head. 'What is it about that place, Jack, that has everyone so intrigued? First Van Heiden pops up there out of nowhere after our balloon landing. Then, later, we find Phillipa furtively tapping away in the barn, and it seems that even Kathy feels some weird connection to it.'

'I don't know yet, but it's time I found out, starting with a chat tomorrow with Van Heiden himself. I'll be interested to find out about his relationship with Phillipa, if nothing else.'

'So, you've actually arranged a meeting?' queried a surprised Audrey.

'Yep, I rang him straight after speaking to Margo Dunbar. I've been suspicious all along of his motive for hanging around here and his connection to Phillipa, so I decided it was time to have it out with him man-to-man.'

'So, where and when is this meeting?' asked Audrey, while wondering why she should be surprised at her dogged husband following up every available lead.

'Norwich Castle museum at 10:30,' said Jack, eyeing up the leftovers.

'Just as long as you go prepared for rain then,' urged Audrey, 'because that's what the forecast is promising for the afternoon.'

'Ah well, the garden needs it,' accepted Jack philosophically while reaching for the bowl of mash. That temptation, however, was thankfully frustrated by the ringing of the study phone and his rush to answer it.

Taking advantage of his sudden absence, Audrey quickly cleared the remaining food out of sight but, by the time Jack returned, he looked too preoccupied to even notice. 'That must have been an absorbing discussion, Jack. Who was it?'

'Bailey, calling to tell me they've just got the DNA results on those skeletons.' Jack sat down again. 'Like I guessed, the bones were so old they'd had to go down the mitochondrial route.'

'And what does that mean?' asked Audrey, trying to show an interest.

'Apparently it involves a process where they somehow use the phylogeny along which the genome is inherited ... or that's what Bailey said.' Jack rolled his eyes. 'Like a foreign language to me, Aud.'

'Quite. Sorry I asked,' laughed Audrey. 'The important thing is, did it work out who those poor souls actually were?'

'Not really. DNA can only do that if you have something to compare it with, and so far they've got nothing.'

'So, in reality, no further forward than before.'

'Not as far as Bailey is concerned, but those results did serve to confirm my own suspicions.'

'How?'

But Jack shook his head. 'I can't say yet, except that instead of showing *who* they were, they did at least show *what* they were.'

*   *   *

Conflicting emotions of a different kind were being faced at the *Watercraft* yard. The last boat had returned hours before, the yard-hands had finished for the day and gone home, but still Stuart Steadmore lingered.

Although dark now, the lights in his office remained off, only amplifying the eerie silence of the yard. Stuart sat at his desk, the beam of the waning moon casting sinister shadows as he contemplated the box of matches before him. In the corner was a can of petrol, drained from an old outboard motor that had been standing unused in the boatshed since last summer. That fuel would give sluggish power but still be flammable enough to start a healthy blaze. Stuart glanced outside at the eerie silhouette of the derelict cruiser sitting just yards away beneath its canvas cover. A quick splash of that fuel, a single lighted match, and the job would be done.

He tried convincing himself that the boat was a wreck that would be broken up and burned anyway, so what harm would it do? He would surely get away with it, but never having broken the law before, could he live with this on his conscience for the rest of his life, even for the love of Kathy Caterall.

And why was it necessary anyway? What possible secrets could that old boat still hold that it needed to be destroyed? There was obviously some connection to the skeletons and, as he pondered, he began to realise that he would be tampering with possible evidence in a murder enquiry.

Murder! Arson was a serious enough offence, but getting involved in murder was something else. Stuart started to feel disgust with himself at even considering such criminality, and even more resentment at being asked to carry it out. Should he instead call the police and report the whole matter?

Stuart let his eyes wander back to the box of matches. He picked it up and turned it over in his hands, knowing that his future could be dictated by the choice he was now agonising over. Then, mind made up, he picked up the can of petrol and headed out into the yard and whatever consequences his decision would bring.

*   *   *

Also suffering second thoughts was Walter Jarvis, languishing in the cold of Brundall Marina while keeping watch on Frazer Dunbar's *Fenland Raider*. And, once again, Walter was discovering that the work of an amateur sleuth could indeed be dreary in the extreme.

It seemed an age since he'd arrived at Brundall Station and made his way through the extensive marina to where Margo Dunbar had told him he would find the boat. Having spent the last three hours in fruitless watch, the only thing he had established in that time was that Frazer Dunbar certainly wasn't short of money, for *Fenland Raider* was an impressive boat, big and sleek with two decks.

This didn't surprise Walter, as he'd already noticed, in the marina car-park, a top-of-the-range Mercedes with its CP1 number plate. It was the same car he'd last seen Frazer bringing Tracy back to her apartment in all those nights ago. Yes, Frazer Dunbar seemed to have it all in terms of material possessions but, more than ever, Walter resolved that Tracy Goldman's heart would not be added to them.

At this late hour, though, that determination was already being severely tested by the sheer monotony of surveillance. With darkness having descended and with it the temperature, Walter was more and more questioning his own resolve. There was little chance Tracy would turn up now, so perhaps he'd call it a night and head for home. Then, at that very moment of indecision, the dilemma was taken out of his hands by footsteps coming down the marina walkway.

Walter ducked deeper into the shadows between two other boats, his heart racing as he recognised a far-from-happy Tracy climbing onto the cruiser's aft deck and immediately banging, somewhat assertively, on the boat's saloon door. In the light behind drawn curtains, Walter saw movement and then the bespectacled, pipe-smoking figure of Frazer Dunbar opening the door to his very agitated visitor.

With Tracy admitted in, Walter edged close to the boat's shining side, eaten up by jealousy and determined to hear what was going on aboard.

His vigil was nearly at an end, but what would be the result?

Chapter Eleven

'Aggh, another lead going almost nowhere.'

It was next morning as Jack wandered into the kitchen after fifteen frustrating minutes on the phone.

'Oh dear.' Audrey looked up from the breakfast table and sighed. 'Who were you calling this time?'

'Firstly, the number of a chap called Bertram Huntworth who was the last registered owner of *Pike Hunter*.'

'Was that the name of the old wreck?' asked Audrey, pouring her husband a coffee.

'It was when it was last tolled thirty years ago. After that, the Broads Authority lost track of it. As far as they were concerned, it had lived its useful life and probably left to rot in some boat graveyard.'

'Well, in a way it had, Jack, but couldn't Mr Huntworth cast any light on its subsequent history?'

'Mr Huntworth can't do anything anymore, Aud, because the poor chap died not long after selling his boat.' Jack sat down and took a hurried gulp of coffee. 'The elderly lady who answered the phone explained they'd bought the house after he died and had kept his number.'

'So, a dead end, love ... in more ways than one?'

'Not completely. I tried looking up other Huntworths in the phone book, found one in Norwich, rang and, hey presto, it turned out to be the late Bert's nephew. Even better, he remembered *Pike Hunter*, which, as the name implies, his uncle used for pike fishing, hence its pretty basic layout. As a lad, he'd often kept the old boy company, but in the end the boat became so dilapidated that Uncle Bert put it up for sale.'

'So ... who bought it?' asked Audrey, eagerly.

'Don't get your hopes up, love, because it was some nameless chap who took it off his hands for a few quid in cash, collected the boat from its Oulton Broad mooring, and no more was heard of it.'

'And there's no chance of finding out the name of this mystery buyer?'

'No, because he never re-registered it. So we're no further forward other than knowing this all happened in the early nineties, just a year or so before his uncle's death.'

'Then let's hope you make some progress this morning and Van Heiden produces *some* answers for you.' Audrey noticed her husband's empty plate. 'Aren't you going to have some breakfast first though?'

'No time, Aud,' said Jack, swigging back the remains of his coffee, 'but, yes, fingers crossed for this meeting because every new fact I've unearthed so far has only served to deepen the mystery, so just a glimmer of truth will be encouraging.' He glanced at the kitchen clock. 'Anyway, time I was off.' He stood up and was buttoning his jacket when the hall phone rang. 'Oh strewth, who's this calling now?' he groaned as he went to answer it.

The kitchen door was ajar as she started washing up and all Audrey could hear were exclamations of 'When did this happen?' and 'Any explanation?' before further discussion and Jack's return with a far from happy expression.

'Oh dear,' she frowned, 'more complications?'

'You *could* say that,' grumbled Jack. 'That was Bailey calling to tell me someone went and torched the boat last night.'

'What, the wreck?'

'Yep, *Pike Hunter*, and with it, any chance of substantiating the new evidence Ted and I uncovered yesterday.'

'Did you tell him it's already enabled you to find out the name of the boat and who owned it?'

'Yep, but it didn't help his mood over what happened last night. It had had a police guard on it until the powers-that-be started worrying about their budget and, reckoning the boatyard was safe enough, withdrew it.'

'Presumably, they have no idea who the culprits are?'

'Probably, local vandals, according to Stuart Steadmore, who reported it first thing this morning. Bailey himself is on his way there now.'

"Knowing that all chance of forensics discovering new leads have now gone up in smoke.'

'Quite literally,' mourned Jack. 'Anyway, Bailey will be back in his office by the time I've finished with Van Heiden, so I've arranged to drop in and see him before I head for Brundall to look up Frazer Dunbar and see what information he can give me.'

'It sounds as though I shouldn't expect you home too early then,' sighed Audrey, wiping her hands and leaning against the sink. 'Goodness knows where this whole business will lead next.'

'That's investigations for you, Aud,' said Jack philosophically, 'and this latest turn has at least given me an excuse to see Bailey and air a theory that I'm beginning to develop.'

'Which is ...?'

'I'll tell you when I've proved it,' promised Jack, grabbing the car keys. 'As it is, our poor old DI is feeling pretty sick at failing to keep a scene-of-crime secure, so my suggesting another source to follow might at least ease his woes.'

'What source is that?' asked an increasingly bewildered Audrey.

Jack only had time to give one of his wry grins as he headed for the door without even noticing poor Spike looking longingly at his lead. 'Wildmarsh Farm, of course.'

*   *   *

Passing between the castellated posts of Norwich Castle's main gate, Jack couldn't help but reflect on the fact that, until 1868, this was the very spot where convicted Norfolk murderers had been publicly hanged. It was a grim thought, but one that took his mind off the episode at *Watercraft* and allowed him to focus on the forthcoming meeting with Hans van Heiden.

After entering the castle proper, buying a ticket and making his way through the central rotunda, Jack found the Dutchman studying a large framed oil painting in the Colman Galleries. Aware of Jack's arrival in an otherwise empty gallery, Van Heiden turned with a warm greeting before pointing to the masterpiece he'd been studying.

'Norwich River by John Crome, circa 1819. Can you see the feint blue lines running through it? That's because, unusually, it was painted on ticking, a woven fabric usually used for the covering of mattresses.'

'I guess, sometimes, we all have to work with whatever material we can lay our hands on,' said Jack, with more feeling than he cared to admit.

'Quite.' Van Heiden gave a nod. 'But still it doesn't diminish the standard of Crome's work or the influence that Van Gogh had on all he painted.'

'Yes, quite striking,' agreed Jack before indicating the museum café. 'How about a coffee while we chat?'

'Good idea.'

While Van Heiden took a seat at a small table, Jack went and fetched two cappuccinos before settling into the chair opposite.

'Thanks.' The art expert took a grateful sip and nodded back to the galleries. 'So, Jack, you yourself are something of an expert on the Norwich school of painters?'

'Well, more an enthusiast really,' hedged Jack, stretching the truth as far as he dared.

'Quite, otherwise you would have corrected me instantly back there on the fact that it was Ruisdael and Hobbema, and *not* Vincent van Gogh, who were the main influencers on the work of Crome.' Van Heiden's mischievous smile quickly faded as he leaned forward and lowered his voice. 'So, Jack, having found out you are not really knowing of the world of art, what is it you really want from this meeting?'

'Perhaps the same as you've just cleverly achieved,' said Jack with a sheepish grin, '... truth and honesty, starting with the real reason you're here in Norfolk and why you are so interested in Wildmarsh Farm ... and don't give me any of your cock-and-bull story of interest in balloons.'

'Ah, yes, perhaps some subterfuge on both our parts,' admitted the Dutchman. Cradling his cup in his hands, he sat back with raised brows. 'Would I be correct in thinking, Jack, that you have more than a passing interest with police work?'

Jack could see this was a morning for total honesty between two equally perceptive investigators. 'You would,' he admitted before briefly outlining his career at Scotland Yard and ending with a shrug. 'Well, that's me, Hans, so how about you? What is it that's *really* brought you to Norfolk and, in particular, what is yours' and Phillipa Keyworth's mysterious interest in Wildmarsh Farm.'

Van Heiden paused for just a few seconds before obviously coming to a decision. 'Yes, Jack, I can see it's cards-on-table time.' He shrugged. 'Well, for a start I really am an art expert ... and with quite a significant reputation in the world of fine arts.'

Jack frowned. 'Strange then that I couldn't find anything about you on the internet.'

'Which is quite deliberate on my part,' continued Van Heiden, 'and you'll understand why when I explain how I now use my expertise.'

'Which is?'

'By attempting to trace lost Dutch art treasures stolen in the war by the Nazis.'

'I half-guessed it was something like that,' admitted Jack, 'once I'd found out what was going on at Wildmarsh during the war. But I seem to recall there once being an organisation purely dedicated to that cause. Wasn't it known as the MFAA?'

'The Monuments, Fine Arts and Archives Programme,' confirmed Van Heiden, 'whose work it was taken over in 2007 by what became known as the "Monuments Men". They continue to do a very fine job on a global scale, whereas me, I have dedicated myself to investigating and recovering just Dutch works of art.' He gave an audible sigh. 'Believe me, just that will be more than a life's work.'

'So, I'm assuming there's still a lot of artwork out there still missing from the war.'

Van Heiden nodded. 'You assume right. The Nazis, they stole an estimated quarter of a million pieces during their occupation of my country, and over a hundred thousand remain unrecovered. These include priceless pieces by Van Gogh, Rembrandt, Renoir and Raphael.'

'You're obviously talking a lot of money there.'

'Billions, Jack, but it goes beyond the value of them. There is an ethical factor that demands as many of these works that still survive should be returned to their original owners.'

'Who were?'

'Various national art museums and collections, but also some of the leading families of Europe such as the Rothschilds, Rosenburgs and Wildensteins.'

'Who are, doubtless, prepared to pay large rewards?'

'Probably, though in many cases, few of the family survived the war ...' Van Heiden leaned a little closer, '... which brings me to the reason I am here in your Broadland.'

'Go on,' urged an increasingly intrigued Jack.

Van Heiden sat back. 'This concerns a prominent Dutch banker called Alfred Vogelsang. Like most wealthy Jews, the occupying Nazis soon had him in their sights when they invaded the Netherlands in May 1940. Very soon, Vogelsang was arrested with most of his family, who then perished in concentration camps.'

'An appalling time,' said Jack, frowning, 'but did you say "*most* of his family"?'

'Indeed, because old Alfred sensed the tragedy that was about to unfold and urged his eldest son, Andreas, to go underground before the Gestapo came knocking at their door.'

'Good for him, and, I'm guessing, this young man also took with him as many of the family treasures as he could.'

'And you guess right, Jack,' acknowledged Van Heiden, 'but young Andreas was not the sort to sit out the war in hiding. Having made sure the Vogelsang collection was safe, he then went on to join the Dutch resistance and fight against the occupying Nazis.'

'Doubtless with a personal score to settle, having seen the rest of his family hauled off to almost-certain oblivion.' Jack leaned a little closer across the table. 'Now, if I may, Hans, can I give you my own take on the rest of this intriguing tale.'

'Go ahead.' Van Heiden took a sip of cappuccino, though his eyes, above the cup's rim, were fixing Jack's with barely-disguised scepticism.

'Right, well, with what I already know, I'm imagining that by 1943 the Gestapo were hot on Andreas's trail, making it necessary for him to take a quick exit from his homeland by way of a moonlit pickup by the RAF.' Receiving no contradiction, Jack continued. 'Except that trip ended in tragedy, didn't it, because the Lysander caught a packet somewhere en route and Andreas was tragically killed before he even reached England.' Jack sat back and folded his arms. 'Please correct any way I got that wrong.'

'No, you were pretty near spot on,' acknowledged Van Heiden admiringly. 'It was a German night-fighter that intercepted them crossing the Zuider Zee, but for me it took years to discover that, thanks to your British time limits on giving up wartime secrets. But yes, Andreas was mortally wounded in that attack and dead by the time the aircraft landed in this country.'

'... at Wildmarsh Farm,' added Jack, 'but I haven't given a full account have I, Hans? There was another important factor in that sad story wasn't there ... one that brings you, a missing-art investigator, here now.'

'Yes, of course, and now I'll complete the story for you ...' but Van Heiden was suddenly distracted by the clatter and chat of a party of school children entering the café, clutching their work books and cheerily looking forward to their own break, '... but perhaps somewhere a little more quiet and discreet.'

Jack suggested outside. 'It's still a lovely day and there are seats around the old moat. Let's get ourselves some fresh air before you confirm the suspicions I've been forming myself on this whole strange affair.

*   *   *

Someone else seeking peace and quiet that morning was Walter Jarvis. In fact, after a more than eventful night in Brundall Marina, he was even contemplating fleeing the county, if not the country.

In the meantime, though, he had settled for the temporary sanctuary of his small council flat, wondering how he had managed to get himself into a mess that could well see him in prison for life. How could he have been so stupid? Of course, he knew the answer to that all too well – that it was purely because of his infatuation for Tracy Goldman.

Last night's jaunt had seemed such a good idea when he first thought of it ... to be her knight in shining armour by saving her from the clutches of a man twice her age. As it was, he now desperately wished he'd never set foot in Brundall Marina where it had all gone so horribly wrong.

It was now a good twelve hours since Walter had had a bite to eat and twice that since he had slept a wink. Not that he had any appetite for either. All he wished was that he could turn back the clock but, as that would never happen, he instead just sat slumped on his couch, watching the door and wondering when the police would come knocking on it.

*   *   *

Outside and beneath Norwich Castle walls, Jack and Van Heiden found themselves a vacant bench seat.

'So, young Andreas had to get out of Holland before the Gestapo got him first?'

'Exactly.' Van Heiden stretched his legs out. 'They knew already he was a successful Resistance leader, but as well that his family owned priceless artwork and a large collection of gold and silver artefacts which the Nazis were desperate to get their hands on. So Andreas had a price on his head and the Dutch Resistance knew it. It was time to get him out, and so it was arranged that he would be collected on the next agent drop-off and brought to England ...'

'... except he tragically copped it on the way out,' completed Jack with a shake of his head. 'Rotten luck all round, but am I right in thinking Andreas brought out more than just his knowledge of Resistance operations?'

Van Heiden nodded. 'Yes indeed. There is only one member still alive now of the resistance group who met the aircraft that night, but certainly he remembered Andreas taking with him a large bag of ... something.'

'The family heirlooms?'

'They had to be, Jack, though that certainly was not something Andreas would have admitted to ... using that extra seat on the aircraft for family wealth rather than the escape of another freedom fighter.'

'Yeah, I can see that,' agreed Jack, stroking his chin, 'but what got you onto his trail in the first place?'

'A request for help from an English girl you already know.'

'Phillipa Keyworth?'

Van Heiden nodded. 'She had met and married Jan Vogelsang while she was working in Holland. His father, Edward Vogelsang, was a distant cousin of the family who, after the war, tried to trace their missing treasure.'

'With any results?'

'I'm afraid not, Jack, and he died accepting the fact they had fallen into the hands of the Nazis. However, after his death, son Jan continued the search.'

'Helped by his wife Phillipa.' Jack looked puzzled. 'But you say her married name was Vogelsang, so why is she now calling herself Keyworth?'

'That was her maiden name,' explained Van Heiden. 'After becoming a widow she reverted to that for reasons I will tell you.'

'You mean Jan is also now deceased?'

'Sadly, yes,' confirmed the Dutchman. 'He and Phillipa had spent all their savings searching for the missing treasure, before bankruptcy finally drove Jan to suicide.'

'This whole business seems to have been cursed by tragedy,' said Jack, 'so it's a tribute to Phillipa's doggedness that she didn't give up.'

'If anything, she was helped by her determination to prove that the death of her late husband was not in vain. There was already suspicion that Andreas had smuggled some of the family treasure out in the escape aircraft so, after the funeral of Jan, Phillipa returned to this, her native country. Here, using her maiden name to avoid suspicion, she pressed on with a search of her own by the scanning of lists at auctions, eventually identifying Vogelsang heirlooms and following their original sale trail back to ...'

'... John Dunbar, the pilot who'd flown Andreas into Wildmarsh,' finished off Jack with disdain. 'Back then, when he realised his passenger was dead, he found the bag of treasure and then got away with stealing and hiding it.'

'We are sure that is what happened ...' Van Heiden raised questioning eyebrows, '... but how did *you* work all that out, Jack?'

'By just a bit of snooping and deduction. So, how much do you reckon Dunbar made from his ill-gotten windfall?'

'A lot of money. Today, just those gold and silver artefacts would fetch near on a million pounds.'

'Phew,' whistled Jack, 'quite a windfall for a humble Flight Lieutenant ... but *you* specialise in paintings, Hans, so I'm assuming there were some of those as well.'

'Just one, actually, but it was the most valuable item in the whole Vogelsang collection and something Andreas would have been sure to try and save.'

'So, a rare piece?'

Van Heiden nodded. 'Very much so ... an early Van Gogh painted, we think, in 1882.'

'Blimey!'

'Indeed.'

'Hmm.' Jack strummed his fingers. 'I can see Andreas managing to smuggle small items onto the Lysander, but surely a painting would have been far too large, and certainly not something Dunbar could have pocketed that easily.'

'It wouldn't have been *that* difficult,' explained Van Heiden. 'You are thinking of the big masterpieces hanging in the galleries, Jack, but this Van Gogh was only forty by thirty centimetres and, taken out of its frame, rolled up and secured in a tube, relatively easy to conceal. And, because his aircraft was too damaged to be flown back to Ludham, Dunbar had plenty of time to hide that and the rest of Andreas's hoard before the ground-crew arrived.'

'... to eventually recover it once the rumpus of his failed mission had died down.'

'That is what we have deduced, and it must have been from the illicit sale of the Vogelsang treasures that, after the war, he had enough money to buy Wildmarsh Farm for himself.'

'Strange that he was so keen to buy the old place ... unless it was to prevent someone else discovering something he knew was still hidden there.'

'Exactly,' nodded Van Heiden. 'The missing Van Gogh.'

'But, how can you be so sure he hadn't already sold that as well?'

'Simply because the discovery and sale of a missing Vincent Van Gogh would have sent shock waves around the whole of the art world, Jack. Dunbar was no fool and soon he realised that was probably -- how do you English say? - one sleeping dog best left lying.'

'And you reckon that Wildmarsh Farm is where the Van Gogh still lies hidden?'

'That's the likely scenario. Why else would Dunbar buy a farm when he didn't have an agricultural background? It was one safe way of retaining his ill-gotten gains without risk of exposure.'

'Content that he'd done pretty well anyway out of his little wartime heist. Just the same, it must have been very frustrating, knowing he was sitting on a potential fortune worth ... how much?'

Van Heiden shrugged. 'When Van Gogh's *Fields near the Alpilles* was recently auctioned by Christie's in New York, it fetched close on fifty-two million dollars.'

'"Fifty-two ...!"' Jack gulped, 'Certainly a treasure worth seeking, Hans ... and even murdering for.'

'Murder?' Now it was Van Heiden's turn to give a quizzical stare. 'What murder?'

'Oh, just another criminal investigation I'm involved in, but which might well be connected to your own quest.' Jack sat back and frowned. 'And you say Andreas would have removed it from its frame and rolled it into a tube to smuggle it out ... which is how it might still be?'

'Probably.'

'And which you and Phillipa have been searching for at Wildmarsh?'

'Absolutely, but so far without success. It was because she needed expert help, that Phillipa got in touch with me for advice and support.'

'But she also recently befriended Kathy Caterall,' pointed out Jack. 'Why was that?'

'Because we suspected Kathy might somehow be connected to the whole business.' Van Heiden shrugged. 'That time you landed there in the balloon and almost caught me searching red-handed ... it was not the first time Kathy had used the old strip. And then, her telling me how she somehow felt a strange affinity with the place made me think that she might well know something of what had happened there.'

'And so ...?'

'... if she did, we needed to find out how much, and that meant getting closer to her.'

'In your case, by wooing the poor girl with your irresistible charm,' said Jack with undisguised sarcasm.

'Yes, I'm sorry I did that,' admitted Van Heiden. 'I had no wish to take advantage of the girl or hurt her feelings in any way but ...' he spread his hands in supplication, '... it seemed the best way at the time. Anyway,' continued the Dutchman, seemingly eager to guide this conversation in other directions, 'dear Kathy's lovely nature soon had me feeling guilty and deciding on another way to find out.'

'By using Phillipa?'

Van Heiden nodded. 'That is correct. Phillipa had some previous experience of PR work, and Kathy's proposed balloon re-enactment offered the perfect excuse for her to make contact. And so she got in touch and offered to help with publicity and fund-raising. However, it too proved not to help, because it did not take long for her to be sure Kathy had no knowledge of either the treasure or what happened at Wildmarsh all those years ago.'

'So, back to square one,' said Jack.

'It looks that way.' Van Heiden shook his head. 'We are rapidly running out of further investigation funds and are all set to write the whole thing off as a dead-loss.'

'Except I'm not sure it is,' said Jack. 'I don't believe in co-incidences when it comes to crime, and now several of them seem to be coming together to form what looks suspiciously like a possible solution.'

'You obviously know something I don't,' probed Van Heiden with a glimmer of renewed hope. 'Can you share it?'

'Not until I have more than just suspicion, Hans, and I'm not sure when that will be. However, my next appointment is with the police to discuss another development, so who knows where that might take us.'

'I was planning on returning to Holland in a few days,' admitted Van Heiden. 'Perhaps I should delay a bit longer yet.'

'It might be worthwhile,' Jack held up cautionary hand, 'but no promises.'

'I'll take that risk.' The Dutchman stood up and held out his hand. 'A worthwhile chat, Jack. Good luck and I hope to see you again soon with some positive results.'

'Let's hope so,' agreed Jack, warmly returning Van Heiden's handshake while glancing at the flag flying atop the castle battlements. It showed the wind now backing easterly and the promised rain on its way. Thankful he'd worn something waterproof, he straightway headed off for his meeting with Bailey.

Chapter Twelve

'Good to see you, Jack, even if it is to discuss a case getting weirder by the day.'

At Norwich CID, Bailey greeted his old friend with an expression as frustrated as it was welcoming.

'This arson's certainly an unexpected twist,' agreed Jack as he sat down to face the DI across his desk. 'What does Steadmore have to say about it?'

Bailey shrugged. 'Not much, actually. Reckons he left the yard last night as usual, but arrived this morning to find the old boat just a pile of burnt wood.'

Jack shook his head. 'A pity, because, under layers of paint, we'd just managed to detect its number.'

The DI brightened. 'Did you get a photo?'

'Unfortunately, no.'

'Which means we never will now,' mourned the DI.

'No, but it did make it possible to trace its old name and owner.' Jack described all he had found out about *Pike Hunter*'s antecedents.

'But none of which explains how it ended up in the reeds for thirty odd years with two bodies on board.' Bailey shrugged. 'And now, whatever else it might have told us, has been lost forever.'

'Hmm.' Jack stroked his chin. 'Anything else damaged in the yard?'

'No, nothing either burned, vandalised or stolen.'

'And Steadmore reckons it was local youngsters?'

'So he says. Apparently the yard has had the odd problem before, but only small stuff like a broken window and a few items nicked.'

'But nothing as serious as a boat burning, Bailey.' Jack frowned. 'Was there any evidence of accelerants being used?'

'Yep. The fire investigation boys reckon the boat had been well-and-truly doused in petrol.'

'Could that have been found in the yard?'

'There were some cans stored for outboard motors, but they were locked away in one of the sheds.'

'Which means the arsonists either brought some with them or …'

'… it was an inside job,' completed Bailey, nodding. 'Definitely an angle to consider.'

'Yeah, I can't see youngsters going to the trouble and expense of buying fuel and carting it there, with plenty more convenient targets to torch if they chose to.'

'Which brings us back to the other scenario … that someone who knew the yard wanted our prime evidence source destroyed for good.' Bailey raised questioning eyebrows. 'Any theories as to who that might be?'

'Possibly,' admitted Jack, 'but before I give it, did Steadmore offer any suggestions?'

'None.' The DI leaned a little closer. 'And, I have to say, Jack, I wasn't totally happy with his whole demeanour.'

'In what way?'

'Oh, just that he seemed slightly dismissive about the seriousness of the whole event. You know, that "just-kids-being-kids" sort of attitude.'

'Which does seem out of character for the decent and competent young man I know him to be,' agreed Jack, 'so I can understand you being a bit suspicious?'

'He's fully aware that arson's a serious offense,' pointed out the DI, 'so would he really risk a hefty jail sentence by destroying police evidence?'

'Not without good reason, but he *is* the sort who'd cover up for someone he particularly cared for.'

'Such as …?'

'Kathy Caterall.'

'This balloon skipper you flew with?'

'Yep, the owner of *Skyrides*, but also someone Stuart's deeply in love with.'

'Okay, but what motive would she have?'

'Good question, and a tricky one,' admitted Jack,' considering that the victims on the boat were probably murdered around the time she was born.'

'But you think she might be directly connected to our investigation,' pressed Bailey. 'In what way?'

'I'm mulling over some theories, but they'll be harder to prove now *Pike Hunter*'s burnt out.'

'And you reckon this Huntworth chap you spoke to has no way of finding out who bought his uncle's boat?'

'No.'

'Well, it really doesn't matter now anyway, seeing as forensics won't be able to search it again for DNA even if we manage to find some corroborating genetic link.'

'True, but all is not lost, Bailey. If we take DNA from everyone else, we can see if those results throw up any surprises. If my theory is correct, they may well do.'

'What, you mean test *everyone?*' groaned Bailey in despair. 'Strewth, Jack, my Super was already complaining about blowing his budget on some long-ago incident that might still be suicide. That was why I pulled the night guard on the blessed boat. If I now go back to him with a request for a dozen DNA tests it'll be more than his budget that blows, it'll be a blood vessel and probably my job along with it.'

'Not if it solves the case,' argued Jack. 'And we're not talking "incidents" here, Bailey, but murder, no matter how long ago it happened.'

'Okay, I go along with that,' admitted the DI, 'but even if I swung it, surely getting everyone to give a DNA sample would only alert whoever you think is behind it all.'

'Ah, that's where this incendiary job on *Pike Hunter* might just be a blessing in disguise,' persisted Jack. 'Have you released any details on it to the media yet?'

'Not yet,' admitted the DI. 'I'm not keen on broadcasting the absence of police security at a crime scene.'

'Good, so best keeping it that way for as long as possible.'

'Suits me,' said Bailey, more than happy to oblige, 'but why?'

'Because we can assess people's reaction to the arson attack and then make out we're taking DNA to eliminate them from our enquiries.'

'Some will already have spread the word though,' argued Bailey. 'I can't see Steadmore keeping quiet about it, and his ex-girlfriend Kathy will doubtless be in the know.'

'Yeah, but if it's not too late, I'll tell them to keep details to themselves for now.'

'Okay, but who do you propose we test?'

'Obviously Stuart and Kathy, and everyone else connected to the case including Kathy's half-sister Tracy, her mother Sandra, Walter Jarvis and also the owners of *Cecilian Promotions*.'

Bailey gave a quizzical frown. 'But I haven't even *heard* of some of these people, Jack. Who's this Jarvis bloke or *Cecilian Promotions* when they're at home?'

'Jarvis is Tracy's minder, but also a lover scorned,' explained Jack. '*Cecilian Promotions* is a musical agency, but with links to the original owners of the *Cecilian* boatyard.'

'But, we've already established this *Pike Hunter* boat wasn't from that yard,' stressed Bailey, 'so why waste time pursuing that dead end?'

'Because I think, bizarrely, everything *is* connected. The chap who founded the agency is called Frazer Dunbar, and he's staying on his boat in Brundall Marina at the moment, so I'm off to visit him as soon as we've finished this chat.'

'Hmm, well if he's that close and you reckon he might have a motive, he could well be in the frame for the bonfire job,' acknowledged the DI.

'I've deliberately avoided letting him know I'm coming, so he won't have time to perfect a story,' explained Jack. 'It's a pity I can't take his DNA while I'm there. The sooner we have the kits, Bailey, the sooner we can move this investigation forward.'

'Yeah, well DNA testing doesn't come cheap, so I hope your copper's instinct doesn't let you down.'

'It hasn't yet,' replied Jack, crossing his fingers.

'Let's hope this isn't the first time then,' said Bailey, glancing at his watch. 'Right now I need to go get authorisation for all those DNA tests, while convincing my Super that I haven't totally taken leave of my senses.'

'Good luck with that then,' wished Jack as he stood up and walked towards the door. 'In the meantime, I'll let you know how I get on with Frazer Dunbar.'

'Yeah, please do,' responded the DI without even looking up from the bulging file he was already re-studying.

*   *   *

By the time Jack reached Brundall Marina, as predicted, the morning sunshine had given way to a dismal blanket of afternoon drizzle that was already making the wooden walkways slippery as he made his way to the jetty where *Fenland Raider* lay.

He found the mooring to be a relatively secluded spot with just two other boats whose dirt-streaked sides and fading woodwork was in sharp contrast to the large steel cruiser lying at the far end, her white hull glistening in the damp air and the name *Fenland Raider* picked out in gold on her wide transom. As he made his way down her side, Jack appreciated the boat's clean lines, neatly stowed deck gear and well-tended mooring ropes. Frazer Dunbar certainly believed in keeping a smart little ship, but as Jack neared the open entry area at the stern and sensed someone was onboard, he couldn't help feeling an air of melancholy about the scene.

Perhaps it was because no lights were showing in the cabin even though the wet afternoon was becoming ever gloomier. Then he saw the probable reason, for lying on the wet walkway was the boat's shore-power cable, one end connected into the corresponding outlet on the quay, but the other end disappearing into the inky depths between quay and hull.

Not a good sign, and Jack went straight on board to check all was well there. As he reached the teak aft deck, there came the sound of footfall coming up the cabin steps. The figure emerging, however, was not Frazer Dunbar's, but a smartly dressed, rather intimidating-looking woman. 'Can I help you?' she demanded.

Jack gave a nod in return. 'I came on board to ask the very same question. I'm sorry I didn't announce my arrival, but ...' he pointed to the trailing shore-power cable ... 'I was afraid there'd been some sort of problem.'

'If you mean the damn lights aren't working, then there is.' She joined Jack on deck. 'Do you know anything about electrics Mr ...?'

'Fellows ... Jack Fellows. I'm a Broads Ranger and know that power cables shouldn't be lying there in the water, so wait here a minute.' Jack disembarked, ensured his hands were dry, pulled the plug from the shoreside socket, coiled the errant cable from the water and took it back on board. 'It probably tripped as soon as it went in, so let it dry before trying a reconnect.' Receiving no thanks, he quickly added, 'but I came here, primarily, to have a chat with Frazer Dunbar.'

'So did I, but he's not here.' Offering no hand, she did at least explain, 'I'm his wife.'

'Ah, yes, we have spoken on the phone, Mrs Dunbar, so could *you* spare me a few minutes.'

'Only if you can then get those damn electrics working.'

'Okay, let me see what I can do,' replied Jack, glancing about the wheelhouse before locating the battery selector switch on the rear bulkhead and confirming it was very definitely in the OFF position for all services. Two seconds had him selecting DOMESTIC and various lights immediately blazing to life.

'There's power for you again, Mrs Dunbar, but only from the batteries, so be sparing with your lights until we've had that shore-power checked.'

Instead of any thanks, she blew a puff of derision. 'Don't worry, I'll only be spending enough time on this thing as it takes to sort out that cheating husband of mine.'

'Yes, well I'd like to talk to you about Frazer myself,' said Jack and indicating the now well-lit saloon, 'so can we go and do that in more discreet surroundings.'

'If we must,' she grunted, leading Jack below and ushering him onto one of the built-in sofas, 'though I can't think how I can help you or when Frazer will choose to return.' She raised questioning brows above dark hardened eyes. 'Was he expecting you?'

'No, and I'm assuming he wasn't expecting you either.'

'You assume correctly, Mr Fellows, but my little surprise hasn't quite worked out as I hoped.'

Jack could well guess the meaning behind that statement and didn't pursue it. Instead he asked, 'How long have you been here on the boat then, Mrs Dunbar?'

'Let's keep it short to "Margo", shall we ... but only ten minutes before you arrived yourself. I came up on the morning train.'

'So, you didn't drive?'

'No, the Merc's Frazer's and it was still there in the marina car-park when I walked through.'

'How about its keys?'

'Still here,' said Margo, indicating a set hanging from a hook below the saloon shelving.

'And you live in the Fens?'

'Yes, that's right.' She gave a concerned frown. 'How did you know that?'

Jack shrugged. 'Oh, just a little research I've been doing on *Cecilian Promotions*.'

'I can't think why ...' Margo Dunbar crossed shapely legs, '... but if I can help you ...'

'I'm sure you could, Margo, but right now I'm more concerned with the whereabouts of your husband. Did he often come to the boat alone?'

'Yes, always. I hate anything to do with boats so never joined him, though I suspect he's not short of female company when he's here. He came this time to apparently sort out a problem in the boat's shore power thing.'

'Which could explain how it came to be disconnected, but you clearly expected to find him here?'

'Yes, and to catch him out with that damned girl he seems to have become obsessed with. Instead I came all this way to find the boat unlocked and open, but him gone.'

Jack chose to ignore the personal connotations of her unexpected visit and instead indicated the pipe lying beside a half-eaten meal on the saloon table. 'Is that Frazer's pipe?'

'Yes, but what of it?'

Instead of answering, Jack stood up and headed for the gangway steps. 'Margo, please excuse me while I go and make a quick phone call.'

On the quay walkway, Jack waited until a familiar, but occupied, voice said, 'DI.'

'Bailey, it's Jack, and I think you need to be here at Brundall a.s.a.p.'

*   *   *

'This had better be good, Jack.' Thirty minutes after the ranger's call, DI Bailey pulled up the collar of his coat against heavy drizzle carried on the easterly wind blowing across the marina walkway. 'My comfy office over a hot coffee would have been a better place to hear what you've got to tell me.'

'Perhaps so, but this is Frazer Dunbar's *Fenland Raider*,' said Jack, indicating the large cruiser at the end of the jetty, 'except he's disappeared.'

'How do you mean, "disappeared"?'

'Just what I said ... he's not here.' Jack explained what he'd found since his own arrival.

'Hang on, Jack ...' The DI wiped some moisture from his eyes, '... are you telling me you've dragged me from a mountain of backlogged paperwork just to tell me this show business bloke isn't on his boat. You told me yourself he wasn't expecting you, so why are you surprised?'

'Because I don't believe he's just popped out somewhere. It's far more serious than that, Bailey.' With Margo Dunbar still sitting in *Fenland Raider*'s saloon, Jack guided the DI out of earshot down the quay and lowered his voice. 'I'm convinced his disappearance has extremely sinister implications.'

The DI gave a cynical smile. 'And what makes you so certain, Jack?'

'Because all the signs indicate that Frazer Dunbar thought he'd be out for minutes at the most, but has, in fact, been gone hours, if not days. There's no way he'd go off and leave his boat unlocked, his meal half-eaten and his pipe on the table in the saloon. And his car and keys are still here as well. No, something ominous has happened here and we need to find out what.'

'Oh, come on, Jack,' the DI gave a half-smile and frown, 'aren't you getting a bit carried away here. Okay, this Dunbar bloke has been detained longer than he thought, but we wouldn't even register him as "missing" for another twenty-four hours.'

'It may be more than that already,' persisted Jack. 'That meal is stone-cold and dried up, so he's already been gone several hours ...' Jack glanced towards the grey waters of the Yare flowing swiftly just beyond the dyke, '... and possibly in there.'

'What, drowned you mean?' There was still an edge of incredulity in the DI's voice. 'What makes you think that?'

'Because I found the boat's shore power connected, but with the live end in the water. His wife Margo reckons he'd come here because of some electrical problem. The way it looks is that he was enjoying his meal when the power failed, so he leapt up and off the boat to fix it and somehow fell in still holding the cable.'

'... probably electrocuting himself.' Bailey shrugged. 'A careless accident, Jack, but not something for CID.'

'I only said that was "the way it looked".' Jack lowered his voice even more. 'Except there are aspects to it that don't ring quite true.'

'Such as?'

'The fact that no experienced boater would connect to the shore outlet before he'd plugged in the boat end. And then there's the system itself.' Jack nodded to the power outlet on the quay. 'They usually have a safeguard built in that would trip if it ever came in contact with water. That's something we can check, but it still leaves the question, where's the body?'

'If there is one, then probably in the river.'

'Yeah, but this boat is in a reasonably confined berth with finger jetties and other obstructions to prevent a body ever reaching the main river. If he fell in by accident, his body, dead or alive, would probably still be jammed between the boat and the quay.'

'Well, we can get the diving boys to have a look.'

'I think you'll need to organise a search, and get Broads Beat involved as well.'

'For a body you don't believe is there?'

'Afraid so, and I'd stake my pension on being right.'

'But you're that sure he *is* dead, Jack?'

'Absolutely certain of it, and that he was murdered.'

'In which case, who's your suspect?'

'Ah, that's something I'm hoping DNA will help us with, but, in the meantime, you can start by talking to ...' Jack indicated the figure behind the saloon windows, '... the grieving widow.'

'Except, she still doesn't even realise she may be one,' pointed out an increasingly confused Bailey.

'Well, that's the impression she gives, but, faced with a husband disappearing off his boat in suspicious circumstances, she's doing an incredible job of controlling her emotions.'

'Hmm ... and you say she claims to have only arrived here a short while ago herself?'

'Yes, and that could be true, though she's really here because she suspects

Frazer of playing away from home, and wanted to catch him in the act.'

'A motive right there then if this *is* murder.' Bailey wiped more drizzle from his face. 'Okay, let's go talk to her and at least get out of this bloody weather.'

*   *   *

'Right Mrs Dunbar, when exactly did you arrive on this boat and find your husband missing?'

Seated in *Fenland Raider*'s saloon, his damp coat laid aside, DI Bailey was trying to make this interview sound sympathetically concerned rather than suspiciously grilling.

It failed, however, to appease the feisty Margo. 'Why on earth are you just sitting here, Inspector? Shouldn't you be out looking for my husband instead of asking futile questions?'

'That side of things are already in place, Mrs Dunbar.' Bailey wiped some rainwater that had dropped onto his notebook. 'Now, can you please just answer my questions?'

Margo gave a little sigh and glanced at the bulkhead clock. 'I suppose about an hour ago now, seeing as I arrived here on the midday train.'

'From the Fens where, I understand, you live together.'

'Correct.' She gave Jack an accusing look. 'What else have you been told?'

'That you'd come here to ... well, to check whether your husband was having an extra-marital affair.'

'Yes, that's also correct ... though I fail to see what business that is of yours.'

Bailey closed his notebook with barely-controlled tolerance. 'Mrs Dunbar, you must realise that there are suspicious circumstances surrounding your husband's disappearance and that you'd do well, at this stage, to be completely co-operative.'

'"Suspicious circumstances"? What's suspicious about it other than he's clearly buggered off with a woman?' Margo straightened up with affected indignation. 'You're talking to me like I'm some sort of suspect.'

'Just preliminary enquiries,' soothed Bailey, 'but just who do you suspect Frazer is having an affair with?'

'That bloody woman we've spent endless time and considerable money promoting ... Tracy Goldman, of course.'

144

'Tracy?' Now it was Jack's turn for shocks. 'But she's a young woman in her late twenties while ...'

'... Frazer is pushing sixty,' completed Margo, contemptuously. 'Yes, I know, pathetic, isn't it, but that's my husband for you ...' she glanced at her reflection in the saloon window and tided an errant lock of her fashionably-styled hair, '... someone who could never resist a pretty face.'

'So, how did you both meet all those years ago?'

'Through his agency,' explained Margo. '*Cecilian Promotions* had just moved office from London to the Fens and I was an up-and-coming professional singer needing an agent. I contacted them, met Frazer, he fell for me, proposed and we married.'

'Amazing the services a theatrical agency can offer,' said Jack with tongue in cheek. 'So did your career then take off?'

'It would have,' flushed Margo defensively, 'before Frazer realised I had management skills as well, talked me into putting aside my glittering career and instead set me sorting out *Cecilian*'s fast-diminishing client list.'

'Why "diminishing"?' probed Jack. 'Frazer had obviously run a successful agency in London before you met.'

'Goodness knows how,' scorned Margo, 'because he was useless and the company started losing business left, right and centre once it had moved to the Fens. He reckoned it was to get rid of City expenses and increase the profits, but instead he started losing so much money he had to sell his boatyard.'

'*Cecilian Cruisers* ... yes, why did he do that?' asked Jack.

Margo shrugged. 'Frazer reckoned the smaller yards had had their day, but I think the main reason was that his sister Alice, who had been managing the place, had now moved on. So it seemed a good time to get out and sell to this Turnberry chap. Frazer still liked boats though, so he used the money to buy this blessed gin-palace.'

'Which means at least the promotions agency is doing well now?' presumed Bailey.

'It is, thanks to me,' said Margo. 'Somehow he'd managed to lose all his old clients, so I used my own show-biz connections to win new ones and make *Cecilian* what it is today.'

'So, it's now worth a tidy sum.'

'Quite considerable,' agreed Margo, smugly, 'of which I'll get half if I prove infidelity in a divorce court.'

'Or *all of it* if we find the worst has happened,' added Jack bluntly, 'including, presumably, Wildmarsh Farm.'

'That dump.' Margo raised her eyes skywards. 'It must have been a lovely place before his father left it to him, and I would have been quite content to live there myself, but Frazer reckoned Norfolk wasn't remote enough for the agency, and so he just allowed it to fall into rack and ruin.'

'Why didn't he just sell it then?' asked Bailey.

'Goodness knows. He does make money from renting the land to farmers,' conceded Margo, 'but as regards the house, he reckons he just keeps it for sentimental reasons. After all, him and Alice did grow up there and she continued to live in it until she gave up managing the boatyard.'

'To go where, exactly?' queried Jack.

'Who knows?' Margo shrugged. 'I don't think even Frazer knew exactly, though he did think a man was involved.'

Bailey stood up. 'Okay, that's all for now, Mrs Dunbar. The diving team and Broads Beat will be here shortly, so I suggest you find alternative accommodation, as you'll obviously want to stay around until we have some news.'

'Perhaps I'll just take the car, go home again, and let you ring me if you find anything,' suggested Margo with no hint of emotion.

'Actually, I'd like you to stay local for further questioning,' said Bailey. 'As regards the car, you can't use that either until our forensics people have given it a going over, so I'm afraid you'll have to find some other way to come to the station tomorrow morning.'

'The *police* station!' Margo's head shot up, wide-eyed. 'For what reason?'

'For a DNA test.'

'DNA? Why on earth do you want *my* DNA?'

'Only for elimination purposes, Mrs Dunbar, in any further investigation of your husband's ... disappearance. And I'd also like something of his from which we could extract *his* DNA.'

'Such as?'

'This pipe would be good for starters,' said Bailey, picking up the item with its blackened bowl and well-chewed mouthpiece. 'I'm presuming it is his.'

'It certainly is,' confirmed Margo with disdain, 'and you'd be doing me a favour to take it. I hate him smoking the thing.'

'Right.' Bailey put the pipe into an evidence bag. 'But just in case it doesn't give us what we need, I'd like something else ... possibly some hair from a comb or hairbrush.'

Margo Dunbar nodded aft. 'The washroom and toilet are back there. If he has them on board, that's where you'll find them.'

Bailey went in search and soon returned with both items, placing them in separate evidence bags and asking, 'Do you also have a photo of your husband that I can circulate?'

'No, I'm afraid I don't.'

'And I noticed there isn't one on your *Cecilian Promotions* website either,' pointed out Jack.

'No, Frazer has always been somewhat averse to having his photo taken.' Margo gave a little snigger. 'Reckons they never do him justice.'

'Nevertheless, a photo would have been a great help,' persisted Bailey, slipping the evidence bags into his coat pocket.

'I'll see what I can find,' mumbled Margo, 'though I'm sure it will prove a complete waste of time, when Frazer turns up safe and well.'

'I hope you're right, Mrs Dunbar, but we have to be prepared for the worse-case scenario.'

Even as the DI said these ominous words and both got up to leave, Jack noticed something at the base of the short stairwell from saloon to the wheelhouse. 'That stain on the carpet there, Mrs Dunbar ... have you seen that before?'

Margo Dunbar looked at the dark red patch on the patterned carpet's otherwise clean surface. 'No, I haven't, but that'll just be red wine. Frazer always had a bottle on the go.'

'Hmm, well, we'll see,' said Bailey as they took their leave. 'In the meantime, let us know if your husband does turn up. Otherwise, I'll see you at the station tomorrow morning.'

*   *   *

Ten minutes after leaving *Fenland Raider*, the two men were sitting together in Bailey's car, overlooking the marina. The drizzle had stopped and the DI was staring at the rows of boats moored in front of them, restlessly tugging at their lines and mainly unoccupied. 'Blimey, Jack, don't you ever get fed up with boats and being on the river?'

'Never,' answered Jack with no hesitation. 'To me, patrolling the river is the best job in the world, and I find boats a never-ending source of pleasure and fascination.'

'Yeah, well I'm not sure if our ladyship back there would agree with you,' replied Bailey with a wry smile as he cast his eyes in the direction of the Dunbar's now-obscured cruiser. 'What did you make of her?'

'Certainly not someone *I'd* want to be married to,' admitted Jack, reflectively, 'but I'm not sure she's capable of murder.'

'Really? I reckon she's hard enough to do anything if there's money in it.' Bailey paused to wipe some condensation from the windscreen. 'You've got to admit her behaviour isn't normal, Jack. Most wives would be hysterical with all that's going on, but she seemed unusually composed and accepting of the situation. And odd that she didn't even have a photo of him either ... not even on her phone.'

'I wouldn't read too much into that,' warned Jack with a grin. 'I'd be hard-pushed to find one of Audrey if I was suddenly asked. Mind you, that's because she's usually *behind* the lens.'

'Well I'm certainly lacking experience on long-term marriage,' acknowledged the DI, 'but, just the same, I wouldn't believe a word our Mrs Dunbar said. I think she's still theatrical enough to spin a convincing line.'

'I'm sure she could ... but I'm equally sure she didn't murder Frazer Dunbar.'

'Why so sure, Jack?'

'Because I've already got a pretty good idea who did.'

'You seem convinced the poor bloke's dead and that it wasn't an accident,' frowned Bailey, opening his side window a crack. 'So, come on, Jack, let's hear your theory.'

'Sorry, but not before I've got more to go on, including the results of those DNA tests I've asked you to get. And, talking of DNA, it'll be interesting to hear the results of that staining on the saloon carpet, because did that look suspiciously like blood to you?'

'Certainly more so than red wine. Anyway, if it is, forensics will soon confirm whether it's Dunbar's from the DNA on these.' The DI tapped the evidence bags in his pocket. 'I must say, Mrs Dunbar was more than happy for us to bag his pipe. Obviously him smoking is a bone of contention between the two of them.'

'Ah yes, the pipe,' mused Jack. 'Very interesting that.'

'Why that in particular?'

'Oh, probably just something of nothing. Hopefully I'll soon hear from one of my old chums in the Met which might tell us more.'

'The Met!' exclaimed Bailey. 'Strewth, Jack, it just looked like a smelly old pipe to me.'

'It is, but it might well give the answer to an anomaly that's been niggling me. If I'm wrong, I'll feel a fool, but I promise I'll explain everything if my suspicions are correct.'

'I'll keep you to that,' warned Bailey, 'but, in the meantime, we'll see if her ladyship's DNA tells us anything after she's been to the station tomorrow.'

'Talking of which, I don't think we want to make the testing of everyone else seem like a big deal,' suggested Jack. 'Remember, they'll be under the impression it's simply to prove they weren't involved in the arson attack and nothing to do with the murder enquiry. Hopefully, this'll put them off-guard and we'll be able to do some gentle probing at the same time. And best we go to them rather than call them in.'

'A lot of running around, Jack, for reasons I'm still not sure of, so will the whole exercise be really worth it?'

'Absolutely, and far better to do it that way than them actually meeting each other.'

'Why's that?'

'Just a hunch, but the proof will be in the pudding.'

'Well, let's just hope that pudding doesn't give my Superintendant indigestion before it's done,' grinned Bailey. 'But as *you* seem to have some idea what this is all about, I want you there with me.'

'Try and keep me away,' chuckled Jack, 'and it might help put them at ease anyway. In the meantime, shall I get an electrician to check that shore-power system on *Fenland Raider* to find out just what, if anything, the problem was?'

'Good move, and I'll leave you to sort out a schedule for carrying out the testing. At least if I join you, I'll finally get to meet some of the characters for the first time.'

Now it was Jack's turn to frown. 'Hang on, Bailey ... what did you just say about not having met them all before?'

'Just that.' The DI looked more confused than ever. 'Unlike you, there are aspects to this strange business I'm still not privy to.'

'Not as much as some of the other players,' muttered Jack, almost to himself, before glancing outside and opening the car door. 'Good, the sun's coming out again, so let's get going, because you'll be glad to know you've just given me the key to this whole mystery.'

149

Chapter Thirteen

'So, how did they all react when you made arrangements with them to have DNA tests?' asked Bailey as he drove Jack along country lanes, en route to the *Watercraft* yard.

It was two days hence from detective and ranger's last meeting and, between patrolling the rivers once more, Jack had found time to contact all those with any connection to the investigation. It was certainly a recollection that had him rolling his eyes.

'Degrees of enthusiasm, as you can imagine. Most wanted to know the reason and some feigned offence at even being asked, while dear Tracy tried to get out of it by saying she hated needles.'

'I presume you reassured her it would be a simple mouth swab.'

'Yes, of course, but did you get anything else besides DNA out of the lovely Margo yesterday? Such as anything added to her account of Frazer's disappearance?'

'Not much other than giving me details of her travel arrangements to Brundall that day, including a good grumble because her train from Ely to Norwich was late getting away.'

'And you checked that out?'

'Absolutely, and she was right. The railway confirmed that the nine-thirty from Ely didn't pull out until nine-forty.'

'Which pretty well backs up her story of only arriving that day.'

'Seems that way, although that would still have left her enough time to be involved in the disappearance of her husband before you arrived on the scene, Jack. To pursue that line, I got the forensic boys to lift that patch of blood-stained carpet from the saloon and sent it off for analysis together with those items of Dunbar's, and his wife's test swab.'

'How long before you get the results?'

'Hopefully, not more than twenty-four hours. Those we plan to take today could be thirty-six to forty-eight.' Bailey turned off the main road towards the boatyard. 'And you reckon the yard at Brundall could find no fault with the boat's shore-power?'

'Nope. It all checked out perfectly, so goodness knows why it was lying disconnected like that.'

'In some ways I wish they *had* found something,' bemoaned Bailey, 'because a simple accident would certainly have made my job easier. As it is, I'm still not convinced any crime has actually been committed anyway. I've had divers down scouring the marina and Broads Beat searching the main river, but with negative results all round. They'll all continue searching though.'

'I know you have to go through the motions, mate, but I'm convinced you won't find him.'

'But you're still sure the bloke is dead, Jack?'

'As sure as I can be without any other evidence as yet.'

'But you agree the missus herself is the prime suspect,' persevered the DI. 'She had the opportunity and certainly the motive, in that she thought her husband was being unfaithful.'

Jack wrinkled his nose. 'A bit extreme, though, to murder your other half just on suspicion, especially when there were no signs of any other woman staying on the boat with him.'

'Does there need to be? When she came to the station she showed more irritation at being inconvenienced than any great concern for a possibly-deceased husband ...' Bailey rolled his eyes, '... which just reinforces my notion that marriage itself can be motive enough for murder.' They were driving into the *Watercraft* yard now before parking close to the charred remains of *Pike Hunter*. 'Well, there's what's left of our prime piece of evidence, and a fat chance now of getting anything else from it.'

'Yeah, it does look pretty sad, doesn't it?' agreed Jack as he surveyed what had once been a classic wooden boat, now reduced to blackened ashes beside the boatyard shed. 'But in the end it'll have given one last good service.'

'Which is?'

'By providing the excuse for these DNA tests.'

'You still think this whole expensive charade will be worthwhile, Jack?'

'Absolutely.'

'Even if our vanishing Mr Dunbar turns up again alive and well?'

'I'm just as sure that will never happen, Bailey.'

'Right,' accepted the DI, climbing out and heading for the yard office, 'let's go and see what the yard manager has to say about it all.'

'I told you, when you first questioned me, it had to be the work of local vandals,' said a somewhat resentful Stuart Steadmore, when the DI and Ranger had settled themselves into his office, 'so why am I having to provide a DNA sample?'

'You're not "having" to do anything, Stuart,' said Bailey with deliberate patience. 'As Jack here has already told you, this is a purely voluntary test to eliminate you from our enquiries.' The DI handed over a printed form. 'This explains both your rights and our requirements in the procedure.'

'It says here that if I don't agree you can get a judge to order it,' declared Stuart after quickly scanning the form.

'That's correct.'

'But only if I'm a suspect in the crime being investigated.'

'Everyone's a suspect until we've eliminated the innocent,' explained Bailey, 'which is what this is all about. If you're okay with that, then just sign your consent on the bottom and we'll get this done.'

'Not much choice have I?' muttered Steadmore, quickly scribbling his signature and then opening his mouth.

'Good, that's done.' Sample obtained and bagged, Bailey carefully placed it in his aluminium case before adopting an even more serious expression. 'As you're probably aware, Stuart, arson is a very serious offence. You've had a few days to think things over since then, so perhaps you've had some further thoughts on the matter?' The DI let his voice drop to a slightly kinder tone. 'If you have something to tell us, now's the time.'

But young Steadmore merely shook his head.

'In truth,' persisted Bailey, 'your suggestion of local trouble-makers isn't too convincing. There was no sign of a break-in, meaning they'd have had to bring a can of expensive petrol, which is pretty unlikely.'

'Who knows what people will do?' shrugged Steadmore.

'Or why?' added Bailey, 'which is another question I aim to get answered. But, whoever it was, clearly had a very personal reason for wanting that boat destroyed.' The DI paused for only a second to let that thought sink in. 'Have you told anyone else about the boat being burned?'

'Only Kathy, the other night.'

'But no-one else?'

'You told me not to.'

'Good. So, assuming it was neither you nor vandals who fired the boat, do you have any idea who else might have?'

'None at all. Why should I?'

'Because you've just given a very quick answer as unconvincing as all your others this morning.'

Steadmore gave no response other than to drop his eyes, but it was reaction enough for the DI to straightway change tack. 'Okay, let me now bring up another line of enquiry. It relates to the disappearance, a few days ago, of someone you might know ... Frazer Dunbar.'

'Frazer ... who?'

'Dunbar,' answered Jack, picking up the questioning. 'I'm surprised you didn't recognise the name, Stuart, seeing as he's the man who originally owned this boatyard.'

'How would I? Way before my time here, Jack, and boss Alec Turnberry himself never seemed to know who'd owned *Cecilian Cruisers*, seeing as they stayed hidden behind their lawyers for the sale.'

'Yes, but that family name would surely ring a bell.' Jack nodded to the aircraft control column mounted just feet away on the office wall. 'The "Flt Lt J B Dunbar", engraved on that plaque, was probably the father of the Frazer Dunbar, who's now gone missing.'

Steadmore frowned. 'Okay I see the connection to the name, but why would I know anything about the Frazer bloke's disappearance?'

'Only because he's Tracy Goldman's agent and the one stopping your Kathy getting her share of royalties for the song they co-wrote.'

'She's not *my* Kathy,' responded Steadmore with feeling. 'You know as well as I do, Jack, that she pretty-much dumped me.'

'Indeed I do, Stuart, but I also know you'd do anything to win her back ... and what better way than threatening the agent standing between her and what she's rightly owed.'

'I might if I'd ever actually met the man,' admitted Steadmore, 'but I'm not stupid enough to murder for love nor money.'

'Who said anything about "murder"?' asked Bailey, coming back into the exchange.

'Well, you didn't,' admitted Steadmore, 'but you did say "disappeared", and why would CID be involved unless you thought this was all a bit more serious than a man doing a vanishing act?'

'All right, we'll leave it at that for now, Stuart,' said Bailey, standing up, 'but be prepared for another chat with us in the next few days.'

'Why ... for what reason?'

Again, it was Jack who answered. 'To clear up some of the mysteries surrounding this very boatyard, Stuart.' Following Bailey through the door, he paused and glanced back to the apprehensive-looking manager. 'I'm sure you'll be as keen as everyone else, to get to the bottom of this whole strange business.'

*   *   *

'So, Jack, you know young Steadmore better than me ... what did you make of his answers and reactions back there?'

DI and Ranger were speeding back down the road the few miles to their next scheduled appointment.

'I think he was telling the truth when he said he knew nothing of Dunbar previously owning the yard or of his disappearance,' conceded Jack, 'but, like you, I'm just as sure he knows more about the boat burning than he's letting on. I don't think he did it, but he certainly knows who did.'

'And the only person he's likely to cover for is Kathy Caterall ...'

'... who we're off to see next.' Already they were nearing Wayford Bridge and the entrance to the marina of the same name. 'Okay, left here, Bailey, and let's see what answers she can give us.'

*   *   *

'There you are, Inspector.' Seated in the cosy saloon of her narrowboat, Kathy Caterall handed back the printed form she had just signed. 'I'm more than happy to get eliminated from any investigation.'

'We appreciate your co-operation, Miss Caterall,' said Bailey, and within minutes her swab sample was taken. 'So, when Jack contacted you to arrange this meeting, you said that Stuart had already told you about the arson attack,' continued the DI, placing the bagged and labelled sample in his case. 'Have you any idea who may have had reason to destroy the boat?'

'No, of course I don't.' Kathy gave a frown. 'My only connection with that yard is that it's where I keep my balloon.'

'Not forgetting, a close relationship you had with its manager,' reminded Jack.

'And why would that be relevant?' fired back Kathy, defensively.

'Because, when feelings are involved, people sometimes do things they later regret ... like another strange happening currently under investigation.' With a nod from Bailey, Jack went on to explain Frazer Dunbar's disappearance.

154

'Sounds a strange business,' agreed Kathy, 'but why are you telling me about it?'

'Because you may have some knowledge of what happened.'

'I don't know why I would. I've never met the man.'

'No, but you were aware that he was Tracy's agent and the one advising her to contest your involvement in writing *Dream Along*. You were also talking to his wife, Margo, a few days ago when she reiterated the fact that *Cecilian Promotions* had no intention of paying you more than a derisory £2000 in royalties.'

'Oh, yes, that's true,' admitted Kathy before adding, slightly ruefully, 'and I did tell her she could stuff it, but that's history, Jack, and I've enough problems at the moment financing this balloon re-enactment without bothering myself with disputes over song rights.'

'But being paid what's rightfully yours would certainly help solve those money problems, wouldn't it?'

Kathy paused as *Balloonatic* heaved slightly in the wash of a passing cruiser. 'Probably, and I'm not saying I won't still pursue my claim at some point in the future, but I promise you, Jack, I had no involvement in the disappearance of this man.' Kathy cast her eyes vaguely in the direction of Norwich. 'If you want to know more about this Frazer Dunbar, then you need to talk to my sister Tracy. He's *her* agent, after all.'

'Don't worry, we'll be speaking to her in due course, Miss Caterall,' said Bailey, standing up to leave, 'and sorry for taking up your time.'

*   *   *

'You didn't need to apologise back there, Bailey,' said Jack as they headed now down the A1151 to Norwich.

'I think we did.' The DI gave a dismissive shrug. 'Personally, I think this whole exercise is becoming increasingly futile. Kathy Caterall wouldn't gain anything by burning that boat and she's not going to murder Dunbar just because he's put a spanner in the works of her royalty claim. It would be counter-productive for a start.'

'I absolutely agree, Bailey.'

'You do?' The DI seemed as surprised as he was confused.

'Of course. I've seen myself that Kathy Caterall is certainly capable of *voicing* her rights, but she just as surely didn't murder Frazer Dunbar.'

'You seem very certain of that, Jack.'

'Totally, and with good reason, although I wouldn't rule her out of having knowledge of who fired *Pike Hunter*.'

'Really! Now I'm totally confused,' grumbled Bailey. 'You seem to have made up your mind about Dunbar's fate, so why are we going through this whole charade anyway?'

'I can understand your doubts,' soothed Jack, 'but I promise it's worthwhile and that I'll share my thoughts just as soon as I have evidence to substantiate them. In the meantime, our chat with Kathy was certainly productive, if only to confirm what she doesn't know.'

'Which is?'

'Something I'll disclose in due course if my theory is correct. Anyway, we're in Norwich now, so head for the Hotel Nelson, which is where I've arranged for us to meet two others in this whole tangled web.'

'Yeah, well talking of webs, I'm still not sure who's the spider and who's the fly anymore,' moaned Bailey, 'Believe me, if I didn't have faith in you personally, Jack, I would've knocked this on the head days ago.'

*   *   *

'Why would I set fire to a boat I've never heard of, in a boatyard I've never been to,' asked a puzzled Hans van Heiden, after Bailey and Jack had explained the reason for this meeting in the art expert's hotel room.

'Just standard enquiries, sir ...' Bailey turned to face Phillipa, standing close by, '... but I understand you *are* familiar with that boatyard, Miss Keyworth?'

'Only because that's where Kathy stores her *Skyrides* balloon. I've only been there once when I first offered to help promote the John Money re-enactment.' Phillipa fixed the DI with a bewildered stare. 'Why on earth would that be a reason for either of us committing arson?'

Bailey gratefully passed the buck on that one. 'I'll let Mr Fellows explain.'

'Actually, I'm certain neither of you did,' reassured Jack, 'but you might just be able to shed some light on another incident we're currently investigating.'

Listening to the account of Frazer Dunbar's disappearance did nothing to ease Van Heiden's growing intolerance. 'And you think *we* could have something to do with that?'

'It's not inconceivable,' argued Jack, 'considering the resentment, particularly you, Phillipa, must harbour at seeing Frazer benefiting from the great wrong done by his father. That theft of the Vogelsang family heirlooms and your search for them, ultimately cost your husband his life and, doubtless, left you with a score you were desperate to settle.'

'Not *that* desperate, Jack.'

'Perhaps not, but another factor is the Van Gogh. If you and Hans found it, Frazer could well have disputed your claim.'

Van Heiden gave a dismissive scoff. 'He wouldn't stand a chance in court.'

'Probably not, Hans, but you and I know how long-winded any civil case can take to settle. Surely better for Frazer Dunbar to be out of the picture completely if you ever do discover the masterpiece.'

'How ridiculous!' It was now Phillipa's turn to defend her corner. 'I admit I've kept my own search a secret from this son Frazer, but he wasn't even born when his father stole and hid the painting, so I'm convinced he's as ignorant as we are as to its whereabouts.'

'Perhaps, but it's probably why he hangs on to Wildmarsh when he has no interest in farming,' suggested Jack.

'Except, I'm becoming increasingly convinced that, even if it is still hidden away somewhere at Wildmarsh, the damp will now have ruined it beyond restoration,' sighed Van Heiden. 'Valuable artwork needs to be con-served if it's to be stored for a long time without being irreparably damaged. Flight Lieutenant Dunbar might have been good at handling aircraft, Jack, but I don't expect he knew much about the preservation of fine art.'

Jack didn't respond to that immediately, but when he did it was to merely shrug his shoulders. 'Who knows how this whole strange affair will eventually pan out. However, I *am* sure that neither of you had anything to do with the burning of that boat so, if DI Bailey agrees, I suggest we save you the trouble and the Norfolk Constabulary the expense, by waiving these DNA tests.'

'Absolutely,' agreed the DI clicking shut his testing case. 'We won't detain you any longer.'

'Common sense prevails,' declared Van Heiden with a sigh of relief. 'So, that's an end to it as far as we're concerned?'

'Not quite,' cautioned Jack. 'There is just a final act in this whole saga I'd like you to be present for.'

'Present for what?' Van Heiden was clearly nearing the end of his pa-tience. 'I really need to get back to Holland where I have work to do.'

'... which can probably wait a few more days, Hans, because it would be good if you could attend a little meeting with all the others involved in this affair.'

'A "meeting" ... where?'

'At the *Watercraft* yard.'

'The place where this boat burning occurred?'

'Yes.'

The Dutchman turned appealingly to DI Bailey. 'Do we have to?'

'Purely voluntary as far as I'm concerned,' answered the DI while giving Jack a puzzled glance.

Van Heiden gave a resigned shrug. 'Well, Phillipa is staying on anyway to help Kathy, so I suppose a few more days will allow me to visit more galleries.'

'Good, I'll let you know the date and time convenient to others,' said Jack as he and Bailey took their leave. 'Until then, enjoy the delights of our fair city for just a few more days.'

*   *   *

'I don't know about the others, but you're certainly keeping me guessing,' admitted Bailey as he and Jack returned to their car. 'And did I read you wrong, or did you have some sort of light-bulb moment back there?'

'Might have,' admitted Jack, 'but I'll explain as we drive to our next participant ... someone you'll actually *enjoy* meeting this time, Bailey ... Norwich's own new star of stage and screen, the delectable Tracy Goldman.'

*   *   *

'You must be coming to take my DNA.'

Answering the door of her penthouse to Jack and Bailey, Tracy Goldman's mood seemed as dark as the rings under her eyes. Dressed in tracksuit bottoms and sweatshirt and with her blonde hair uncombed and greasy, she was looking anything but the glamorous singer of ascending stardom.

Bailey, for one, was taken aback by the sorry sight in front of him. 'I realise this probably isn't a good time, Miss Goldman, but if we could just have a few minutes ...'

'You'd better come in then.'

Guessing that this starlet had not long rolled out of bed, Jack was quite prepared for the cluttered and untidy state of Tracy's otherwise-luxurious penthouse, but not for the presence of another female in her lounge.

'This is my mum,' explained Tracy, indicating the thin, slightly greying woman sitting on the large L-shaped sofa. 'I told her you were coming, so she came to give me a bit of support.'

'I'll simply be taking a mouth-swab that'll be done in seconds,' said Bailey, turning to the mum, 'so you won't have to give *too* much support Mrs ...'

'Caterall ... Sandra Caterall ... and it's "Miss", actually,' she corrected, standing up to exchange Bailey's handshake.

'And I'm Jack Fellows,' said Jack, introducing himself. 'We were with your other daughter just a few hours ago.'

'What, Kathy?' She shrugged. 'A year less than *I* last saw her then.'

'That's a shame,' remarked Jack, 'but you must be very proud of two such successful girls.'

'I suppose.' Sandra smiled towards Tracy, now lounging on the other end of the sofa. 'Certainly this one's done okay for herself.' Her eyes narrowed slightly. 'So what's this business of needing her DNA?'

'Just part of an investigation in progress,' answered Bailey, noncommittally, while opening his testing case and taking out the packet of swabs.

'What investigation?' asked Tracy, suddenly alert and sitting upright.

'A recent incident in a boatyard ten miles north-east of here.'

'Which can't be anything to do with my Trace,' said Sandra, jumping to her feet. 'Why would she want to go burning some boat?'

It was an outburst sufficient to have the DI's eyebrows rising suspiciously. 'Who said anything about the burning of a boat, Ms Caterall?'

'I ... well ... I must have read it in the paper.'

'Hardly, seeing as it hasn't been reported in any.'

'I ... I ...' Sandra's rounded shoulders seemed to sag with awkwardness as she sat down again, '... I don't know then.'

Further mortification was diverted by her daughter. 'I certainly don't know anything about a boat being burned ...' there was an element of relief now in the young starlet's voice, '... I thought this was about ... about something else.'

'What else?' asked Bailey.

'Oh... I don't know ... all sorts of things are happening these days.' Tracy ran a hand nervously through her dishevelled hair. 'Anyway, I've got nothing to hide, so let's get this test done and you gone so I can make myself presentable for tonight's gig.'

As Bailey took his swab, Jack went over to the room's large picture window overlooking the slow-moving waters of the Wensum. 'A lovely view your daughter's got from up here, Sandra.'

'Yes, isn't it gorgeous.' The mother seemed to relax slightly. 'Trace wants me to come and live here, but I don't like to impose. A girl like her, on the start of a good career, doesn't want her mother cramping her style.'

'Oh, I don't know,' said Jack, scanning the discarded clothes, food-encrusted plates and well-thumbed fashion magazines that littered the lounge, 'I'm sure she'd welcome someone taking care of the domestic side of her life while she concentrates on ... what do you call them? ... gigs?' He turned to Tracy, swab taken and now wiping her mouth with a paper tissue. 'Do you have a gig every night?'

The starlet frowned. 'Not every night. Why do you ask?'

'Oh, just curious to know what you were doing two nights ago.'

'I can't remember. Is it important?'

'Very much so. It's in connection with another on-going police enquiry ... the disappearance of a man called Frazer Dunbar that night in Brundall Marina.'

'Who?'

Jack turned back to face the young singer. 'Oh come on, Tracy, you know as well as I do that Frazer Dunbar is ... was ... your agent.'

'So ... what of it?' The tissue had now gone from mouth to eyes that were rapidly filling with tears. 'He was alive and well when I left him.'

'Trace, just shut up,' ordered her mum.

'No, don't stop, Tracy,' said Jack gently as he saw the colour drain from the young singer's face. 'Just relax and tell us what you know of the night Frazer Dunbar disappeared?'

'She didn't say that she knew anything,' interrupted Sandra, edging closer to her daughter and putting an arm around her now-shaking shoulders. 'I think it's time you fellas left us in peace.'

'Actually, I think it's time we heard more,' said Bailey, now *extremely* interested in the way this interview was evolving. 'Clearly you were with Frazer Dunbar that night, Miss Goldman, so can you tell me why?'

'I ... I had to sort out an allegation made against both him and me.'

'Allegation? What sort of allegation?'

Tracy gulped back a sob. 'That he and I were having some sort of affair ... or at least that's what his wife reckoned. So I rang him on his mobile, and that's when he said to come and see him on his boat that evening to talk it over.'

'Which you did?'

'Yes. He seemed as perturbed about it as I was, so having a face-to-face meeting seemed the best way to sort it out.'

'And did you ... sort it out?'

Tracy shook her head and began to cry again. 'No ... just the opposite, in fact.'

'Just collect yourself and then tell us exactly what happened,' advised Jack, softly.

'Not what I expected. I'd been hoping Frazer would dismiss the whole ridiculous suggestion as some stupid misunderstanding. And things did start off friendly enough, with him pouring me a large glass of wine and telling me to sit down and relax.' Tracy looked crestfallen at what was obviously a painful memory. 'But, then, when I'd drunk half my wine, he started telling me I didn't understand his feelings for me and that there was something he needed to disclose.'

'Which was ...?' asked an increasingly intrigued Bailey.

'I didn't wait to find out, Inspector. Obviously he was going to tell me he loved me, but that was the last thing I needed to hear. So, I just stopped him in his tracks and went to get off that boat as quickly as I could.'

'Probably, the wisest course,' said Jack, 'although I'm guessing it didn't quite work out that simply.'

'No, it certainly didn't ...' Tracy sniffed and wiped her eyes, '... because, as I went to hop ashore, Frazer, grabbed me and gave me a hug. More than ever, I knew I had to get away, and so I just hit him across the face.'

'In self-defence, Tracy, so I wouldn't worry too much about that,' consoled Bailey.

'You would if you'd been in my shoes,' replied Tracy. 'You see, in my haste to get away, I'd still got that glass of wine in my hand and, without thinking straight, smashed it into his face, and the next thing I knew he was backing away, streaming blood.'

'What, back into the boat or onto the jetty?' asked Jack.

'Back into the boat, but clutching his face.' Tracy put her hands over her own face. 'And now you tell me he's disappeared and I'm thinking he might have fallen overboard in pain and that I'm responsible.'

'Did you see him come back out after you?'

'No, all I wanted to do was get away from the whole mess as soon as I could, so I fled back up the marina to my car and drove straight back here.'

'Okay,' soothed Bailey, 'but did you see anyone else around at the time?'

'I might have ...' Tracy frowned, '... because, somehow, I got the impression that there *was* someone there, lurking in the shadows, as I ran back up the walkway.'

'You say "impression", Tracy,' persisted Bailey, 'but did you actually *see* someone?'

'Only vaguely ...' she rubbed her forehead, as though trying to stimulate more recall, '... just the shape of a figure hanging back there as though they didn't want to be seen.'

'Man or woman?'

'I can't even say that for sure. Whoever it was, wasn't very tall, but my only thought right then was to get as far away as I could.' Tracy looked appealingly at both men. 'Do you really think I might have been responsible for Frazer's death?'

'We don't even know if he is dead,' said Bailey, 'but from what you've just told us, we have to keep an open mind until we know one way or the other.'

'It's obvious, isn't it?' intervened Sandra, giving her daughter's shoulder a loving hug. 'Trace might have hurt that agent of hers, but she didn't kill him.'

'I agree,' said Jack, 'but I'm thinking it all runs a bit deeper than that, doesn't it, Sandra?'

'What do you mean?'

'I mean there are factors here than even Tracy isn't aware of, aren't there ... something that the DNA we've just taken from her is going to show up when we get the results.' Jack lowered his tone until it became almost fatherly. 'Sandra, I really think now's the time to come clean on that secret you've been guarding all these years.'

There was a long silence as that advice sank in but, ultimately, it was her own daughter's confusion that broke it. 'What, mum? What is it that I don't know?'

'I should have told you years ago, Trace, but, in the end, I left it so long that I thought you'd hate me for it.'

'What?'

'That Frazer Dunbar is actually your father.'

Chapter Fourteen

'My ... what?' Tracy Goldman turned to her mother with an expression of utter disbelief. 'Tell me you're joking. Are you actually saying that Frazer Dunbar, my theatrical agent is actually ...'

'... yes ... your father.' It was Sandra Caterall's turn now to shed tears. 'I'm sorry, Trace. I know I should have explained everything to you and Kath years ago, but there were certain ... well ... complications.' Sandra shuffled closer to her daughter and again put a comforting arm around her shoulders. 'The thing is, the other night when Frazer told you he had something special to say, he was probably simply wanting to tell you ...'

'... he was my dad,' completed Tracy, 'and that he really did love me, but as my father, which made a nonsense of Margo's suspicions of us having an affair.'

'I think you owe us all, but particularly Tracy, a full explanation,' advised Jack.

'I suppose I do.' Sandra wiped her eyes. 'As you've probably guessed from my accent, I'm actually a London girl. When I left school I trained as a secretary and, soon after qualifying, got a job with a London agency.'

'*Cecilian Promotions?*'

'That's right. I'd always been interested in the theatre, so you can imagine how thrilled I was to become part of it and on speaking terms with some of the big singing stars of the day.' She paused to try and regain her composure. 'Frazer was so good at managing people's careers in those days and we got on really well ...'

'... to the extent you became lovers?'

'You're right, Mr Fellows, and not long after that I fell pregnant with Kathy.'

Tracy gave another big sniffle. 'So, why didn't you marry?'

'Good question.' Sandra briefly shook her head. 'We wanted to, but things were changing in show-business at that time ... theatres were closing all over the country, the costs of running the London office were going up and jobs for our client list going down. The only solution was to up sticks and move somewhere with cheaper overheads.'

'Which explains why *Cecilian Promotions* moved to the Fens,' accepted Jack, 'but why didn't you go with them?'

A shadow seemed to flit across Sandra's face as she shook her head. Only because someone needed to stay in London a few more weeks to wind things up, and I volunteered.'

'And ...'

'And, before I could join Frazer in the Fens, that awful, but glamorous, Margo woman had signed on with the agency and got her claws into him.'

'In other words, you were jilted.'

'Something like that.' Sandra's sunken shoulders heaved slightly with emotion.

'So, why did you come to Norfolk, Mum,' asked Tracy, starting to come to terms with these mind-blowing revelations while giving her mum an encouraging hug of her own.

'Basically, I just needed to get out of London and start afresh. I'd come up here before with Frazer, and it seemed such a lovely place to live, away from all the hustle and bustle of London.'

Jack cast Bailey a knowing glance. 'So, you actually visited *Cecilian Cruisers?*'

'Oh yes,' confirmed Sandra, her face lighting up, 'and went out on Frazer's lovely old cruiser a few times.' She smiled at the recollection. 'That boat was his pride and joy and probably the reason he set up the boatyard in the first place. It worked out well at first, because his sister, Alice, who was a lovely girl, happily ran the yard while Frazer concentrated on the agency.'

'Why did he then go and sell it?'

'Probably because he needed the money to keep the agency going ... that and affording Lady Margo's expensive tastes.'

'So, what happened to Alice?'

'Apparently she moved on to pastures new but, as we had split up, that was his business, not mine.'

'But Mum, there's one crucial thing here that I still don't understand,' persisted Tracy. 'You reckon you left London for here when you were pregnant with my sister Kathy, but I didn't come along for another eighteen months. You've always led us to believe we had different fathers, but now you're saying that Frazer was my father too ... so how did that happen?'

Clearly, Sandra was beginning to find this grilling about her past a bit overwhelming and Jack could tell she was becoming slightly flustered. 'It was when Frazer still came here to enjoy his boat that he secretly visited me and Kathy in Norwich. I'm ashamed to say, one thing led to another and ...'

'... you became pregnant again and had me, even knowing he'd dumped you once and was now married to someone else?'

Sandra blew a breath of derision. 'From what he told me, being married to Margo was no bed of roses and, I suppose in my mind, it was one way of getting back at her for what she did to me.'

'So, all the time I was thinking I'd done well having *Cecilian Promotions* take me on as a client, it was just my dad trying to help me out,' said Tracy as the penny dropped.

'Only to help you get onto the first rung of the ladder, love' consoled Sandra. 'It was your own genuine talent that won you *Stars*.'

'Maybe, Mum, but now, just when it's all working out and I find out who my real dad is, he's disappeared and is probably dead ...' Tracy started crying again, '... because I went and hit him, cut his face and probably caused him to fall into the water and drown.'

Once more, her mother tried to assuage a burst of sobbing. 'I'm so sorry, Trace.'

'You mustn't start condemning yourself before we know the full facts,' counselled Jack. 'We've yet to have any proof that ... your father ... came to any real harm.'

'No, but I can tell you think he was murdered, and if it wasn't me, who do you think killed him and why?'

Bailey stood up to leave. 'They're questions I'm hoping we'll soon have answers to, Miss Goldman, though not until we have more evidence ... and to help with that, I'll also take a DNA sample from you, Sandra, while we're here.'

'Me? Why would you think I had anything to do with what's happened?'

'Don't worry, this is only for elimination purposes,' assured the DI, taking out another sample kit.

While Sandra reluctantly opened her mouth for the swab, it was Tracy now voicing their discontent. 'What a waste of time and money when you ought to be out finding who really murdered Fra ... my father.'

'Which is what we intend doing, I assure you,' promised Bailey as he bagged the sample.

'Well, I'm sure you'll tell us when you have,' said Tracy, pulling herself together and showing both men to the door.

'Which might even be in just a couple of days,' said Jack, 'because we're planning a meeting then at the *Watercraft* yard, which we'd like you both to be present for.'

'Why us?' asked Sandra. 'Who else will be there?'

'You'll see on the day,' replied Jack, before both men said their goodbyes and set off for their next appointment.

*　　*　　*

'Well, a few disclosures there, Jack,' said Bailey as they drove off to the southern suburbs of Norwich, 'though why did I get the impression that you weren't altogether surprised?'

'Because they fitted in with the theory I was already forming on this whole business,' admitted Jack, '... but I'm glad you took a sample from the mum while we were at it.'

'Well, at least we now know that stain on the carpet was blood and that it was Frazer's.' Bailey turned and glanced at Jack. 'And a few revelations there from Mum Sandra, so did they at least clear up one aspect of your secret theory.'

'Yes and no,' confessed Jack, 'because, even then, I don't think dear Sandra was being totally straightforward with us.'

'In what aspects?'

'All of them, actually. For a start, you heard her blurt out about the boat arson ...'

'... before we'd even told her about it,' remembered Bailey with a nod. 'She certainly dropped herself right in it there, didn't she? What did you make of that?'

'That she was the one who fired *Pike Hunter*.'

'*What?*' The DI swerved slightly as his focus momentarily waivered. 'For crikey's sake, Jack, she's old enough to be a granny. What would she want to go torching boats for?'

'Perhaps to purge some old demons,' suggested Jack, 'or, possibly, self-protection.'

'From whom?'

'I'll tell you as soon as I'm sure, but don't go writing Sandra off as an innocent in all this. Remember she was once secretary to a leading London agency and that daughter Tracy's success is largely due to her initiative.'

'By calling in a favour from her old lover ... but I'm still struggling to think she was capable of the fire job ... though she did seem less than enthusiastic when you said you wanted her there for the proposed meeting at *Watercraft*. And I'm assuming you think this Walter Jarvis we're seeing next, is another one in the frame?'

'Not for arson, Bailey, but I think he might shed some light on the shadowy figure Tracy saw lurking near Dunbar's boat that night ... and why I haven't warned him about our visit this morning,' added Jack with a smile.

'Good ... we'll be a nice little surprise for him then,' grinned Bailey as they neared Norwich's southern outskirts, '... but why so sure he might be the one, Jack?'

'Because I saw him myself arriving at Brundall by train the very night of the incident.'

*   *   *

Walter Jarvis's humble home was situated in an extensive council development in one of those parishes that had once been an outlying village until nineteenth century expansion had seen it swallowed into the city's urban sprawl. Here, upriver of an old mill, the River Yare became a mere stream-like shadow of the navigable waterway that joined Norwich to the sea, leaving just mill and church as sole reminders of the parish's rural past.

'Those three bunking off school will doubtless soon be making the acquaintance of the Norfolk Constabulary,' predicted Bailey, eyeing a trio of loitering youngsters already giving his parked car appraising looks as he and Jack headed up the rough concrete stairwell of the three-storey block of flats.

Following him to the top floor, Jack could only agree when their knock on Walter's door was answered by a suspicious, 'Who's that?'

'Are you Walter Jarvis?' demanded Bailey.

'What if I am? Who wants to know?'

'Police ...' in the presence of what he now regarded as his chief suspect, Bailey was at his most intimidating, '... so open up because we need to talk to you.'

There came the sound of a lock being turned and then the door opening to the extent of its chain. Through the small gap, a frightened face peered out. 'Why?'

'You'll find out soon enough, so buck up and open this door,' ordered Bailey, showing his warrant card. With the chain reluctantly slipped and the door ajar, the DI didn't waste any time in pushing it wide open and stepping inside. 'Okay, Walter, let's go and talk.'

Jack followed the DI into Walter's small sitting room that, apart from a general untidiness, had little in common with the penthouse luxury they'd just left. There was no apparent recognition from their previous brief encounter at the balloon launch site, and the young man himself, of small stature, ashen-faced and anxious, now seemed almost overwhelmed by the situation he found himself in. It was a time for a softer approach. 'Sit down, Walter,' requested Jack quietly. 'We just think you can help us with a couple of enquiries.'

'What ... what enquiries?'

'The burning of a boat a week ago at a yard near here,' said Bailey, bluntly.

'A boat ... burned ...' Walter shook his head in confusion, '... I don't know of any burned boat.'

'No,' said Jack, 'but you do know of a much more luxurious one at Brundall Marina, don't you?'

'Do I?' stammered back Walter, licking his lips nervously.

'Yes, one owned by a man who's now disappeared ...' joined in the DI again, '... a man called Frazer Dunbar.'

'... Tracy Goldman's agent,' added Jack, 'who you thought was paying too much attention to the girl you yourself had set your sights on and wanted to help ... which is what you were doing that night.'

'... except your planned minor surveillance got out of hand, didn't it, Walter?' pressed Bailey, 'because you saw Tracy come off that boat in a distressed state, decided to have it out with Dunbar, and ended up murdering him.'

'Murder! ... what you mean, murder?' Finally faced with the reality of all his fears, Walter's face was a picture of pure trepidation. 'I didn't murder him.'

'Then, perhaps, you'd better tell us what really happened,' advised Jack, kindly.

'Alright ... but I tell you I didn't really mean to harm Dunbar,' stammered Walter. 'You're right, I was really angry when I saw Tracy come off that boat crying and distressed and, after she'd gone, I went and jumped on board to have it out with him.'

'And ...?'

'And ... I was taken aback at first, because he looked a bit of a mess. His face was all cut about and he'd obviously been bleeding badly. Anyway, I still had a go at him, but instead of being angry, he told me to sit down and listen, and said that, like Tracy, I'd got it all wrong, and then dropped the bombshell that he was actually her dad.'

'That must have been almost as big a shock to you as it was to her,' said Jack.

'Too true. I felt a right idiot, actually, and even ashamed when he poured me a drink and asked about my own ambitions regarding Tracy's career.'

'Which were?' asked Bailey.

'I said I wasn't sure anymore since his *Cecilian* agency seemed to have taken over her management. But he said there was still a place for me in it all, and seemed to take an interest, asking what I'd done in the past and what I was best at. When I explained I'd started by looking after the lights and sound systems he really perked up and said if I knew electrics, there was a problem on his boat I might look at.'

'Which you agreed to do?'

'Of course I did,' said Walter, showing a shadow of his old self-importance. 'He was making out he could help me, wasn't he, and I felt I owed him one. And not just job-wise either, because he also hinted that he'd like to see me and Tracy together.'

'He hinted that, did he?' asked Jack, trying not to show his scepticism 'Okay, so did you fix his electrics?'

'I guess I didn't,' admitted Walter in a barely audible whisper. 'He reckoned the shore power was what had been giving the problems, meaning he was having to rely on the boat's batteries. I said I'd take a look and went and gave the main panel and fuses a good looking over. I couldn't see a problem there, so I told him to go and plug in again to see if that showed up anything.'

'... while you monitored the main panel,' said Jack while guessing where this was going. 'So you couldn't actually see Dunbar plugging in on the jetty.'

'No. I just shouted to him to plug in and a second later heard a big splash.' Walter's voice began to quiver. 'Of course, I dashed straight out to see what had happened and ...'

'And ... what?' demanded Bailey as Walter's voice faltered.

'And ... and nothing.'

'What do you mean, "nothing"?'

'Just that. There was nothing there anymore. He'd gone ... into the water, from the sound of that big splash.'

'Well, did you search for him?'

'Yeah ... course ... I dashed back on board and found a flashlight ... shone it on all the water around the boat but, apart from a lot of ripples, he'd just vanished.'

'So what did you do then?'

'I didn't really know what to do,' admitted Walter, downcast, 'except to think how bad this would look on me. I guess I panicked a bit because, in the end, I just legged it away from that boat as quick as I could.'

'... making no attempt to call the police or rescue services or anyone else who might have helped?' scorned the DI.

'No ... like I said ... I was in a sort of shock.'

'How about the electrics, though?' asked Jack. 'Was the shore power actually connected?'

'At the shore end, yes,' said Walter, 'but he hadn't plugged it in on the boat. Instead it was trailing there in the water.'

'... into which he'd fallen?'

Walter merely nodded again.

'So, assuming he'd electrocuted himself, this is going to be a case of technical negligence at the very least,' said Bailey sternly. 'On top of that, failing to report a death is a serious ... a very serious ... offence, Jarvis, which we must now investigate further.'

'But I was only trying to help him,' pleaded Walter, almost in tears.

'On the contrary, you admitted yourself that you initially went to that boat to confront him on other issues,' reminded Bailey, 'so I've yet to be convinced that what you've told us is the whole truth, and that you might well have pushed Frazer Dunbar over in the course of a struggle.'

'No ... no it was all an accident,' wailed Walter.

'We'll, see about that,' warned Bailey, 'but I'm going to require you to come to the station later to make a full statement. In the meantime, we'll take your DNA.'

'Why?'

'Because I'm not entirely satisfied with your account of what happened, Walter, and suspect you might well have committed a far more serious offence,' Bailey opened his testing case and removed a kit, 'so open your mouth.'

*   *   *

'Well, what do you reckon?' asked the DI when he and Jack were back in the car. 'Was it just an accident like Jarvis said or did he actually murder Dunbar?'

'I don't think either, Bailey.'

'What!' Once again, the DI shook his head in bewilderment. 'Strewth, Jack, I was sure we'd got this one well-and-truly nailed. So now you don't think Dunbar was murdered?'

'Oh, he was murdered all right, but not the way it seems.' Jack gave an apologetic grin. 'Sorry I can't be more specific at this stage, Bailey, but with these DNA results and once I hear back from my old colleagues at the Met, I hope to have the proof I need to confirm my theory.'

'Which I can't wait to hear, Jack, but, in the meantime, how about the arson on *Pike Hunter*?' Bailey nodded vaguely back up to the flat where they'd left the deeply troubled young man. 'Do you think he was involved in that?'

'What would his motive be?' Jack shook his head. 'No, I think he was telling the truth when he said he'd never even been to the *Watercraft* yard.'

'So, he's not going to help us solve the wreck mystery either then?'

'On the contrary, I think he's going to be a great help in that ... so let's get all these samples back for testing so you can give me the results a.s.a.p. If they prove I'm on the right lines I'll tell you all I know.'

Chapter Fifteen

The two days Jack waited impatiently for both calls were, thankfully, once more spent on the river doing a job he loved, though, he had to admit, one all the more fulfilling when there was a mystery to solve.

Despite this, thoughts of DNA tests were soon put on the back-burner as he slowly piloted his patrol launch up the meandering River Ant on the sort of fine morning that had him honestly assessing his life. Watching twelve newly-hatched ducklings swimming in close formation behind their mother caused him to reflect that perhaps this really was the time to finally hang up his hat on the past and leave detective work to others. It was idyllic enough for him to have just decided that this was all he needed to fill his waking moments, when a ring on his mobile showed it from his old colleague in the Met.

Broadland wildlife, momentarily put on one side, Jack eagerly took the call and listened intently to the information being relayed, while jotting down details in his notebook. Finally, he drew a line beneath the most pertinent item of all.

'And that's a fact from an indisputable source is it?'

'Absolutely, and I hope it's helped.'

'It's done more than helped,' said Jack, 'it's absolutely clinched my case.'

It wasn't often that Jack short-circuited a previous arrangement but, as he clicked in the DI's number, this seemed one time worthy of it.

'Bailey, I know I said I'd await your call, but I thought you'd like to know I've just heard back from my mates in the Met.'

'... and ...?'

'They've confirmed my hunches were spot on. I'll give you the details, but first, have you got those DNA results back yet?'

'Just his morning, so you've saved me a call.' Bailey paused. 'Just confirm there's no-one there with you.'

'Only a family of ducks and a couple of moorhens,' quipped Jack before again becoming deadly serious, 'so give me the gen.'

'Okay, but stand by for some real eye-openers in what they've revealed.'

Bailey straightaway related the results. 'So there you have them, Jack. I don't know about you, but these are nothing like I expected.'

Jack smiled smugly to himself. 'Actually, Bailey, they were *exactly* what I expected. Do you want to hear why?'

'You bet ... I'm all ears.'

'Right ...' Jack related all his suspicions and conclusions, backed now by the DNA results and the morning's findings from the Met.

'Phew, that's pretty specific, Jack,' acknowledged the DI, completely staggered by Jack's evaluation. 'And you really think that was the scenario?'

'Absolutely ... I'd stake my pension on it.'

'Yeah, well it might be my pension that goes down the tubes if you're wrong, Jack ... but you seem to have the facts behind you, so let's stick our necks out and go ahead with that meeting of yours to back them up.'

'Right, I'll call all those involved tonight and hopefully get something organised very soon.'

'Good luck with that then,' sighed the DI, 'because I should think getting all that lot in one place at one time is going to be like pulling teeth.'

'Not if I tempt them with enough intrigue,' promised Jack with a chuckle. 'Let's face it, everyone likes to hear the solution to a mystery.'

'Except the ones who *are* the solution,' pointed out Bailey, 'because, if you're right, this meeting could be the last time some of them enjoy freedom for a long time.'

'Hmm.' Jack promised to confirm the final arrangements, rang off and continued his patrol up the Ant. Dedicated as he always was to truth and justice, he couldn't help mulling over the thought that the next few days would see several lives changed forever.

*   *   *

'My goodness, I thought you were going to be on the phone all night,' said a sleepy Audrey as, that evening, Jack finally joined her in the lounge.

'Yeah, a bit of a marathon session that was,' he agreed, slumping into his favourite armchair just short of midnight. 'But well worth it, seeing as I've finally got everyone coming to a meeting at the *Watercraft* yard at ten tomorrow.'

'I don't know how you managed that at such short notice, Jack,' complimented Audrey as she handed across a large tot of whisky, 'but I'm guessing it's earned you this nightcap.'

'Thanks, love ... I think I'll need something to get me to sleep tonight. My mind's buzzing.'

'It sounds like tomorrow's going to be a big day, Jack.' Audrey put a comforting arm around her husband's shoulder. 'I don't know the details – and don't really want to – but I assume you've once again taken it upon yourself to finger the wrongdoer.'

'Yep. Like they say, Aud, it's always easier to do nothing than something, but we've been married long enough for you to know that there's no way I'll sit back and let a crime go unpunished.'

'So we are talking "crime" here are we, Jack?'

'Yes, and a particularly evil one at that.' Jack glanced at the lounge clock. 'By this time tomorrow, some people will be happier, while others contemplate the years ahead being the worst they've ever known.'

'It's *your* future years I'm more worried about,' admitted Audrey. 'Isn't it time you just sat back, love, and enjoyed your life of semi-retirement simply policing the peaceful waterways of Broadland, and left crime investigation to those still in the force.'

'You may well be right, and something I was actually considering myself on the Ant this morning.' Jack gave an apologetic smile. 'This case needs closing first, though, Aud.' As if in agreement, the clock on the mantelpiece started pinging its last bells of the day. 'But not before a good night's sleep, so come on, love, because this new day's not going to be easy for anyone.'

174

Chapter Sixteen

'Good morning everyone, many thanks for coming, and sorry if we're a bit squashed in here,' apologised Jack.

In the *Watercraft* office, filled with a collection of mismatched chairs, he and Bailey were facing eight unsmiling and nervous faces whose general air of resentment was now being voiced by Hans van Heiden.

'It is inconvenient enough delaying my return to Holland, Jack, but I still fail to see what an act of vandalism ...' the Dutchman glanced through the office window to where the burnt-out remains of *Pike Hunter* still lay in sad dereliction, '... can possibly have to do with us.'

Beside him, Phillipa Keyworth could only nod her own agreement, while Stuart Steadmore also had something to say. 'I think this is all way over the top just because some old wooden boat got burned. If it was that important, it shouldn't have been left unguarded anyway, so don't try and blame us.'

To a background mumbling of assent, Jack scanned his assembly.

In one corner, huddled in overalls and fleece, arms crossed in intolerant protest, Kathy Caterall remained quiet, but seemingly resigned. It was the only thing she appeared to have in common with Tracy, fashionably dressed, hair and make-up immaculate, sitting as far away as possible in the other corner. Between them, their mother Sandra seemed a picture of unkempt anxiety, an impression matched by Walter Jarvis, twitching nervously on her other side. A little apart from them all, Margo Dunbar added her own dissatisfaction. 'I agree, and surely the police could better occupy *their* time by stepping up the search for my poor Frazer.' She put a tissue to her eye in a way that lent more to drama than real emotion.

Stepping forward, Bailey sought to defend his force. 'We've already expended considerable resources in time and manpower searching for your husband, Mrs Dunbar, but all to no avail. And, as for the act of arson on that boat out there, then I'm pretty certain the perpetrator is sitting here right now.'

As everyone glanced nervously at their neighbour, Jack did a quick count of heads. 'Hmm, not quite all here yet ... but ... hang on ...' he paused as a small hatchback pulled up beside the office, '... here's our last attendee ...' Jack glanced at his watch, '... only slightly late.'

Seconds later, the man entered, clearly not expecting the group now facing him open-mouthed. Stopping dead in the doorway, he seemed all set to turn and run before a white-faced Margo broke the shocked silence. 'Frazer ... what are you doing here? ... where on earth have you been?'

'Who cares,' exclaimed Tracy, jumping up to embrace her father. 'The important thing is that my dad is alive and well.'

'... and not dead as we all thought,' added a clearly-relieved Walter Jarvis.

But it was Stuart Steadmore who voiced the confusion of the others in that room. 'What do you mean "Frazer" and "my dad"? This is my boss, the owner of this yard.'

The only one to move, though, was DI Bailey, who stepped forward to confront this startled man, clearly about to bolt. 'Alec Turnberry, I'm arresting you on suspicion of the murder of Frazer and Alice Dunbar. You don't have to say anything, but ...'

*   *   *

Within seconds of this arrest, a police car had driven into the yard and now, just ten minutes later, it was leaving with Alec Turnberry in the back between two officers. Watching from the *Watercraft* office in stunned silence, the group suddenly erupted into a cacophony of voices demanding an explanation. Understandably, most vocal of these was Margo Dunbar's.

'What is all this madness? You surely can't arrest a man for murdering himself,' she half-sobbed, through tears that Jack couldn't decide were ones of relief, anger or disappointment.

'No, we certainly can't,' agreed Bailey, holding up his hand for a return to silence. 'I can understand you being upset, Mrs Dunbar, and that you certainly deserve an explanation ... in fact, you all do, but I'm going to ask Jack Fellows to give it, since he's the one who's been unravelling this strange case from the beginning when ...'

'... from Kathy's balloon, I spotted a derelict boat hidden in the reedbeds,' began Jack. 'However, it's a story that goes back many decades before that, to 1943 when Frazer Dunbar's father, John, was serving as a pilot in the RAF and secretly flying black ops out of Wildmarsh Farm. On one of those missions he picked up a brave man from Holland and flew him to what he hoped would be safety in this country.'

'Except that resistance worker was killed by a German night-fighter before they even crossed the North Sea,' broke in Phillipa Keyworth. 'That man was Andreas Vogelsang, a distant cousin of my own late-husband.'

'Who brought with him the most valuable of his family's heirlooms,' added Van Heiden. 'It was indeed a treasure worth saving and one the occupying Nazis were desperate to get their hands on, especially as it included a small but priceless work by Vincent van Gogh.'

The audible exclamation from the others showed confusion being replaced by intense interest. 'So, where is it now?' asked Walter Jarvis with almost-schoolboy excitement.

'Ah, if only we knew,' sighed Van Heiden, 'because on landing and finding his passenger dead, John Dunbar simply helped himself to all that treasure, hid it until after the war and then sold it to buy Wildmarsh Farm. But the Van Gogh never surfaced and remains missing to this day.'

Jack could detect the lure of hidden fortune in Margo's expression, though she masked it with feigned indifference. 'All very fascinating, I'm sure, but how does this involve my husband?'

'Because the real Frazer Dunbar, John Dunbar's son, was more interested in music than farming,' explained Jack, 'and so went to London and founded an agency called *Cecilian Promotions*. But I suspect he still missed boating on the Broads and, when his dad died, rented out the land at Wildmarsh to local farmers and used his share of the inheritance to set up *Cecilian Cruisers*, to be managed by his sister Alice. Meanwhile, the London agency was doing well and he eventually needed to employ a secretary ... which was you, wasn't it, Sandra?'

All eyes followed Jack's gaze to see the girls' mother give a slow nod of agreement.

'Clearly an enterprising man,' observed Van Heiden.

'But not a particularly discerning one,' countered Jack, 'because he also took on another employee at that time by the name of Alec Turnberry.'

Amid the gasps, it was Stuart Steadmore who voiced the other's doubts. 'Are you sure of that?'

'Very much so, Stuart, seeing as it was confirmed just a day ago by the Metropolitan Police.' Jack shook his head. 'But goodness knows why he hired such a character, because it was the worst thing he ever did and a decision that ultimately cost him his life.'

'*I* can tell you why.' It was an ashen-faced Sandra Caterall speaking up for the first time. 'Because it was me who got him the job.'

Amidst a room full of shocked faces, Jack's was perhaps the most astonished. '*You*, Sandra?'

'Yes, Lord forgive me. You see Alec Turnberry was my boyfriend before I even got my job with *Cecilian*. I soon realised he was a bad'n and horribly controlling but, stupidly, I stuck with him.'

'Am I hearing you right?' gasped Kathy in disbelief. 'That you actually went out with that scumbag Turnberry?'

'I'm ashamed to say I did, love ... that is until I started working for Frazer Dunbar who was the kindest man I'd ever known. That was when I found out, for the first time, what real love was really like.'

'And you became lovers?'

'Oh yes ... but not before I'd opened my big mouth and boasted to Alec Turnberry what a wealthy man my boss was and how he owned a farm and boatyard in Norfolk.' Sandra paused to wipe a tear. 'Soon after that I told Alec I'd had enough of his bullying ways and that I wanted to end our relationship and make a new start with Frazer.'

'Which must have enraged a man like Turnberry,' presumed Jack, 'and probably the catalyst he needed to start planning, not only the ultimate revenge, but also to become very rich in the process.'

'I can see that now,' admitted a distraught Sandra, 'but at the time Alec even pretended to support my new-found love and talked me into seeing if Frazer would give him a job.'

'Which I presume Frazer went along with to please you and, hopefully, allay Turnberry's wrath,' surmised Jack.

'Probably. He had reservations, certainly, but in the end agreed to give Alec six months trial as a handyman.'

'Thereby giving Turnberry every opportunity to study Frazer's finance and banking details.'

'And which you probably helped him access,' said Tracy, glaring accusingly.

It produced another sob from her mother. 'Yes, but Alec could be really threatening if I didn't do what he wanted. And I honestly had no idea what he was planning to do with that information.'

'But *he* certainly did,' pursued Jack, 'but not before he'd got rid of the man whose identity he planned to assume.'

'By "got rid of" you mean ... murdered?' asked an increasingly horrified Tracy.

'I'm afraid so,' affirmed Jack, 'and, in preparation for that felony, he'd already purchased an old motor boat called *Pike Hunter*.'

'But that's the boat out there that got burned?' registered Phillipa Keyworth, glancing through the window and into the yard.

'The very one,' continued Jack. 'Turnberry's plan was simply to wait until Frazer went on one of his regular weekend trips from the yard with his sister Alice. Then he arranged a rendezvous on the broad for what they probably assumed was just a pleasant meet-up.'

'And instead he murdered them,' gulped Tracy.

'... cold-bloodedly by shooting them both in the head,' confirmed Jack, grimly, 'after which he transferred their bodies onto *Pike Hunter* before driving the boat hard into the reedbed where he hoped it would never be found. Then he took their cruiser back to the yard.'

'Wouldn't that have aroused suspicion?' asked Van Heiden.

'Not really, Hans. All he had to do was invent a plausible reason for both brother and sister being unexpectedly called away and them asking him to return their cruiser.'

'I can't believe I'm hearing all this,' said Tracy. She turned to her mother. 'And you knew that creep had murdered the man you loved and yet made no effort to shop him.'

'But I *didn't* know at first,' wailed Sandra, 'until later when I queried Frazer's absence. That was when Alec, needing me to help cover his tracks, told me what he'd done while making it quite clear that if I reported him to the police he'd take me down with him as an accomplice. By that time I knew I was having Frazer's baby and realised a conviction would see me jailed and our baby taken into care.'

'And that baby must have been me,' whispered Kathy, 'so thank you, Mum, for keeping us together and doing what you did in the face of an awful dilemma.' She shuffled closer to put a loving arm around her saddened mother.

'No doubt Turnberry was already proficient at forging Frazer's signature,' reasoned Jack, 'so he simply assumed his identity, his business and all his bank accounts.'

'Yes, but, surely, there was no way he could do that without raising some suspicions in London?' asked an incredulous Tracy.

'That really wasn't a problem to a man as devious as Alec,' explained Sandra, 'because virtually all communication with our clients had always been done by either phone or correspondence. But just to ensure his tracks were well-covered, and to avoid coming into contact with any others who'd known the real Frazer Dunbar, he straightway moved *Cecilian Promotions* and its office to the Fens.'

'Where, I'm guessing, he got even more into Frazer's character by wearing glasses and smoking a pipe,' added Jack. 'Of course, there were still a couple of problems in his grand plan, one being that he knew nothing of the entertainment business or running the agency.'

'Well, we know how he solved that one,' stated Kathy, 'don't we, Margo?'

The woman herself leapt to her feet. 'So, you're telling me I was married to a cheating, impersonating murderer for all those years. No wonder he got me to run the agency. He was nothing but a bloody conman.'

'You're certainly correct on the last bit,' assured Jack, 'which, in turn, makes the former null and void.'

'What, you mean we weren't actually married?'

'Not on the basis of a false identity, you weren't,' confirmed Jack, 'but if it's any consolation, he only married you in the first place for your experience in the world of entertainment. When you contacted him to act as your agent, he knew you'd be the perfect manager to keep *Cecilian Promotions* going, and so he lost no time in seducing you.'

'The manipulating bastard,' cried Margo.

'And that's not all he manipulated,' added Sandra, 'because his other problem was that *Cecilian Cruisers* was somewhere everyone knew and liked the real Frazer and one place he wouldn't get away with his false identity. So he got around that by going through the act of buying the yard as himself, Alec Turnberry.'

'Achieved by simply forging poor Frazer's signature and having the whole deal enacted by London solicitors,' explained Jack. 'That also served to allay any suspicions the boatyard might have had at Alice suddenly ceasing to manage the place. It was now under new management and they accepted the sale and just got on with it.'

'Let me get this right,' queried Stuart Steadmore, trying to get his head around these revelations about his boss. 'That it was only while he was here at *Watercraft* that he was correctly known as Alec Turnberry, whereas everywhere else he took on the false identity of Frazer Dunbar. But surely, Jack, no-one could lead a double life like that for all those years without being sussed.'

'Ah, but you are talking about a very devious man, Stuart. You see he was ensuring he didn't come into contact with anyone, except Sandra, who knew the real Frazer, so his identity went unchallenged. That is everywhere other than the local area around Wildmarsh Farm and the boatyard where Frazer was a familiar face, so it was here he had to retain his real name, Alec Turnberry.'

'No wonder he kept such a low profile at the boatyard,' realised Kathy. 'It was the one place his dual life could be easily exposed. I guess that's why he kept his cruiser on the southern rivers at Brundall and miles away from here.'

'Indeed, *Fenland Raider* was the perfect base for his visits to Norfolk and where he could live his other life with no-one to question his background while you,' said Jack, turning back to Sandra, 'made a new life for yourself and Kathy just down the road in Norwich.'

'It's good to know my father was the *real* Frazer Dunbar,' smiled a relieved Kathy, 'meaning that the brave pilot flying into occupied Europe must have been my grandfather. So now I can see where I inherited my love of flying and why I always felt a connection to Wildmarsh Farm and that control column of his on the wall there.'

'... which your father or Aunt Alice must have proudly brought from the farm as a memento of a distinguished father with a gallant war record,' presumed Jack.

'... but one who, in reality, had so easily succumbed to temptation,' accepted Kathy.

'Yes, but what about *my* father, Mum?' broke in Tracy. 'You told me *he* was Frazer too, but now I know he was already dead when I was conceived, so who really is or was *my* dad?' But, even as she asked the question, an unthinkable realization slowly dawned. 'Oh God,' she cried, 'don't tell me it's that murdering Turnberry.' She covered her face with her hands and let out an anguished sob as the enormity of this possibility began to hit home.

'I'm afraid so, love,' admitted Sandra, shamefully. 'He turned up every time he came to Norfolk, giving me money to keep my mouth shut and threatening what he'd do to me if I ever dared let the cat out of the bag. He tried it on sometimes too, for "old time's sake" he said, and I hate admitting I was too scared to refuse his demands.'

'And so you became pregnant again, and this time by that vile man,' groaned Tracy, now red-eyed.

'Try to understand, Trace,' pleaded Sandra. 'Things were tight and that money helped.'

'It at least explains why he was always so keen to bugger off to that boat of his, leaving silly me to run things in the Fens,' seethed the ever-wiser Margo.

'Exactly,' said Jack, 'and that's how things just ambled along for thirty years until, ironically, a nosey ranger in Kathy's balloon spotted that death boat in the reedbed.'

'Yes, and isn't it poetic justice that I played a part in getting my father's murderer finally caught,' added Kathy, triumphantly. 'An evil man who deserves all that's coming to him.'

'Amen to that,' agreed Sandra, 'and I hope you realise I was almost as much a victim in all this as dear Frazer and poor Alice.'

'Nevertheless,' said Bailey, stepping forward, 'you're going to have to accompany me to the station now to further help with our enquiries.'

Sandra blinked and nervously gripped her youngest daughter's hand. 'What, you mean, after all these years of fear, I'm still going to be charged with something?'

'That'll be up to the CPS, but you did fail to report a crime and helped cover it up. So, come on,' said the DI, helping Sandra to her feet, 'let's go and get all this off your conscience once and for all.'

'I'll come with you, Mum,' said Tracy, pulling herself together and standing up.

'And me,' offered Kathy.

But it was their mother who shook her head and said, 'Thanks anyway, girls, but this is one fix I need to sort out for myself.' She paused and smiled. 'But it's good to see you both wanting to do something together again.'

Minutes later, and Bailey's car was disappearing out of the *Watercraft* yard, leaving two watery-eyed girls hugging each other and Jack pondering his next move. Finally he took both Kathy and Stuart Steadmore to one side. 'I know this isn't a good time for either of you, but can I have a quick word in private.'

*   *   *

'Well, what a turn-up for the books this has been,' said Margo after Jack, Kathy and Stuart returned to find everyone still somewhat shell-shocked.

'You don't sound particularly grief-stricken for someone who's just seen her husband arrested for murder,' observed Kathy, returning to Tracy's side.

'Why should I be?' huffed Margo. 'I'm just too angry to care what happens to the lying, murdering toad. Even before this horror came out today, I suspected he was cheating on me, spending so much time on that boat of his up here in Norfolk, but I didn't for a minute think he was seeing your mother, his old girlfriend from London, and even getting her pregnant.'

'How do you think I feel,' groaned Tracy, 'because the media are going to have a field day when this all comes out and they learn my agent is my father, who wasn't even who he said he was, and who murdered my half-sister's father ...'

'... before I even had a chance to know him,' reminded Kathy, 'so yours won't be the only story making headline news.'

But far from this causing any rancour between the two girls, Jack was pleased to see them embrace again in mutual sadness.

'And now we seem to have lost our mum as well,' added a tearful Tracy.

'But we've got each other again,' said Kathy, quick to comfort her.

'And even if you've lost your agent, Tracy,' piped up Walter Jarvis in a slightly self-satisfied voice, 'you've still got me.'

'No she hasn't,' came back the ever-businesslike Margo. 'It's me who always kept *Cecilian* going anyway, so nothing has to change regarding Tracy's management.'

'I wouldn't be so sure of that,' intervened Jack. 'Actually, the law in this country is pretty clear in that no-one can benefit financially from a criminal act. So the courts could well decide that all Turnberry's ill-gotten wealth be confiscated and handed back to the next-of-kin of his victims.'

'You mean that I might be left with ... with nothing?' stammered Margo.

'Exactly, because the real Frazer did have a daughter, and that was ...' Jack turned to face the girl standing close by, '... Kathy here.'

Margo's manner seemed to change as quickly as her financial expectations. 'Not on the say-so of that promiscuous mother of hers, it won't be,' she snapped back.

As Kathy's eyes blazed, Jack stepped between the two women. 'There's no question now of "say-so", Margo, because we have DNA proof of who fathered Kathy, which makes her the legal beneficiary of Frazer's estate.'

'So, you mean that, when all the paperwork's done, I will actually own ...' Kathy waved her hand over the *Watercraft* yard, '... all this?'

'This and Wildmarsh Farm and anything else that Alec Turnberry criminally claimed.'

'What even his Mercedes?' wailed a desperate Margo. 'You mean I can't even drive home?'

'Oh, you can keep that, because I certainly don't want it,' declared Kathy, 'and, anyway, we wouldn't want to delay your departure.'

'Hang on,' interrupted Phillipa Keyworth, stepping into the fray. 'Before you all start dividing up the spoils, you're forgetting something here ... that everything in the Dunbar estate itself came from ill-gotten gains ...'

'... originally stolen from the Vogelsang family,' added Hans van Heiden.

'... and quite a mess for the courts to sort out,' agreed Jack, 'which could well take years.'

'And see our fortune gobbled up by the lawyers,' reasoned Phillipa before pausing and adding, 'unless we reach an amicable settlement between ourselves. Of course, I'll need to talk to surviving members of the family in

Holland, but I'm thinking, what with the help we've received from you all, they'll agree to splitting things between themselves and Kathy here.'

'Oh, that's fairer than I could ever hope for,' grinned Kathy, giving her new friend a big hug.

'Too bad we never found the Van Gogh then,' said Hans van Heiden, 'because that would have given you some real wealth to share.' He sighed with regret. 'A pity *that* aspect of this whole business came to nothing.'

'I'm not so sure it has,' said Jack with a slight twinkle in his eye, 'because a remark you made the other day, Hans, got me thinking about where that painting might actually be hidden.'

Van Heiden's eyes narrowed sceptically. 'I can't think what that remark was, Jack, because we'd already decided that wherever it was hidden in Wildmarsh, the damp conditions there would have made it beyond renovation anyway.'

'That's right, but it was you referring to John Dunbar being "good at handling aircraft" that set me thinking about something in particular ...' Jack nodded towards the memento still hanging on the *Watercraft* office wall, '... Flight Lieutenant Dunbar's old Lysander control column.'

'You mean that ...?'

'Let's see,' said Jack, grabbing a screwdriver from a nearby toolbox and setting to work removing the control column from its varnished base before laying it on the desk. 'Here, hand me that hacksaw, Stuart, and hold this thing steady for me. It's only aluminium, so it shouldn't be too hard to get the end off.'

Jack began sawing, an action that caused Van Heiden to wince. 'Careful! If what you think is in there, for God's sake don't cut into it.'

'I won't,' promised Jack. 'You can see that this base was welded on to here before the joystick was mounted so ... yes ... it's coming off.'

The cut off section fell to the floor and went rolling away, but all eyes now were on the remaining tubular column. 'Right,' said Van Heiden with barely suppressed excitement, 'the moment of truth.'

'A truth that I hope is in our favour,' said Jack. 'But this is something you've spent years looking for, Hans, so I'm going to let you make the final move.'

Van Heiden simply nodded and the tension was electrifying as he gingerly probed inside the column. 'I can feel something ... yes ... give me some long-pointed pincers, Stuart.'

Carefully, as though a brain surgeon extracting vital tissue, Van Heiden slowly eased what appeared to be a roll of plastic sheet from the innards of the column before then laying it on the desk and, almost reverentially, unrolling it in front of an emotional Phillipa.

'What is it? Is it ...?' she whispered as the art expert carefully removed the plastic covering, to reveal a small rectangle of curling canvas.

'Yes,' whispered Van Heiden, struggling to control his own euphoria, 'it's the missing Van Gogh.'

Epilogue

A few weeks later

'Oh gosh, Jack, how wonderful to see so many people enjoying themselves.'
'Yep, and for such a good cause.' It was the day of the Norfolk and
Norwich University Hospital's summer fete and the weather gods had
indeed smiled on this annual fundraiser. Jack paused to take another bite of
his oozing hot dog, with a slightly-slobbering Spike begrudging his every
mouthful. 'And perfect weather for Kathy, too.'

He was indicating the scene being enacted just two-hundred yards away
in the open hospital grounds, where the brightly coloured *Skyrides* balloon
was slowly inflating under the watchful eye of Stuart Steadmore. Over the
roar of the burner, Kathy, attired in period costume, was explaining to a
group of local journalists the significance of re-enacting John Money's own
fund-raising flight almost two and a half centuries before.

Audrey smiled and nodded. 'Yes, and it's good to see those two together
again.'

'What, Stuart and Kathy?' Jack wiped away some errant ketchup from
his chin. 'Yes indeed. They've been sorely tested these last few weeks, but I
guess true-love won in the end.'

Further away, as crowds browsed the numerous stalls, watched displays
or inspected an impressive collection of vintage vehicles, a brass band
suddenly struck up a rousing melody.

'That must mean Tracy's just finished her performance,' realized Audrey.

'And, judging by the crowds watching and applauding, it was going
really well,' said Jack, who'd made a fleeting visit to the live music spot
before queuing at the hotdog van. 'I think we can safely say her career is
now well-and-truly on the up. And without any more rancour over royalties
either, because Kathy, now financially secure, has said to forget that whole
derisive business.'

'Thank goodness for that, Jack, and Tracy has no agents to worry about
now either.' Audrey gave a relieved sigh. 'I have to say, I'm glad she's wasn't

tempted to take up Margo's offer. From what you told me of that woman, I can't help thinking she would have milked Tracy's talent for all she was worth, not to mention being a constant reminder of the girl's murderous father. But how sad, that having at last found out who her real father was, she now just wants him out of her life forever.'

'Which he probably will be,' said Jack without a trace of sympathy. 'The magistrates remanded Turnberry until the next Crown Court, where I'm guessing he'll be sent down for good.'

'Instead of living the high-life off his evil gains ... which he might still have been doing if you hadn't nailed him,' added Audrey. At this point their conversation was stalled as Spike, becoming bored with all this chat and lack of action, started pulling at his lead. 'Looks like we're on the move, Jack, but we can still keep his Lordship happy and carry on walking while you explain a few things I'm still in the dark over ... like, when did you first suspect Turnberry and Frazer being one and the same?'

'Not immediately,' explained Jack, 'though I was puzzled by just a small thing early on.'

'Which was ...?'

'That, when I first met Turnberry, I noticed a brown nicotine stain on his right forefinger. In the past I'd noticed that same stain on pipe-smokers as a result of their regularly tamping down the tobacco in their pipe bowl. Do you remember I popped back to ask Stuart a question when we visited the boatyard with Spike? It was to ask if Turnberry was a pipe-smoker but, according to Stuart, he definitely wasn't. So why was his finger stained like that? Then Bailey later phoned me with the initial DNA reports on the two skeletons.'

'Which you told me didn't show *who* they were,' remembered Audrey, 'but *what* they were ...'

'... which was that they were brother and sister ... a significant finding, because the only siblings with a connection to Wildmarsh Farm and the boatyard were Frazer and Alice Dunbar. Initially, Bailey agreed the skeletons had to be theirs until Frazer appeared to be alive and kicking ... that is, until he disappeared off his boat at Brundall.'

'So, a ruse that almost worked,' said Audrey.

'Almost, and wife Margo clearly didn't suspect him of being other than who he said he was, which made Bailey think twice about that first identification. But, having found an old pipe on board *Pike Hunter* and then seeing a pipe left behind on *Fenland Raider*, reminded me of Turnberry's stained finger. I added that to another factor that had already raised my suspicions.'

'What other "factor"?'

'That immediately after *Cecilian Promotions* moved to the Fens, the business started going downhill. Now, why would a previously-successful agency start to fail? Margo said it was down to Frazer's incompetence, but he'd never shown that before, so why had he suddenly changed? Right there I started to consider the possibility that it wasn't the real Frazer at all, but that it was Turnberry taking on his identity. The trouble was I couldn't think of anything to link the two men until I called my old chums at the Met and asked them to delve more deeply into the sale of the yard and the working arrangements of the agency in London.'

'That can't have been easy, seeing as *Cecilian* had moved thirty-odd years before.'

'Not that difficult really, Aud. All they did was go to the old solicitors to elicit the fact that there'd been a general assistant employed at *Cecilian Promotions* by the name of Alec Turnberry.'

'The missing link you were looking for.'

'Exactly, and confirmation of what I was already sure was the solution.'

Audrey shook her head. 'So, when you assured Bailey that Frazer was murdered, you weren't referring to his disappearance at Brundall, but to the *real* Frazer's death whose remains, together with his sister Alice, you'd found in the old wreck.'

'Correct. Until we discovered *Pike Hunter*, Turnberry must have thought he'd ticked all the boxes. Then we started making enquiries ...'

'... and he realised the game would soon be up and that his double life would finally be exposed,' completed Audrey. 'I guess that's when he began thinking of an escape clause by faking the death of his "Frazer" persona at Brundall. Bad luck on poor Walter Jarvis, though, that he almost ended up carrying the can for a murder that didn't actually happen.'

'Yes, dear old Walter fell right into that one,' agreed Jack, 'because I'm sure Turnberry had little compunction in using him as the fall guy in his disappearing act.' Jack shrugged. 'I think it safe to assume that, after faking that accident with the shore-power, Turnberry simply slipped away into the darkness and probably got a taxi to some hotel in Norwich. Until the time he walked into our meeting at the boatyard and realised his double-identity really was blown, he probably planned on maintaining his real self as owner of *Watercraft* for a few more days until he carried out the rest of his plan.'

'Which was?'

'Probably to hot-foot it abroad. But it wouldn't have been an impulsive act, because it seems he'd been transferring money from the Dunbar account to an overseas one for quite some time, obviously preparing to dump Margo and vanish abroad at some point in the future.'

'Well, all that money's not going to do him much good now, Jack, and it will, presumably, all go to Kathy?'

'In time,' concurred Jack, 'plus *Watercraft* and Wildmarsh Farm.'

'So, a very well-off girl?'

'Yep, and with a good man to help her manage it.' Jack was pointing towards Stuart Steadmore, now completing the final preparation for the balloon launch. 'They'll make a good and competent team even if they won't be inheriting the Van Gogh.'

'Ah, yes, that lost masterpiece of the Vogelsang family,' remembered Audrey. 'What's actually happened to that?'

'Returned to Holland where it belongs.'

'And what then?'

'I don't know, Aud, but, perhaps, *she* does,' said Jack, suddenly eyeing an upright young woman sitting on a straw bale watching therapy dogs being put through their paces, waving recognition and happily beckoning them to join her.

'Jack ... Audrey ... good to see you,' said Phillipa Keyworth with a smile for them and a stroke for Spike, who had perked up considerably at the sight of some canine friends.

'And you too, Phillipa.' Jack settled himself down beside her while trying to get Spike to calm down and not spoil the display. After shuffling along to make space for Audrey, he glanced about. 'Is Hans here too?'

'No, he's busy in Holland sorting out the provenance of the painting.'

'How long will that take?'

'Probably ages, but we've been told there'll be an interim reward paid to us for having recovered such a priceless work ...' Phillipa frowned, '... some of which should be going to you, Jack. After all, it was you who actually discovered it.'

'Only because of that casual remark of Hans's,' said Jack dismissively. 'No, you'd both been searching for that masterpiece for years and my reward is just knowing it's back where it belongs and that justice will be done.'

'But don't *you* feel at a bit of a loose end now your search is over, Phillipa?' asked Audrey.

'Oh no, I've got plenty to keep me occupied ...' she pointed towards the balloon, now fully-inflated and swaying gently in the light breeze, '... because I'm investing some of my reward money in *Skyrides* as a co-owner with responsibility for marketing.' She gave an excited smile. 'I'm sure, working together, Kathy and me will literally rise to new heights.'

'If what you've done to publicize today's event is anything to go by,' said Jack, 'then I'm sure you will.'

'And that's not all,' continued Phillipa, 'because Tracy seems to have been impressed enough with my marketing skills to ask me to represent *her* as well.'

'Oh, that's wonderful news,' enthused Audrey before having one slightly-sad thought, 'but where will this leave poor Walter Jarvis?'

'Oh, he'll be okay,' reassured the new agent. 'Tracy is officially making him her manager, so he'll still be very much a part of her life.'

'... practically, if not romantically,' added Jack with a grin.

'Yes, well there he is now doing his thing,' said Phillipa, laughing as she watched Jarvis ushering Tracy through the crowds with his usual slightly-officious manner. 'I'll have to cure him of that,' she said with a wink.

'Good luck,' wished Jack, 'but is that period costume that Tracy's wearing?'

'Yes, because she's going in the balloon with Kathy.'

'So they really have made up their differences,' sighed a delighted Audrey as crowds made their way to the launch-site to watch. 'Come on, Jack, let's go and wave them off.'

'Don't worry, I wouldn't miss it for anything.' Hurrying to get a good vantage point, they went striding off with Spike, but it was only as they got closer that Jack pointed out a thin, rather lonely-looking woman standing near the public barrier. 'Gosh, there's Sandra.'

Audrey had never met the girls' mother before, but was glad Jack didn't hesitate to walk straight over to this ill-used woman.

'Sandra ... what a nice surprise.'

Startled, she spun around. 'Oh, Mr Fellows, I didn't expect to see you here.'

'Nor me you, Sandra,' replied Jack, smiling. He glanced towards the balloon basket where Tracy, encumbered by her 18th century dress and holding on to her straw boater, was being helped into the basket to join Kathy. 'You must be very proud of your two girls.'

'Oh, yes.' Her face lit up. 'They haven't done too badly really have they, considering everything?'

'They've done great and they'll both now be going on to even better things,' assured Jack before asking, sympathetically, 'but how are you doing, Sandra?'

'Oh, okay I suppose, under the circumstances.' She gave a long sigh. 'Inspector Bailey charged me with "perverting the course of justice", so

I'm on bail and only here to see the girls off on their big day.' And then, noticing both Kathy and Tracy waving her over, she smiled again. 'Looks like they want to say some goodbyes so ... will you excuse me?'

'Of course,' grinned Jack. 'Off you go.'

'Ah, that's nice for her,' said Audrey as Sandra scuttled across the grass to receive heartfelt hugs from her daughters, 'but what I still don't understand, Jack, is how she could have continued seeing Turnberry, and even end up having his child, while knowing he'd murdered Frazer, the man she really loved.'

'I don't think she had any choice, Aud,' replied Jack, shaking his head, 'because I'm sure she was scared stiff, knowing what the man was capable of doing. So she submitted to his demands and just put up with it.'

'... resulting in the poor woman falling pregnant with his child. I can see how, as a single mother striving to make ends meet she had little choice other than to go along with it all,' conceded Audrey, sadly, 'but I just hope they take all that into consideration at her trial.'

'I'm sure the girls will get her a good lawyer and that the courts will be lenient ...' Jack gave a little chuckle, '... especially if they never learn about Sandra's other misdemeanour.'

'Other ... what are you talking about, Jack?'

'I'm talking about burning a boat.'

'What, *Pike Hunter*? So it really was Sandra who did that?'

'Oh yes, and very effectively stymied Bailey's hopes of getting some more DNA evidence.' Jack gave one of his most disarming smiles. 'Of course, she gave herself away when we first went to interview Tracy on the subject, and blurted out about the fire at the *Watercraft* yard, when the police still hadn't released details. I knew then she must be involved, but needed proof. When we talked to Stuart and Kathy I realised they knew more than they were disclosing so, after Turnberry had been arrested and Sandra taken in, I had a quiet word with them both.'

'And ...?'

'And ... they admitted the full facts. First, Turnberry had called Stuart and tried to bribe him to burn the boat on the pretext of it doing harm to the yard's business. That was a step too far for Stuart and he drove away from the yard that night, glad he hadn't carried out his boss's wishes. But what he *had* done, ironically for safety reasons, was to take the can of petrol from his office and leave it outside.'

'Only for Sandra to conveniently find it when she came to the yard herself.'

'Unfortunately, yes. I imagine she was only planning to use matches until she stumbled across that can. Either way, she'd been there and waiting for Stuart to leave before she leapt into action. She should probably have waited longer because he was only a few miles down the road when he glanced in his rear-view and saw the glow of a fire. Suspecting it was the boatyard, he did a quick one-eighty back just in time to catch Sandra making her exit. Even as he collared her, Kathy arrived on the hopeful mission of reconciliation, but instead was confronted by the sight of *Pike Hunter* well alight and her mother being apprehended by Stuart. Thinking quickly and realising they had to get well away from the boatyard before the emergency services arrived, she and Stuart took Sandra back to *Balloonatic* and spent the rest of the evening talking things through and making up the story of vandals firing the boat.'

'But why on earth did Sandra do such a stupid thing?'

'Because that morning, a distraught Tracy had called her, explaining how Margo Dunbar had accused her of having an affair with husband Frazer. Sandra was petrified that, with his wife making waves and the skeletons being discovered, the whole story would soon be coming out and she could well be ending up in prison with Turnberry. She was a desperate woman and there-and-then decided to take action of her own.'

'By burning all the evidence.'

'Which of course she did,' explained Jack. 'But in covering up for her mother's recklessness, Kathy implicated herself in the arson attack as did the ever-faithful Stuart.'

'Ah well, that's love for you, Jack, but I'm surprised you never discussed any of this with Bailey.'

'Actually I did, after Sandra had dropped herself in it at Tracy's flat. But we reckoned that the poor woman had probably got enough running against her without a charge of arson.' Jack shrugged. 'And now, with a result for an old murder case in the bag, Bailey is more than content to let that embarrassment be written off to mindless vandalism.'

'And a good thing too,' agreed Audrey, before glancing in the direction of the flight area and seeing Sandra making her way back to the public enclosure. 'Looks like the balloon's about to lift off, Jack.'

Indeed, as the band struck up a rousing fanfare, Kathy could be seen adjusting the burner to a steady roar and the basket lifting slowly off the ground while Tracy waved with enthusiastic joy. From the onlookers came a big cheer, spontaneous applause and much waving in return.

'What a lovely sight,' extolled Audrey as the balloon climbed higher and higher while slowly drifting ever northwards on the light breeze, 'especially after all the heartache our own flight triggered.'

'But which cleared up a lot of family angst in the end,' pointed out Jack.

'I suppose so.' Audrey was still watching as the balloon cleared the city limits and drifted away over open country. 'Don't you wish you were in it, Jack?'

'Not really, Aud. That's one thing from my to-do list well and truly ticked off.' Jack gave a token lick of his lips and bent down to fondle Spike. 'Instead, I reckon a nice cup of tea together and some of your scones would be a perfect way to end this very pleasant day.'

THE END

Printed in Great Britain
by Amazon

44051923R00116